THE RISING OF THE 18 SHIELD HERO

Aneko Yusagi

Naofumi Iwatani

Glass

Kizuna Kazayama

"Formation One, Formation Two: Glass Shield!"
I shouted, creating glass shields imbued with sufficient
life force to impede the movement of the magic unleashed
by the Demon Dragon.

Table of Contents

Prologue: The Meeting to Discuss Efficient Eating Enhancement.06

Chapter One: Sloth...20

Chapter Two: Library Search.....................................37

Chapter Three: Fishing Fool's Determination.....................71

Chapter Four: Sisters and Jealousy..............................90

Chapter Five: Ultimate Soup Stock...............................120

Chapter Six: Seya's Restaurant..................................130

Chapter Seven: Contentious Cooking Battle.......................157

Chapter Eight: Medicinal Cooking................................179

Chapter Nine: Resolution via Violence...........................200

Chapter Ten: Dragon of Ultimate Magic...........................233

Chapter Eleven: Volunteer Soldiers..............................269

Chapter Twelve: Double Reflection...............................294

Chapter Thirteen: The Reborn....................................325

Epilogue: The Game Knowledge Pitfall............................343

Prologue: The Meeting to Discuss Efficient Eating Enhancement

"Hey, the food is ready!"

"Oh God . . ." L'Arc looked at the food I laid out on the table and pressed his hands to his mouth as he made a burping sound. I wasn't especially impressed with his reaction—he almost made it look like I was trying to poison him!

"I hate to say it, Mr. Naofumi, but this is making for a pretty big breakfast," Raphtalia objected.

"What are you talking about? You will—quite literally—not grow up big and strong if you don't eat up!" I reminded her.

In that moment we were in Kizuna's world, eating breakfast in the refectory in L'Arc's castle. Everyone gathered there—with just a few exceptions—had pretty sickly expressions on their faces.

"You should be taking notes from Filo, S'yne, and the killer whale sisters," I commented.

"More food! More food!" Filo was chanting.

"This really is delicious," S'yne added.

"More food this morning! Any chance I can get a drink with this?" Sadeena asked.

"I'd love some of those snacks from yesterday . . ." Shildina said. Those four basically sucked up everything placed in front of them. If only everyone in the group were so gluttonous!

"You were practically force-feeding us last night, and now you want us to eat more?" Glass said, also looking a bit green around the gills.

"I think having any kind of appetite left after dinner last night is the issue here," Raphtalia opined.

"Raph!" Raph-chan agreed. Even she didn't seem very hungry. I pondered for a moment. This was definitely an issue we were going to have to resolve in order to enhance the strength of everyone across the board.

"Then shall I make my morning performance one to enhance digestion and promote hunger?" Itsuki stood up and started to play the instrument in his hands.

"Fehhh!" Rishia exclaimed. "Itsuki! Please, don't do that!"

"Rishia, if we aren't greedy about getting stronger, we won't survive the trials that lie ahead," Itsuki chided her.

"I understand your reasoning, but, Mr. Naofumi . . . please, just give us some more time." Even Raphtalia was asking me to hold back. It was starting to feel more and more like I was torturing my allies rather than just feeding them.

"Hmmm. You weaklings leave me no choice. I'll just go make some more while you rest up," I decided. Glass gave an audible gasp at my words.

"I had no idea it was possible to kill people using food, without the use of poison," she exclaimed.

"Please don't make me sound like some kind of serial killer!" I retorted, unable to stop myself from responding.

There was a reason why I was piling all these dishes so high with food. Quite a long and complicated reason, actually. But if I were to provide an abridged version . . . after we defeated Takt, a beaten and battered Ethnobalt had appeared from Kizuna's world, seeking our help. Three holy heroes in Kizuna's world had been killed. Kizuna herself survived. Her remaining allies were in a pretty sticky situation.

During our troubles with Takt, Raphtalia's katana vassal weapon sent her to Kizuna's world. So to come rescue Raphtalia, I had crossed over to this world with a party that included Itsuki and some of my other companions.

After that, we had become embroiled in a conflict with the Musical Instrument Hero, Miyaji, a vanguard of the waves. We had faced him, Bitch, Itsuki's former party member Armor, and S'yne's sworn enemies from her own world in a big battle. To make matters worse, the holy weapons in Kizuna's world had been captured, and our enemies had access to a mysterious power that sealed away the holy weapons from our world—my shield and Itsuki's bow—as well as our magic.

Amid these dire circumstances, the mirror vassal weapon lent me its strength and I became the Mirror Hero. I was ultimately able to use that power to defeat Miyaji and also successfully rescue Kizuna. Itsuki was even chosen by the musical instrument vassal weapon after it was released from Miyaji.

It wasn't all good news, however. We failed to capture Bitch, Itsuki's former party member Armor, and S'yne's older sister, who had been among the forces from S'yne's world. There was also the issue of three of the four holy weapons from Kizuna's world still being held by the enemy.

We clearly had more battles ahead. It turned out that the mirror vassal weapon housed the ability to boost stats via eating, using a separate kind of experience. So in order to prepare for these battles, I have been stuffing everyone with as much food as possible. They had to understand the reasons why—just eating any food was enough to earn experience, but the food that I made was the most efficient. Bonus experience and imbued abilities—just eating could provide things like a permanent plus 1 to magic. It makes total sense that I would stuff them like prize turkeys.

"Shall we get into the main topic for today?" Glass suggested with a pretty serious expression on her face as she sat at the table. I'd been told that the treatment Kizuna was receiving—who had been turned to stone—was going to finish either today or tomorrow, so maybe that was what Glass wanted to talk about.

"You mean how we can't possibly eat so much of kiddo's

food efficiently enough without our stomachs popping like balloons?" L'Arc quipped. I couldn't tell if L'Arc was trying to make a joke or not.

"Whatever are you talking about?" I snapped at him. This from a guy who had three shades of snot beaten out of him by a vanguard of the waves, Bitch, and S'yne's sworn enemies. He'd been right on the ropes before we showed up to bail him out! There were clearly more important issues to deal with than—

"He is correct," Glass stated flatly. "At this rate we are looking at either the aforementioned balloon situation or becoming so obese we will be sitting ducks in battle. Either one of these is too high a price to pay for further strength." Pretty much everyone who had gathered nodded at Glass's assessment.

"What the hell are you all joking around about?" I asked.

"You may think it's a joke, Mr. Naofumi, but for the rest of us, this is a pretty serious issue," Raphtalia said. Even she was siding with Glass on this issue.

"That is exactly why I am playing my support music, to soothe your distended stomachs—" Itsuki started.

"We've already heard enough from you, Mr. Musical Instrument Hero. We know which side you are on! That's not what we are talking about here!" L'Arc's sharp tone cut deeply into Itsuki. I shook my head, wondering if this was really something worth devoting so much brainpower to.

After all . . . everyone involved with Kizuna had this side to them, influenced—"poisoned" might be a more apt term—by her into being a bit airheaded. I wished they would just get a bit greedier—literally—about getting stronger without having to debate the method so intensely.

"The recipes contained in the weapon also display how much experience they provide. Let's search for the best recipes to have Naofumi make. If possible . . . those that allow for a large volume of experience with just a small volume of food," Glass continued.

"I bet those recipes will require rarer ingredients. I thought experience was energy for a Spirit, anyway?" I asked her. I'd even heard that it would spill out if too much was obtained.

"Naofumi, this enhancement via cooking also applies to Spirits. The experience is provided in a different format from normal," Glass explained. That was interesting—it meant Glass also had a lot to gain from this enhancement method.

"I'm with Lady Glass on this one," L'Arc said.

"Master, more!" said Filo.

"I'm coming!" I moved over to refill the plates of those who were happy to actually eat. "Maybe I'll cook up something with a stomach-expanding effect?"

"Mr. Naofumi, we don't really need your input on this matter. Please just enjoy your never-ending meal with Filo, S'yne, and the killer whale sisters until we are finished with our discussions," Raphtalia told me. So it sounded like I was definitely going to be the one doing the cooking. I stood back and watched their discussions. The very issue on the table was absolutely ridiculous, and yet everyone was completely serious.

Based on how such things normally worked, it seemed highly likely that dishes with carefully selected ingredients, or that took longer to prepare, would offer better effects. If they didn't want to just shovel in platefuls, the only option was to increase the quality of each dish. That also sounded like a real pain in the ass though. It would make my life much easier if everyone was like Filo and just ate whatever was put in front of them.

"Master! I'm feeling so full of energy, although I'm not sure exactly why !" Filo chirped.

"I might have some ideas," I replied. Left with few choices, I moved over to sit with Filo and the other eaters. The group of gluttons was piling it away in astounding fashion. It almost felt good to watch them at work. It was still a pain to make the food, sure, but I didn't feel so bad about it when it was being so heartily enjoyed.

Of course, not everyone could eat like these guys, and yet it was also true that we needed everyone to eat as much as possible in order to get the ability boosts. Maybe how to proceed was an important question after all.

I'd have to give it some thought myself.

"I'm not going to lose this time. That's why—" S'yne had

been roundly thrashed by her older sister and didn't seem very happy about it—she had been doing nothing but eating since. Getting stronger just by eating sounded like a pretty good deal to me. An extremely easy approach. That said, it was also a little worrying that just boosting specs and then not having the follow-through could lead to trouble when the actual fighting started. Some earnest training surely provided additional benefits over just wolfing down a plate of food.

"I have to say . . . you whale sisters can pack it away too, can't you?" I said. Not to the extent of Filo, but they were maintaining a steady pace. Many of the others in the village were hearty eaters, but these four could more than hold their own.

"Oh my. Do you dislike women who eat a lot, little Naofumi?" Sadeena asked.

"What? You do?" Shildina chipped in.

"Not really," I responded. I didn't let myself get hung up on stuff like that. Eating a lot was proof of being healthy—but eating too much could damage one's health. That was the whole reason for the meeting the other group was having.

"I must say, little Naofumi, it feels like your cooking has really helped the smoothness of my skin and luster of my hair," Sadeena stated. I took another look at her—she did indeed seem more luminescent than normal.

"You're definitely smooth and lustrous in your therianthrope form," I quipped. She was a sea creature, after all—a freaking killer whale.

"Your breasts have gotten bigger too," Shildina mentioned. At that comment, I felt eyes glancing over at us. I turned around to see Glass and Raphtalia looking over. It had started to feel like something from a love-comedy manga—I almost expected the girls to start comparing bust sizes, with the bigger cup attaining the upper hand. Not that such a thing was in any way realistic.

"How do you feel about breasts, little Naofumi? Lean in and whisper it just to me, if you're embarrassed to say," Sadeena said.

"Excuse me?" I retorted with some hostility.

"My breasts in particular," she continued, thrusting them out with what looked like the intent of getting me to touch them. I might have loosened up a little after the whole Atla business, but that didn't mean I liked talking about this stuff now.

"I think nothing of them. If you have time to worry about your bust line, spend it obtaining something more practical—some muscles for battle," I told her. Breasts weren't really something one had any control over, anyway. It was pointless to compare them. If big ones provided some kind of advantage in battle, great, but I'd never heard of that either. It didn't matter what men thought about them. The only requirement was some kind of practical application.

Then, for some reason, Raphtalia gave a sigh.

"I don't think you have any real cause for concern in that

regard, Lady Raphtalia—if I may be so bold, of course," L'Arc ventured.

"That's not the issue here . . . Ah, forget it," she replied.

"Kizuna has a considerable fixation on breast size," Glass mentioned. "I should share this information with her as quickly as possible." This meeting was really starting to get off track. They were never going to solve the cooking crisis like this.

"Those guys over there are trying to resolve issues of getting too fat or eating too much, but what about you, S'yne? Killer whale sisters? Do you have any concerns?" I asked them. Filo, of course, didn't really come into it—and whether she was a filolial or a humming fairy, she would look fine even if she was a bit fat. I mean, she was just going from a fluffy ostrich to one of those plump yellow video game birds from that endless fantasy. She might even attain a weight more in keeping with her plumped-up appearance.

"Ah! Master, you're thinking something rude about me!" Filo chirped.

"Go ahead, then. Do you have any worries, Filo? Like what might happen if you get fat?" I asked her point-blank.

"Huh?" she responded in a very Filo-like way. As far as I could tell, in her monster form Filo was almost all muscle, with no fat at all—and yet she was the biggest glutton in the village. She did run around a lot, so she was always burning energy. "I'm not sure what you mean," she continued.

"Me neither. I've never been fat so I wouldn't know," Sadeena added.

"Same here," Shildina said.

"Me too—" S'yne managed to get out. It seemed none of my semi-pro eaters had ever really worried about their weight at all. As for S'yne, I couldn't really comment on her, but the killer whale sisters' natural habitat was underwater, a place with heavy resistance to the slightest movement, so their bodies were likely just clumps of muscle. They surely burned a lot of calories swimming around in the cold too. I was sure some women would be pretty jealous to hear all this—but those two also did naturally look pretty plump when in their therianthrope or monster forms.

"When you get older, I bet you'll be all fat and saggy," I said. Women often worried about how what they were doing now would make them look in the future. Then I noticed Sadeena winking over at Raphtalia for some reason.

"Little Naofumi, would you not like me anymore if I was fat? . . . What about Raphtalia?" Sadeena asked.

"Hmmm . . . I can't imagine either of you being overweight," I replied. I had seen images of Raphtalia's mother, and she had been—if I had to pick one—on the plump side. Raphtalia herself currently took after her father, but there was no reason she couldn't take after her mother in the future. "It's better than being all skin and bones," I finally managed. I'd seen some skeleton-looking women in college, girls with the goal to just be as thin as possible. I knew that some people liked it, but I certainly wasn't one of them.

I was starting to feel that maybe physical appearance didn't bother me at all. When it came to romance . . . I didn't feel like forming an actual relationship with anyone—even with those I felt a kind of love toward, like Filo and Melty. Back when I was in Japan, I was something of a connoisseur of those two-dimensional Lolita types, but simply touching a real Lolita was out of the question. I tried to think of Atla in a sexual way for a moment, but couldn't. Raphtalia's young appearance also bothered me. Mentally speaking, there might have been something . . . but all the young ones, apart from Raphtalia and Atla, were definitely out of the picture.

I snapped back to myself, wondering what I was even thinking about. I really needed to get off this topic.

"In fact, I think big and fluffy might be best. Like Raph-chan," I said.

"Raph?" the cutie questioned. Raphtalia slumped down, seemingly drained of all her energy.

"It looks like you've still got a while before you truly comprehend the female mind," Sadeena said wistfully.

"Indeed. Sweet Naofumi needs to work out what he likes," Shildina agreed. I was just shaking my head at what a completely annoying answer that was when I saw S'yne nodding in agreement too. Like I cared at all about comprehending the female mind!

"If you really don't want to end up fat, maybe I can use some ingredients suited to dieting," I said, trying to find a compromise. This being a pseudo-fantasy world, there were apparently magical ingredients that would actually let you lose weight as you ate them. Sure, they were also apparently pretty rare, but we'd only need them to take the weight off. There were also recipes for dishes that boosted metabolism. In other words, these problems we were discussing had already been taken into account.

"So that's the conclusion we come to, is it?" L'Arc said, accusation in his voice.

"I'm not going to allow you to run from eating simply because it's going to make you fat!" I retorted, somewhat sharply. The heads of every member of the conference group drooped downward in stunning synchronization.

In the end, we came to the conclusion that we should consume food as efficiently as we could without overeating. Personally, I wanted everyone to become as strong as absolutely possible. One of the most wonderful aspects of this power-up method was that it took effect on all allies, not just other heroes. That meant an overall boost to the strength of our entire force. There was no reason not to jump at such a chance. I also had plenty of experience with my own research into cooking that

I could now bring to bear, including such things as adding medicinal herbs to dishes. It would definitely be worth trying to make recipes other than those in the weapon's recipe book.

Chapter One: Sloth

After finishing breakfast, we started our activities for the day. Those who hadn't been present for the meal—including Ethnobalt and Therese—were already off starting work or training.

Meanwhile, I headed with Glass and Raphtalia toward the medical facility where Kizuna was being treated. I'd been told that they had almost reached the next stage of her treatment for being turned to stone: the removal of the complete paralysis of her entire body.

We entered the magical treatment room inside the facility. The room itself had lots of ofuda plastered over the walls, making it look like the site of some scary ritual. Kizuna was standing transfixed in the middle of all of that, her fishing rod out in front of her. She looked like she was only sleeping.

I had to wonder, not for the first time, how she got herself turned to stone like this. As I was thinking, a professional in this world that was called both a curse master and a healer spoke up.

"The paralysis will be broken soon," he said. We remained quiet and just watched as the ofuda around Kizuna started to glow with a faint light. That light proceeded to gather around the unmoving Kizuna. A moment later the light scattered again, and with a shudder, the paralysis was broken and Kizuna started to move.

"Kizuna . . ." Glass, concern in her voice, started forward at once, but immediately after being released, Kizuna's entire body started to give off a flickering purple aura. I recognized it at once—I'd used curse series gear myself. Glass had surely worked it out too, because she readied her fan and had a stern look on her face.

"Ah . . . so listless," Kizuna whimpered. Keeping her fishing rod in front of her, she simply dropped to a horizontal position and started sleeping.

"Kizuna?" Glass ventured. The response was little more than a moan, Kizuna barely opening her eyes and looking in our direction. She looked totally doped up.

"Are you okay?" Glass asked.

"I guess . . ." Kizuna replied. "Where am I?"

"A medical facility in our base," Glass told her.

"Oh . . ." Kizuna responded, completely without engagement. She wasn't even surprised to see me here! She definitely seemed very different from the Kizuna I had known before—listless was one way of putting it, or another way would be to say she looked like she was just annoyed to be having to do anything.

"She's acting a lot like you, Mr. Naofumi, when you don't want to do something," Raphtalia observed.

"You think I act like that?" I replied with a suitable note of incredulity.

"Yes, you do." Raphtalia quickly put me right. "But maybe not quite as openly as this." They say that seeing your faults in others can be a way to correct them in yourself . . . but I always get things done in the end. No correction necessary.

"Kizuna, pull yourself together! We've finally managed to save you!" Glass pleaded with her.

"Good for you," came the lethargic reply. It looked like Kizuna just wanted to be left alone to sleep, and all she did in response to Glass was roll around.

"Is this the cost of the curse? Something like that?" I asked. Kizuna was generally unable to attack humans, but just like me, she should have gained that ability by using a cursed weapon—of course, only as a last resort. Glass and the others had told me about it and that the cost of the curse was to make her weaker.

"No . . . the cost for that weapon is a simple, direct reduction in level and power-ups. I can't imagine it would turn her into this pathetic creature," Glass bemoaned.

"Hmmm," I responded. We proceeded to carefully check the condition of the weapon that Kizuna was holding. It was a fishing rod with a peculiarly twisted aura to it. The reel, which was a bit bear-like, definitely caught my eye. I was also quick to notice a strange black accessory—like handcuffs, almost, connecting Kizuna to the weapon.

"Kizuna! Pull yourself together!" Glass tried again, this time with an added light slap to the cheek. Kizuna moaned, and then something like smoke started to well up around her. With a brief sound of surprise, Glass almost slumped to the floor, even as she still held onto Kizuna. The smoke continued to swell, filling the room.

"Stardust Mirror!" I used the mirror version of Shooting Star Shield to create a barrier, fencing off the smoke, and then lifted Glass up. Kizuna was currently not one of my party members and so she had been pushed out by the barrier.

"Glass, are you okay?" I asked. I held her, and Raphtalia tried to wake her by slapping her on the cheek.

"I'm . . . still here." Glass rejoined us, rubbing her cheek as she stood up.

"You okay?" I asked again, now that she could hear me.

"Yes, I think so . . . but what happened?" she asked.

"That strange smoke emerged from Kizuna. You were the closest, and it made you collapse," I told her.

"I'm not sure what this is inside me . . . a feeling of complete lethargy . . ." Glass reported, her face looking pale.

"Kizuna, excuse us. I need to talk to Glass. You just wait here," I said. Kizuna only groaned a bit in reply, unable to even do that properly.

We left Kizuna on the ground in the room full of smoke and headed back outside. Then we called in one of the curse masters and had them take a look at Glass. It turned out she was suffering from a light curse—one that, thankfully, could be

treated quickly. Just in the time since we left the room, Glass was already fully conscious and standing on her own two feet.

"What's going on with Kizuna?" Glass managed to ask.

"She did attack you, didn't she? Someone who is meant to be her ally," Raphtalia said, clearly worried.

"No. From what we saw in there, I'm not sure I'd call that an attack by her," I responded. It certainly didn't look to me like Kizuna had instigated the action herself and much more like her weapon was to blame.

I spoke to Kizuna through a glass window in her room.

"Kizuna, can you stop using that weapon? It's causing all sorts of problems," I said.

"What? Did you say something?" she replied lazily. Kizuna was still lying down with her back to us. A few more seconds passed and it was like I'd never even spoken.

"Kizuna! What are you lying around for? Hurry up and change your weapon!" Glass chided her.

"Bah . . . such a pain," came the response. Kizuna continued to lie on the floor, even as the mysterious smoke continued to fill the room. At least it looked like we'd managed to contain the smoke in the room, but now strange vibrations in the air, strange pulsations, started to pass through the walls and come at us.

"I'd put good odds on that weapon being the thing making Kizuna all loopy," I said.

"I agree," Raphtalia stated.

"Remember, Kizuna was being held by a vanguard of the waves and S'yne's sworn enemies. I wouldn't put it past them to booby-trap her in case she was ever saved," I continued. We already knew they had used some kind of strange corruption on the four holy weapons and brought the holders under their control. Kizuna was now the only one of the holy heroes left on this world—it made sense they would do something to her that wasn't going to kill her but would also prevent her from getting back into action even if she did escape.

"We should have destroyed that accessory before we turned her back," I lamented.

"We did try," Raphtalia responded.

Indeed, we had given it a try.

"So just what kind of curse is this?" she asked. We all looked at Kizuna again. It was like the pollution was spreading out from her. I didn't like it.

The curse masters had placed new purification ofuda on the walls and closed the room up again.

"If it's another curse based on the seven deadly sins . . ." I thought back over the trend we had seen in the past. I had been wrath. I still wasn't sure what it would have been like if the rage completely overtook me, but the urge to destroy stuff and kill people had been overpoweringly strong. Ren the Sword Hero, meanwhile, had suffered from greed and gluttony. Itsuki the

Bow Hero had been pride, but his had been a bit of a different curse, making him more righteous than anything else. Then there was Motoyasu the Spear Hero, suffering from lust and envy. Looking at Kizuna lying on the floor, complaining about doing anything at all, the one that seemed to apply was . . .

"Sloth. You think this might be a sloth-curse weapon?" I asked. If it was sapping her will to do anything, while also polluting the space around her, sloth seemed pretty appropriate. "Whatever it is," I continued, "we need to get her to change it."

"Kizuna! Please, change your weapon at once!" Glass pleaded. "That weapon is even influencing your mind!"

"Huh . . . okay . . ." she responded. It almost sounded like she was going to actually make an effort! Kizuna placed a hand on the fishing rod and tried to change its shape . . . but nothing happened, and she just slumped lazily back to the ground.

"Can't change it . . . what a pain . . ." she managed to say. I met her eyes and swallowed hard. They looked like the eyes of a dead fish, blank and lifeless and horrible.

Did she love fish so much she was starting to become one? If you bumped into her in a dark alley at night, with those eyes, you would run for your life.

"It seems she can't change her weapon . . . and she's also completely lifeless and listless," I summarized.

"So even though we 'saved' her—even though we have her here—she hasn't actually been saved yet?" Glass lamented.

"That's the short of it. They really did a number with their booby-traps." I shook my head, wondering how they forcefully turned one of the holy weapons into a curse weapon. When I thought about it, she had been in a strange pose—fishing rod out and all—and so we should have been a bit more alert. We needed to break the curse before we restored her to normal.

"How to break this curse, then? Can we break the accessory with, what . . . some hot spring water that works on curses or some holy water . . . something like that?" I asked. I tried to break the accessory using magic, but it was just repelled. This one was far tougher than the accessory they had been using to control the vassal weapons.

"Ah, this is all such a pain . . ." Kizuna reached out, took a steamed bun I'd put in the room for her, and started stuffing her cheeks while lying on the ground. At least she could work up the concern to eat, if nothing else.

"We'd better go report this to the others," I said.

"Okay," Raphtalia agreed. We proceeded to gather the others.

"Bah! This situation sucks!" L'Arc muttered, clicking his tongue.

"Therese, is there anything you can do?" I asked.

"I'll give it a try . . ." she replied. She gingerly moved over toward Kizuna and started to intone some magic. The effects of the accessory that Imiya had made for me were providing

Therese with a considerable amount of protection. L'Arc had told some pretty wild tales of her exploits in battle, so if this problem was rooted in magic, maybe she could resolve it. However . . . "It's not good," she eventually said. "It feels like they've fused the holy weapon and accessory together and are forcing it to retain the shape of a cursed weapon."

"Which means maybe Lady Kizuna can overcome it by getting stronger," L'Arc said.

"I can't say if that would work or not. It's using the power of Kizuna and the holy weapon as its medium. If Kizuna gets stronger, the accessory will just get stronger too," Glass explained.

What a freaking pain! That said, we couldn't just leave Kizuna like this. We had no idea when Bitch, S'yne's sworn enemies, or the remaining enemy vassal weapon holders would show up to attack. We needed to bring Kizuna back into action as quickly as possible.

"Fehhh . . ." Rishia murmured, her only contribution.

"How about if I played some magical purification music?" Itsuki asked.

"Shall I sing?" Filo suggested, joining in with proposing how to break the curse. That had worked in the world we'd come from . . . and in the Cursed Lands, for example.

"I'm sure you could purify the area around Kizuna. It would likely work to protect us, but I think it's unlikely to do much to Kizuna herself. The seat of the disease lies within. It's likely you would just delay the spread of the corruption a little," Glass explained. The more I heard, the more annoying this entire curse was turning out to be.

Then Ethnobalt raised his hand with another proposal.

"My home, the Ancient Labyrinth Library, has copies of almost all of the books ever written in this world," he explained. "We might find some clues there as to how to deal with this." Ethnobalt had been the ship vassal weapon hero when we first met him, but during the battle with Miyaji he had been chosen as the holder of the book vassal weapon. He was a race called a "library rabbit," so a book definitely suited him better than a ship. "There are legends saying that impossibly difficult problems of the past were solved by searching Ancient Labyrinth Library archives," he continued. That didn't sound like much to go on, but it was probably better than doing nothing at all.

"I'll remain here and continue to play a purification song, in order to impede the spread of the curse," Itsuki said. "Naofumi, you and the others can use that time to go and find a way to save her. How does that sound?" I didn't really have any choice but to nod to this proposal.

"Itsuki . . ." said Rishia, a little concerned for him.

"No need to worry, Rishia. We simply have to do the best that we can," he replied.

"I guess having you guys here, watching over and protecting

Kizuna, will make it easier for us to leave," I reasoned. It would not be amusing in the slightest if our base of operations was attacked and fell to the enemy while we were all out trying to find a book. The base being occupied would be bad enough, but it would also mean that we'd need to rescue Kizuna a second time.

Filo's singing would probably be good backup for Itsuki, and so I decided to ask her to stay too.

"I should also tell you that the Ancient Labyrinth Library is located some distance from the closest dragon hourglass. The round trip will take a while even if we use Return Dragon Vein. We need to choose the people to leave behind quite carefully," L'Arc added.

"Just what kind of place is the Ancient Labyrinth Library?" I asked. I had passed by it before but not really seen the place in any detail.

"You were dropped with Kizuna into the never-ending labyrinth, right, Naofumi?" Ethnobalt confirmed with me.

"That's right," I replied.

"The Ancient Labyrinth Library is a similar place . . . a massive maze that continues on forever. It is said to be the place that all knowledge in this world gathers . . . the destination of all books," Ethnobalt explained. I still couldn't really imagine a building housing what he was describing, but as a video game lover, I thought it was really ticking some boxes for me. It sounded something like the Akashic Records, a pretty common trope in my chosen forms of entertainment.

"Library rabbits are monsters who live in the library. We have the power to feel, somewhat vaguely, the location of books that people are searching for," Ethnobalt revealed. Now that sounded super convenient. They also seemed to be thinking that not having the ship vassal weapon was going to slow us down, but they seemed to be forgetting someone. Me.

"As far as getting there goes, I'm thinking the mirror vassal weapon's skill Teleport Mirror will get the job done. If my memory serves me correctly, I should be able to take us there as it's somewhere I've been before," I said. The mirror vassal weapon was pretty tricked out with movement skills using the medium of mirrors. It had a selection of various similar movement skills. The mirror was a pretty capable weapon when it came to movement abilities. Sharing traits with the ship vassal weapon, it had skills like Portal Shield and Scroll of Return. To say I had "been there before" was maybe a stretch, as I'd just dropped in briefly by way of Ethnobalt's ship. But I was pretty sure it would work out. "So there's no need to worry about movement time," I continued. "We just need to work out who is going to come along."

"Monsters will appear in the labyrinth areas, so we're going to want people who can fight," Ethnobalt added.

"Right here." S'yne immediately raised her hand. "In a special dungeon—"

"Lady S'yne is explaining that she has the perfect skills for use in a deep-level labyrinth," came the translation from her familiar. But it sounded a bit inconsistent to me. I wouldn't categorize a special dungeon and deep-level labyrinth as being the same. Surely "deep-level" meant a labyrinth that specifically went down many floors.

"You didn't say anything when we were in that labyrinth beneath the city where the music vassal weapon holder was hanging out," I commented, just a little snidely.

"In that dungeon—" S'yne started.

"Lady S'yne is saying that that place felt different from one in which her skills would apply," her familiar explained. I wondered for a moment if I'd be able to obtain that "feeling" if I trained harder.

"It's true that the underground labyrinth and Ancient Labyrinth Library have a similar structure, but the rules that apply to them are a little different. In terms of depth . . . I should think the Ancient Labyrinth Library goes deeper," Ethnobalt assessed. Reflecting on my own experience in the never-ending labyrinth, there had been different rules there, such as restrictions on transport skills.

"So what's this 'perfect skill' she has access to?" I asked. In response, S'yne turned her vassal weapon into a ball of thread.

"The labyrinth skill, Ariadne's Thread—" she replied.

"Using this skill will auto-map the area being explored. If the dungeon has rules that interfere with transportation, it can also ignore those and instantly transport you directly outside," her familiar said. That actually did sound really convenient. The kind of standard return skill that always showed up in RPGs.

"But isn't transporting a large number of people difficult for you, S'yne?" I asked. I recalled that when she used that skill to jump to a pin, she had said it was dangerous to take a group with her.

"That will be fine—" S'yne said.

"This skill is purely used for escape, so the burden is only about the same as when transporting alone," the familiar explained for her.

"I must say . . . the vassal weapons from other worlds have some truly incredible powers," Ethnobalt said, clearly impressed. Seeing as he was born there, he was probably impressed to hear about circumventing the building rules that he had been dealing with his entire life.

Still, Ariadne's Thread . . . That was famous in my world as the means used to escape the minotaur's labyrinth.

"So you'd be fine even if you got cast into the never-ending labyrinth, S'yne," I commented.

"Yeah," she replied. That really was convenient. If we'd had S'yne with us back then, we wouldn't have had to use the bioplants.

"That makes S'yne a fixture then. Add in Raphtalia and Ethnobalt . . . Glass, what about you?" I asked her. "Do you want to stay and keep an eye on Kizuna?" Glass glanced at Kizuna's room for a moment but then looked back at me.

"No. I need to prioritize finding a way to cure her," she replied.

"Pen!" Chris chimed in, moving toward Itsuki and displaying an intent to help him resist the curse. He was a shikigami, making him pretty resistant to this kind of problem. So Glass was going to leave Kizuna with Chris and come help search for the solution.

"Okay, that's fine with me," I said. "Anyone else?" I was pretty sure the killer whale sisters would want to come along—and indeed, they raised their hands next.

"Right here, little Naofumi. We don't want to miss out on the fun!" Sadeena said.

"That's two more!" Shildina added. I didn't see any major problem in taking the two of them along.

"L'Arc, what about you guys?" I asked.

"I'd love to tag along, but there's going to be a wave in a neighboring nation soon, so I need to go take part in their strategy council," he said. Of course, with most of the holy heroes gone, the frequency of the waves was really ramping up. Those nations working in cooperation with Kizuna and her allies had been bolstered by our recent deeds and were now tackling the waves very seriously. L'Arc taking part in such a council meeting was completely natural—and a good thing.

"Any chance it's some kind of trap?" I asked, just to be sure.

"That's my biggest worry, but I can't always fall back to relying on you when something happens, can I, kiddo?" L'Arc responded. Good point.

"The power of this accessory you have given me, Master Craftsman, will allow me to overcome any peril we face," Therese offered. I decided to just let her be.

S'yne proceeded to place a small needle into L'Arc's sleeve. She could use that to move around or spy on events at a distance.

"If this gets jammed—" she started.

"Lady S'yne says that if this pin is jammed or something happens to it, she will immediately inform you, Master Iwatani," her familiar relayed.

"That sounds like a good idea. If you can hold your council meeting in a place I've visited before, that would be useful too," I suggested.

"Sure thing. We're intending to hold it in the place Kyo controlled," L'Arc replied. I immediately knew the place he was talking about. When I was here before, I dropped in there by way of Ethnobalt's ship just before my departure. I should be able to travel there just using Return Dragon Vein.

"Okay then. Let's all get started," I told them.

"Sure thing!" L'Arc seemed pretty full of beans for some reason. And so Raphtalia, Raph-chan, Glass, Ethnobalt, S'yne, Sadeena, Shildina, and I all headed straight for the Ancient Labyrinth Library.

Chapter Two: Library Search

A mirror close to the entrance to the Ancient Labyrinth Library started to glow, and then my party and I leapt out from it.

"Looks like we made it," I said.

"It seems you've mastered control of them at will . . . but it feels a bit different from a transport skill, doesn't it?" Raphtalia commented. I just nodded. I'd used Transport Mirror to get here, which seemed like a unique skill for the mirror vassal weapon . . . but there was something that felt a bit odd about it. It wasn't like I had much choice right now, anyway—even with access to Scroll of Return or Return Dragon Vein, I couldn't use Portal Shield. I was just going to have to make do with these slightly more annoying skills until I could finally regain use of my shield.

Knowing that most of the holy weapons from this world had been captured continued to leave a bad taste in my mouth. The holy weapons were like the pillars that supported the world, and so having three of them in enemy hands was not good. Even worse, that had also led to the holy weapons from other worlds being sealed away. In regard to that point, Rishia used one of the seven star weapons, so maybe we should have brought her along. Too late now, anyway.

"Wow . . . that's a lot of books," Sadeena breathed.

"You said it. The library in Q'ten Lo has nothing on this place," Shildina added. Both of the killer whale sisters were looking around, eyes wide, like they just swam in from the boonies.

"I have returned," Ethnobalt proclaimed, to which a bunch of nearby library rabbits hopped over. They twitched their noses and seemed to be discussing something with Ethnobalt.

"Yes. Thank you for looking after everything while I was gone. Of course. I completely understand," Ethnobalt said.

"Who's that I see there . . . hey!" Just as we were about to start into the Ancient Labyrinth Library, someone called out and so I turned around—to see Altorese. This guy was another ally of Kizuna's, a merchant—or more like an information broker. He had a pretty androgynous appearance, probably more suited to being a poet or something along those lines. In our world, he would have held a position much like a slave trader.

"I heard that we had some heroes from another world over. I guessed it might be you and your crew, Naofumi," Alto said.

"Nice to see you again. Have you not heard that we rescued Kizuna?" I asked him.

"Of course, and I've been in touch. Your friends were really on the ropes for a moment there! It might sound cold-hearted, but I was seriously thinking about cutting all ties to avoid getting dragged down myself." Alto's tone was light, but

Glass gave him a real glare as he spoke. Merchants were loyal to money, first and foremost. They went where the wind blew rather than resist it. "That said, it's not like I've been selling information to their enemies either," Alto assured us.

"You sure about that?" I asked, only half joking. He replied with nothing but a chuckle.

"Which is it?" Glass was less inclined to stay quiet on the matter. "Depending on your answer, you may feel more than just my wrath." Raphtalia was also nodding at these words. The jokes of a free-spirited merchant clearly didn't mix with the two deadly serious girls.

"That response meant that he's done nothing of the sort. If you get all serious when interacting with a merchant, they will just mock you to pieces. Trust me," I told them.

"You do know a lot of merchants, don't you, Mr. Nao-fumi?" Raphtalia said. That sounded like a really loaded statement from her, but I wasn't about to get into that now.

"Alto, tell us what you're doing here," I said, moving on.

"I'm here for a periodic survey of the place. Kizuna has requested a long-term survey of this whole library thing. I've hired some adventurers who are in there as we speak, getting the job done," he informed us. It sounded like they were surveying the labyrinth, then, in an endeavor sponsored by Alto. This was a place packed with a serious volume of knowledge, after all.

"Have you found much of anything yet?" I asked.

"Regrettably, what with the wars and the waves, there aren't many adventurers showing up anymore. Best I've been able to do is sell off materials—at grossly inflated prices—to those who do stop by," Alto admitted. Business as usual, then.

"Tell me, did you see a bit of a flashy redhead, an arrogant guy in a suit of nobleman-looking armor, and a woman who looks like a bigger version of this girl here?" I asked while pointing at S'yne.

"Mr. Naofumi, I'm not sure that's enough information for him to go on," Raphtalia said.

"Right, you mean those three who L'Arc put a bounty on after that little encounter you all had? There are descriptions of them going around, but I definitely haven't seen them," Alto replied. Raphtalia looked at Glass and nodded. It sounded like information was getting around.

"I wondered if the descriptions we sent out would have got this far yet, but I clearly underestimated you, Alto," Glass said.

"When the wind is blowing, you can bet I'm riding it," he replied, almost making being a complete opportunist sound like something to be proud of.

"Oh my," said Sadeena, looking at Alto. Without Therese here, Sadeena probably didn't understand much of what we were saying, so it seemed wiser to me if she just kept her mouth closed. "Oh my, oh my!" Perhaps noticing Sadeena's gaze and attitude, for some reason Alto looked at me, seeking backup. Shildina also seemed to have noticed something and tilted her head while pointing at Alto.

"Is he the same as Keel?" she asked.

"Huh? Keel?" I replied. Why would she think Alto was the same as Keel? "Where exactly do you see similarities between that greedy little puppy and Alto here?"

"This is all your fault, Mr. Naofumi." Raphtalia rounded on me. "It pains me deeply that people can say whatever they want about Keel, and you've created that environment."

"Little Shildina. Sometimes it can be kinder to pretend not to notice something," Sadeena said—but she had made quite the show of noticing it herself! Whatever "it" was!

"I'm sorry, why are they all pointing at me and what are they talking about? I don't even understand the language they are speaking," Alto said, somewhat flustered.

"The killer whale sisters here are saying that you're the same as this little doggy we know, Keel, who kinda walks the line between being a boy and being a girl," I told him. Alto's smiling face suddenly gave an unexpected twitch. "Dammit, Alto . . . are you a woman?" I asked. He was pretty slender to be a guy and definitely had a feminine side to him . . . Keel was proving to be a successful merchant back in the village, so if Alto shared the same gender question mark, the two of them would really start to overlap in my mind.

"Huh?" Glass and Ethnobalt, meanwhile, were looking at Alto with puzzled expressions.

"Whatever are you talking about? You think I'm a woman? If you want to make a joke, at least try to make it a believable one!" His merchant's smile was quickly back in place, but that just made it all the more suspicious. Then there were the killer whale sisters! I couldn't help but wonder how they had seen through his masculinity so quickly.

"It doesn't really matter if Alto is a guy or a girl. Let's just put that aside and move on," I said.

"That would be a big help for me, no doubt, but I presume you want some information?" Alto asked.

"Even you can't possibly know that once we freed Kizuna from her paralysis, she was corrupted by a curse. And so, we've come here to find a way to treat her," I replied.

"Sounds like you've got a pretty serious problem on your hands. This place certainly is a repository for information from around the world . . . and they also copy and replicate documents here, so it's definitely a good place to search," Alto told us.

"Do you want to come with us?" I asked.

"I'll be waiting here, thank you very much. I don't like to get my hands dirty—or bloody, at least," he replied with a smile. He was a merchant, after all. His was a different battlefield.

"Let's head into the Ancient Labyrinth Library," Ethnobalt

said, leading us deeper into the building. We soon came to what looked like fairly provisional facilities: something that looked like an inn and then a tavern. I remembered seeing a row of shops in here before. Proceeding further inside, we came to a pretty fearsome-looking door. Beyond here lay the stairs down to the underground.

"Beyond here lies a labyrinth created by an ancient civilization. As I'm sure you are aware, Naofumi, it is an extremely dangerous place, so please steel your hearts before we enter," Ethnobalt explained, perhaps laying it on a bit thick.

"I've got a parting gift for you all," Alto said, passing us discs that looked like CDs. These were the same kinds of tools that Kizuna had used previously in the never-ending labyrinth. So they could be used here too. "Do you know how to use them?" he asked.

"I have some idea. They can take you to a registered spot inside the labyrinth, right?" I said.

"That makes this easier, then. Ethnobalt . . . do you have any idea where the book you are looking for is located?" Alto asked.

"Give me a moment." Ethnobalt gripped the book vassal weapon, spreading its pages out around us and focusing his concentration. It looked like he was using some kind of power of the book vassal weapon.

"The book has increased the accuracy of my ability to

search," Ethnobalt explained. "It's a big help. That said . . . our desired item appears to be pretty deep down."

"That might work out, then," Alto said brightly. "Those tools I gave you will currently take you to the deepest floor that we have reached. There's a door there that I wanted to get Kizuna to try and open—I'd appreciate it if you could give that a try. If it still won't open, just take the other path you see there."

These tools really were going to help us out.

He continued. "I'll also try collecting information on the people you are looking for and anyone else acting suspiciously. Having said that, we have gathered quite a lot of information already."

"Do you mean . . . about the harpoon vassal weapon hero?" Glass asked, to which Alto nodded. They say the one who controls the flow of information can control the world . . . but I had to wonder just how much information would sate Alto.

Even if we knew the location of S'yne's sister, we still didn't have any means to properly resist her. We needed to find any possible way to get even a little bit stronger—and in order to do that, we needed to heal Kizuna as quickly as we could.

"I need to say something else first," Ethnobalt said. "Please do not use fire magic under any circumstances. That is one of the rules of the Ancient Labyrinth Library." There had to be a good reason for that. In any case, I couldn't use fire magic.

"Let's get moving," I said. Everyone nodded. We tossed out our discs together, and they started to spin and create pillars of light. Then the discs passed through their respective pillars, and we headed after them.

When I thought about this world just in the context of this scene, it really was like being inside a video game.

Passing through the pillars of light, we emerged into a kind of passageway almost completely buried in books. One of the books was even flying around in the air like a butterfly. It was a monster called a Demon Magic Book. I was pretty repulsed by it already, and then the flying book bared its fangs and attacked.

With a surprised gasp, I quickly incanted Stardust Mirror and created a barrier, but the book spread its pages and spat water.

"Hah!" Raphtalia drew her sword from her scabbard and unleashed a slice in Haikuikku before sheathing it again. That took care of the closest of the book monsters, but a reinforcement flock was already heading toward us. *This was why you had to stay quiet in the library!*

"Yah!" Now Glass whacked one of the books with her fan.

"Formation One: Glass Shield!" I let one of the incoming books bite onto my Glass Shield. The fragments of glass that broke off weakened it.

"Hah!" S'yne used her scissors to chop up the books. We seemed to be defeating them pretty easily.

"Little Naofumi! Flying books? These really are fun monsters!" Sadeena enthused, getting a bit excited again.

"This is the big city now! Stop acting like some kind of country bumpkin!" I told her. Shildina seemed to be taking things a bit more in stride.

"There's a lot of them, so we'd better help out too!" Sadeena said.

"Count me in!" Shildina said.

"Just don't go too wild," I cautioned them. Sadeena proceeded to pierce a book with her harpoon, while Shildina imbued magic into an ofuda and then activated a spell. A blob of water emerged from the ofuda, drenching a book and finishing it off. From Ethnobalt's warning, it seemed fire wasn't allowed, but water was okay—I wasn't sure about the criteria there.

"There are some pretty freaky monsters out there, huh?" I said. These things were almost like those balloon monsters. I flicked through the pages of a defeated one to see what was inside. It was written in a language I couldn't read. Ethnobalt also picked one up.

"Are you going to copy that?" I asked him. This place was basically a locker of weapons for the book vassal weapon. There were countless potential weapons just lying around on the ground.

"... As I suspected, I can't copy monsters. Also, books have quality and category ratings. Every single book isn't handled as an individual weapon to be unlocked. Haven't you seen that too, Naofumi? A weapon that turns into something else when it's copied?" Ethnobalt asked.

"Yeah, I have," I responded. One example was the Spirit Tortoise Carapace. Maybe because it was connected to the Spirit Tortoise Heart Shield, it had turned into something other than the weapon the old guy had made for me.

"It has to be a book functioning as a weapon, and also the content of the book makes a difference," Ethnobalt explained.

"Hmmm . . . it's that simple, is it?" I said. It sounded like I'd be fine putting one into the mirror, so I tried it. The result was a mirror that looked like a folded book with the name "Mirror Demon's Book." The unlocking effect was magic plus three. This category of monster looked like it would have multiple types. Appearance-wise, it overlapped with the Book Shield.

The monsters also dropped a material called "intellect powder." Potions created using it could be sold for a large amount, and they had some kind of doping effect too. It was an item that was something like those seeds in that old RPG. Once per each material type, a hero could obtain levels just by unlocking the weapon from them. Even pennies can eventually become a fortune if you save enough of them. These were materials that adventurers who had reached the level cap hoarded like treasure. Maybe that explained why there were some pretty strong people in this world, even when those people didn't have a vassal weapon. I wondered if I should be collecting them for enhancement myself. There was probably an upper limit in place.

I got my mind back on track and checked out my surroundings. Just as Alto had said, it looked like we had arrived at a fork in the road. One branch had a large door, which was locked. The other one was open to carry on.

"Are we going through this large locked door?" I asked.

"Yes. That's what Alto seemed to suggest—that maybe Kizuna could open it," Glass said.

"So we're here to rescue Kizuna, but we need Kizuna to do it? We'll have to deal with that later. What's down there?" I pointed at the path without the locked door.

"There's a big maze down there. It hasn't been completely explored yet," Ethnobalt said.

"I'd say we're in a pretty big maze already," I commented. This place is a labyrinth, right? What is the difference? Additional pointless twists and dead ends?

"What's beyond the door . . . is what I'm getting at. Why did Alto think Kizuna would be able to get inside?" I asked.

"Just take a look at the door," Ethnobalt replied, pointing at large lettering written on it. It was pretty worn and I couldn't really read it, but it looked like some kind of relief. I'd seen a similar relief—or symbol—back in our world. The Church of the Three Heroes—or actually, it was the Four Holy Pillars—had a symbol a bit like this.

"It says 'four holies' in ancient letters," Ethnobalt revealed.

"I see. So the idea was that one of them might be able to open it?" I asked.

"That's right," he replied. There was a large gemstone in the place that looked like the lock. This definitely looked like something only one of the four holies could open. In that moment, the gemstone part of the mirror started to glow as though it was trying to say something.

This "something" was linked to my shield. Did that mean Atla's consciousness was trying to impart something to me?

"Do you think failing verification is going to trigger some kind of trap?" I asked.

"Honestly . . . I don't know," Ethnobalt admitted, somewhat reluctantly. I guess that was asking too much.

"We only just got here. If a monster comes out, we'll just have to defeat it. If something happens we can't handle, we can just leave," I reasoned. S'yne was already prepping to leave at a moment's notice. I stood in front of the large door and raised the mirror. The gemstone in the door started to glow and a shaft of light reached toward the mirror. Once that light reached the gemstone on the mirror, there was a clinking sound, the lock on the door unlocked, and the door swung heavily outward.

Another scene just ripped right from a video game.

"Looks like one of the holies from another world can still open it," Raphtalia said.

"Probably any holy or vassal weapon user," I said.

"It all seems to have worked out, sweet Naofumi, which is all that matters," Shildina said.

"A little optimistic, but okay. Can't you feel anything, Shildina? You can read stuff from old things, right?" I asked.

"Hmmm . . . unfortunately my precision has been falling a bit, and I'm not exactly omnipotent. This looks too old to extract any residual memories from—in fact, it's not really something that would collect them anyway," Shildina assessed. Okay, so that sounded like a complete bust.

"Let's get moving," I said.

"Sure . . . if you're sure it's safe," Raphtalia said, worried.

"Raph," said Raph-chan.

"Raph-chan is sensitive to these kinds of traps, right?" I confirmed. She struck a confident pose in response. This all looked legit to me. Just had to hope that things kept going this smoothly.

Beyond the door, we quickly reached some stairs that headed downward.

"Watch out for monsters," Ethnobalt said, cautiously looking all around. "I'm also going to investigate our surroundings a little as we proceed. We might be able to find some useful information."

"Sure thing," I replied. As for the monsters . . . they looked like nothing we couldn't handle. They were strong, but no match for some of the most powerful vassal weapon holders in this world. The only thing that did look of interest was what looked like a trashcan just casually placed along the path. It filled with what looked like a bunch of useful items. Glass and Ethnobalt said it was a treasure chest, but it really looked like a trashcan to me. There were other boxes that looked more like actual chests, that much was true, as well as little tricks and gimmicks with a treasure-hunt kind of vibe to them.

I looked at one of the bookshelves on the wall.

"With so many books, I bet there's some juicy info on the waves somewhere in one of them," I commented. Maybe something easier to understand than those ancient texts that even Rishia and Trash couldn't decipher. "Just what kind of books can we expect to find down here?"

"Well . . . stories written by unknown authors, and all sorts of varied materials. There are even some books mixed in that current world administrations are not especially pleased about the existence of," Ethnobalt explained. I gave a low whistle. I guess that came with the territory when talking about a library this size. "There's also a whole bunch that are so encrypted there's almost no way to read them at all."

"They won't be any help, then, even if they do talk about the waves," I mused.

"No need to worry on that score. You have a library rabbit with you; I can get the general gist," Ethnobalt replied.

"Really?" I questioned.

"Yes. I'm capable of determining if any texts that we encounter will suit our purposes or not," Ethnobalt replied. I mean, there was a bird whose greatest pleasure was to pull a wagon, so I guessed there could also be a rabbit with a book-searching function. "On that note, having investigated the immediate vicinity, I don't see anything that can be of any help to us, so let's carry on. It feels like it is a little deeper inside."

We continued onward, checking the books as we went.

In video games there were sometimes dungeons set in libraries, but I was now realizing that they really didn't capture the utter banality of looking for that one needle-in-a-haystack book in real life. Even when we relied on Ethnobalt's instincts, this was going to take quite a long time.

"Can't we just push forward as deep as possible first and then search as we come back out?" I suggested.

"That's not a bad idea . . . but we could easily walk right past the very thing that could end this entire expedition," Ethnobalt reasoned, even as he took down a book, leafed through it, and then returned it to the shelf. As he did so, the books from a nearby shelf whirled up into the air, forming . . . a dinosaur . . . perhaps. No, a dragon. The monster's name was "Magical Tome Dragon." Now things were really getting a bit crazy. A dragon created from books! Was this some kind of joke?

"Another pile of books. Another dusty old monster. Let's fight," I said with dry enthusiasm.

"Here we go!" Raphtalia said, a lot more eagerly than me. The battle itself . . . was hardly worthy of mention. Another resounding victory. Ethnobalt picked up the book that had formed the most vital organ of the Magical Tome Dragon and checked its contents.

". . . This one talks about the Demon Dragon. It also describes techniques it used through a complete understanding of the magic of the world to draw power from distant subordinates and form powerful magical spells," Ethnobalt said.

"Yeah, I remember that guy," I muttered. Back in our world, the Demon Dragon had taken over Gaelion, absorbed Filo, and then even hacked my shield.

"There's a chance that my library rabbit search ability latched onto this book because the Demon Dragon knows the way to break the curse on Kizuna," Ethnobalt mused. Then he wiped the dust from the book and placed it back on the shelf. The other books that had formed the dragon proceeded to also return to their shelves. Some of them were pretty beaten up now—I wondered for a moment if that would be a problem.

We continued to explore the labyrinth. However, the monsters that opposed us also continued to become stronger. We were still yet to face one that could break through my defenses, but Stardust Mirror was getting broken more often than when we arrived. It should be pretty enhanced by now . . . and S'yne was starting to breathe hard too . . . We clearly still were not up to full power in this world.

"Shall we take a short break?" I offered.

"Yes. That sounds like a good idea," Raphtalia replied.

"I can keep going," Sadeena said. "I've been getting lots of experience from this."

"Me too!" added Shildina. I mean, for those among the party who weren't vassal weapon holders—Raph-chan and the killer whale sisters—the experience in here was probably pretty tasty. For vassal weapon holders, having two or more of them fighting together meant they didn't earn any experience. With Raphtalia, Glass, Ethnobalt, and me here, we had a total of four. It did feel like a bit of a waste.

In any case, everyone accepted my proposal, and we decided to take a break.

"I'm not sure how these things work down here, but it's starting to get dark. We're not even allowed some kind of campfire?" I asked. We had been told that fire wasn't allowed, but I still didn't understand why. A little warm food right now would go a long way.

"No, not even a campfire. No flames of any kind in the Ancient Labyrinth Library," Ethnobalt replied, taking out a lantern that glowed with a magical light and placing it in the center of our circle.

"You said that when we came in here, but why? Lots of the monsters in here look pretty weak to fire, so it feels a bit unfair to say we can't use it at all," I reasoned.

"Well . . . take a look at this." Ethnobalt opened his book and muttered something, and a small flame appeared in the air. There was immediately a loud noise, and text started to float in the air all around him. It almost looked like something from a horror movie. Amongst all the text, there was some in Japanese that I could read. "No Fire Under Any Circumstances!" Ethnobalt extinguished his fire and the text faded away. It was like we were under complete surveillance, which was somewhat worrying.

"First you just get a warning. The next time your magic is sealed away for a while. Continue to ignore the warnings and powerful monsters are drawn to you. Persist even then and you will be forcefully ejected and unable to return for a certain period of time," Ethnobalt explained.

"I see. Just as you said, Ethnobalt, this is a labyrinth with a complete restriction on the use of fire," I said.

"Exactly. You can use pretty much anything else you like though," he replied. Water magic was going to get the books wet, so why was fire completely off the table? There was no asking for reason from a bizarre place like this, anyway. All this otherworldly junk could eat shit for all I cared.

"What a fun place," Sadeena said. "It's like fighting using the special rules back at the coliseum."

"Well, I'm glad you're having fun, but that doesn't resolve this issue," I said.

"It's not an issue for me," said Shildina dismissively. "I'm no good with fire anyway." She also made a good point—we didn't really have anyone with us who was particularly skilled with fire. Maybe my Shield of Wrath would fall under that category, but my weapon was currently the mirror and I didn't have access to that shield.

"Take turns keeping watch," I told them.

"I'm presuming that even you can't cook without fire, Naofumi?" Glass said. I wondered why cooking was coming up again now. Was she that scared of being force-fed more of my dishes?

"There's actually quite a lot of things I can make without any fire at all. I'm not Kizuna, but there's sashimi and other raw dishes, for a start," I replied, a little vindictively. And that was only if you strictly avoided foods that required a flame. "All I really need is some heat. Maybe have Sadeena . . . Hold on, we can't use magic from our world. I'll have Shildina use one of her ofuda to create lightning to heat a metal plate. Then I could cook on that." Shildina immediately looked excited to give it a try, probably due to me saying that it was something she could do and not Sadeena.

"Oh my," said Sadeena.

"Shall we do it?" Shildina asked.

"No need. What do we have here with us? Vassal weapons. No need to worry about how it tastes, just make some food," I told them.

"You aren't very choosy, are you, Mr. Naofumi?" Raphtalia said.

"I've no problem with people being choosy about eating delicious food, but that kind of defeats the point if you collapse from starvation," I countered. We could create food using recipes and our weapons. It always turned out as just regular food, not delicious, but not disgusting either. "I'll ask for your help if I need it, Shildina . . . but this will all be pointless if we eat too much and can't fight. Now take turns resting and then we'll get moving again."

"Definitely best to avoid eating too much," Glass said with a sigh. We proceeded to take turns resting.

After finishing our little library camping trip, we started to explore the labyrinth again. Both sides of the way forward continued to be lined with bookshelves, which appeared to stretch off into infinity ahead of us. Every now and then we came to an open space stacked high with bookshelves all around or had to climb a ladder to continue. At other times we found ourselves turning left, then right, then left again, but with S'yne's Ariadne's Thread and the killer whale sisters' ultrasound, we never got lost. Solving a maze was always easiest when looking at it from above. Expanding the range that could be seen, even just a little, could bring you closer to the exit. We also had Raphtalia and Raph-chan along, with their resistance to the kind of magical traps we were facing, so they were a big help too.

By the evening of our second day, however, I was really starting to wonder just how big this place was.

"Ethnobalt, is there still no sign of a book that could help cure Kizuna?" I asked. Ethnobalt proceeded to use his search skill again.

"We are getting very close," he reported. "Just a little more, I think." We proceeded to clear the maze and continued on a little further. Then Raph-chan, the killer whale sisters, and Ethnobalt all reacted at the same time to a bookshelf ahead of us.

"Raph!" said Raph-chan.

"Oh my?" said Sadeena.

"There . . ." said Shildina.

"There's something about that bookshelf," Ethnobalt confirmed. I moved over and stood in front of it.

"I wonder if we are going with a classic trope here," I muttered—referring to the old chestnut of pulling a certain book to make a secret passage open. Of course, this could all just be a trap—or pulling out a certain book might provide some kind of key or hints for a future puzzle.

"Right! I'm taking out the books!" I said.

"Go ahead," Ethnobalt told me. I proceeded to roughly

pull the books down from the shelves and quickly found one that seemed to be fixed in place. Upon close inspection, it wasn't even a book. It was a switch shaped like a book. I pulled it, and with a clunking sound, the bookshelf slid backward, away from me. *Okay, that was pretty cool.* It was my first time seeing such a setup in action. Beyond the new opening, however, was another large and decorative door like the one we had first entered in the labyrinth. Another shaft of light extended from the gemstone and touched the gemstone on the mirror, but then it flashed away with a crackle and was gone.

"Huh? It failed? Maybe this one needs a particular weapon to open?" I wondered.

"That could be the case," Raphtalia answered.

"I hope there's a way we can get this open . . . but I have a sneaking suspicion that we won't be able to," Ethnobalt muttered worriedly. He was from here originally, so he would probably know—and as it turned out, after we tried all of our weapons, none of them opened the door.

"This is a tough nut to crack," I bemoaned. "Not much we can do if we have to get all the vassal weapons or holy weapons together in order to proceed." All these annoying tricks and traps were finally getting on my last nerve. I started to wonder if we could just bust it down. Considering the steps taken against those using fire, we'd probably just get kicked out.

I looked at the relief on the door again, hoping for some

hints of some kind. It appeared to be depicting some kind of tree blossom.

"That looks like a flower," I said.

"Indeed it does . . . but what kind of flower is it?" Ethnobalt commented, seemingly puzzled.

"Sakura lumina," Shildina whispered quietly. I looked again and indeed it did have the same kind of look to it.

"Sorry, but probably not. That isn't a sakura flower," I said. It was definitely some kind of plant though.

Then I realized something.

"In our world, the closed-off nation of Q'ten Lo played the role of pacifier if the four holy or seven star heroes ever started acting out, right?" I confirmed.

"Yes, that's right," Raphtalia said.

"So even though this is a different world, they also have four holy heroes—meaning we may also find nations, technology, or roles similar to our world here as well, right?" I continued.

"You think the tools of someone related to that is the key here?" Raphtalia asked.

"Could be," I replied. At my response, Raph-chan clapped her paws. Then she leapt toward Raphtalia and pointed with a cry of "Raph!" It looked like she was about to start something.

"Why don't you try using your own power as a pacifier, Raphtalia?" I asked her. Regrettably, I was unable to use the power of the Sakura Stone of Destiny Shield in this world, but

Raphtalia should still be able to use her powers as Heavenly Emperor.

"I can use them as a skill . . ." she said.

"If you can do something to back up Raph-chan, we might be able to get this door open," I said.

"Very well. I'll give it a try," Raphtalia agreed. She proceeded to sheathe her katakana and hold it in front of herself. She regulated her breathing to match Raph-chan's and started to focus her power.

"Raph!" Raph-chan stamped down on the ground with one foot. A magic circle proceeded to appear on the floor, rippling out in sync with Raphtalia. It looked like she could definitely use the power of the Heavenly Emperor.

"Five Practices Destiny Field Expansion . . ." With a groan, Raphtalia staggered to her feet. Then Raph-chan let out a long and protracted "Raph!" Both of them were clearly doing their best, but the door didn't budge at all. I could tell they were pushing themselves harder than they should be. It seemed there was no way to just force this door open.

"Raphtalia," Glass said and moved over to the staggering Raphtalia, stepping into the magic circle in the process. That caused the pattern of the magic circle Raph-chan and Raphtalia had created to shake and quiver for a moment. Glass herself shone softly.

"Ah!" Glass, thinking she had—literally—put the wrong foot forward, attempted to move back from the circle.

"You're okay there, Glass," Raphtalia told her.

"Raph!" agreed Raph-chan. As Raphtalia smiled, Raph-chan collected something to create a ball of magic and pushed it into the door. With a faint clicking . . . the door quietly opened.

"I can't believe it actually opened," I said. In video game terms, it felt as strange as using the key from one dungeon to open the door in a totally different dungeon—like something that should never be allowed to happen was unfolding right before my eyes. It would have been just like me to think that the result was all that mattered, but in this case, even I couldn't quite accept it.

"Glass, what's your intuition here? Do you have any idea what just happened?" Raphtalia asked.

"Don't tell me, Glass is like the Raphtalia of this world? Could we really get that lucky?" I said. Could she really be the Heavenly Emperor of Kizuna's world? It sounded pretty implausible, but then there was Raphtalia herself—someone with the blood of a pacifier, right by the side of one of the four holy heroes.

". . . No, I'm sorry, but I've no idea how this happened," Glass replied.

"Maybe that happened because you are a Spirit," Shildina said. Yes, that could have been it. The requirements might just have been met by coincidence.

"Once we've saved Kizuna, it might be worth looking into

your family tree," I said to Glass. If we were lucky, we might find weapons close to those of the sakura stone of destiny or other useful information. Who knew where the hints Ethnobalt needed might be hiding, after all. "In fact, maybe some information like that is lying around somewhere in this library?" I said.

"There is a truly astronomical number of books stored here, so even with my searching instincts . . . I can only sense an approximate location," Ethnobalt explained. "It is quite a bit deeper in from here too." If there was something to be gained from it, we had to give it a try. It seemed like too obvious a hint to pass over. Half filled with expectations, half with anxiety, we pushed onward.

The first thing we found was a spiral staircase, which looked as though it headed away into infinity. The lack of bookshelves was a jarring change.

"Looks like we're going down," I said.

"Indeed," agreed Raphtalia.

"I can't wait to see what's down there!" Sadeena exclaimed.

"No need to get so excited about it!" I retorted. We weren't here on some kind of fun field trip. Even as I had that thought, however, I also wondered if being able to enjoy whatever this world—these worlds—threw at you was the only way to survive them. I wasn't quite on the level of the other three heroes, but it was possible to enjoy this experience a bit like a video game. You just had to be careful not to think of it as actually being one.

We headed down into what felt like an infinite pit. One piece of luck, at least, was that there were no monsters down here. We had no idea when this place had been created, after all, and it had been pretty tucked away behind the bookshelf and the door—it seemed unlikely monsters would be just hanging out back here. We continued downward and finally reached the bottom of the spiral.

That led to another corridor, which led to a switch. Flipping the switch made the wall slide open. I wondered if it was safe to think we were now leaving the secret passage. Having done so, anyway, we came out into a room. On the right side there was what looked like the inside of a closed door. On the left side . . . I did a double take. There were books floating like steps in the air, leading up to a floating chamber created from bookshelves.

"This place . . . might be the chamber of the master librarian. The legends do speak of such a place," Ethnobalt breathed.

"It feels like a pretty nasty monster is probably waiting up ahead," I commented.

"I sense it too, but that's no reason to consider giving up," Raphtalia said.

"That never crossed my mind. Everyone, just be ready to fight if we have to," I told them. Everyone nodded or voiced their agreement, and with me in the lead, we climbed the floating book steps and proceeded toward the chamber above.

"It doesn't look like there's any monsters here after all," I said, looking around. Nothing of the sort caught my eye. I was taken with the scary thought that the "boss" might only appear once we actually touched or took something. The chamber contained a glowing bookshelf . . . and, beyond that, a small red vial placed on a wooden table. The vial had a barrier surrounding it, seemingly indicating its importance. And the vial was also glowing. The walls of the chamber were rare for this place. In spots without bookshelves, there were murals or something painted on the walls. They looked like the walls of the pyramids, very symbolic. One showed a cat-like creature with wings. I wondered what that could be. The tail was too reptilian for it actually to be a cat. It even looked like it was wearing clothing. What was it, some kind of monster unique to this world?

It also looked like there were pictures of the holy weapons . . . and the vassal weapons too. They were depicted as though they were shining.

The small vial, meanwhile, contained a red liquid that looked like blood. I touched the barrier and it instantly dispersed. Picking up the vial, I gave the contents a sniff. It smelt like blood too.

"What is it, the holy grail?" Another trope that turned up frequently in this kind of fantasy setting—the blood of an ancient holy man.

"That might be the special poison written about in the notes left by the first master librarian," Ethnobalt pondered.

"That's also a thing, is it?" I asked.

"Yes, but the only record is in those notes left by the first master librarian. It looks like this is where he kept it," Ethnobalt replied. Shildina was looking at the vial with an incredibly suspicious look on her face, and then she spoke.

"I don't think it's either good or bad . . . but this vial has something incredible about it. Something other than residual thoughts," she explained.

"This vial?" I asked. I decided to try appraising it . . . and was shocked by the result. Maybe the information was too dense, or there was too much of it, because my appraisal failed. This really was something out of the ordinary, that was for sure.

"This stuff looks pretty dangerous," I said.

"The notes of the first master librarian described it. One drop means eternal pain, two drops means eternal loneliness, and three drops . . . means something truly terrible," Ethnobalt revealed.

"This is a totally hazardous substance," I commented, and whistled, wondering if it was intended to be used for suicide. Maybe this first master librarian rabbit took his own life using it, but why then leave it so carefully for those who would come after him? That said, it didn't look like there was much left. "Enough with the toxicology. What about the bookshelf?"

The moment I touched it, however, my fingers sparked away, rejected.

"Maybe we can't—" S'yne started.

"Lady S'yne says that maybe we can only take one of the two," her familiar relayed. "She has seen treasures like that in the past."

"What? So I've screwed things up by getting hands-on too quickly?" I said. It would be a real pain if that was the case!

"No . . . I think I have a different explanation," Ethnobalt interjected, reaching for the bookshelf himself. In the same moment, writing from the bookshelf started to crawl toward him across the walls.

"Watch out!" I pushed Ethnobalt aside and raised my mirror, but the writing passed right through me and flowed on toward Ethnobalt. He gave a gasp of surprise.

"Are you okay?!" I shouted. It looked like the writing was practically mobbing him, and then it just faded away.

"I'm fine. It looks like it was some kind of library rabbit verification device, and now I have the correct authority displayed in my field of view," he reported.

"Okay then," I replied. That sounded promising.

"Now I will use the authority of the master librarian to break the seal on the bookshelf," Ethnobalt said. He turned into his rabbit form and extended a paw. The light around the glowing bookshelf proceeded to scatter. It looked like the barrier had been removed. Then Ethnobalt took down a few books and started to read them.

"It looks like . . . this is what we came for. It explains how to break curses placed on the four holy weapons, among other things."

"Sounds good," I said.

"Also . . . there's an ancient text here, much like the one I gave Rishia," Ethnobalt reported.

"She said she couldn't decipher that one . . . but maybe she needs this book first?" I guessed. Ethnobalt showed me a page. The images on it did look very similar. There was also the winged cat thing that was on the walls of this room. It looked like it was attacking something that had a halo, but I couldn't really make anything out.

"Please decipher it with Rishia once we get back," I requested.

"Of course. When we discussed this matter before, it seemed she was further ahead than we are. If we work together, I'm sure we will proceed with uncovering the truth of the waves," Ethnobalt said.

"I'm counting on you," I told him. Ethnobalt continued to read the book about curses.

"Okay . . . it looks like that vial you picked up is also effective in removing any problems placed on the four holy weapons," he reported.

"Really?" I asked.

"Yes. It has multiple applications. It seems we have completed our mission," Ethnobalt said. He proceeded to take out his CD disc from his bag and imbue it with some kind of magic. "That completes registration of this location. Now we can come back here at any time, meaning we can leave at once."

"That didn't take as long as I was expecting. A bit anticlimactic for me," Sadeena mused.

"The faster we find it, the better, if you ask me," Shildina responded, quick to oppose her sister.

"That's right," Raphtalia added. I also thought it best that we reach our goal as quickly as possible.

"But there is still a path that goes deeper. It looks like this isn't the bottom floor," Sadeena said suggestively.

"In a video game, that would be optional content. There might be more powerful magic or better weapon recipes or materials down there, but also a tougher challenge," I told them. Raphtalia and Glass turned to look at the path downward, their eyes suddenly intense. I had to admit, I felt the temptation too. We did need to boost our strength as much as possible. "If it looks like we might have time, we can come back with Itsuki, Kizuna, and the others," I said.

"Good idea," Raphtalia said.

"We do need to concentrate on making some better food recipes first," Glass chipped in. She was still bringing that up.

"Searching for treasure is so exhilarating, right, little Shildina?" Sadeena said.

"I do enjoy searching for old casks of wine in sunken ships," Shildina agreed.

"Raph!" Raph-chan added. Sadeena and Shildina also worked salvage, so they probably had some idea how this felt. Raph-chan was now up on Sadeena's back, pointing the way forward.

"Are we not going back—" S'yne said.

"Are we going to continue deeper?" her familiar asked, rephrasing. S'yne's question all brought us back to ourselves, anyway.

"We're going back first. We've found what we came for, and I can't really see anyone else coming down this deep before we come back. S'yne, take it away," I said.

"Okay. Ariadne's Thread!" S'yne used her skill, instantly transporting us back to the dungeon entrance, and then we headed outside. Thus, we found the information required to treat Kizuna and escaped from the Ancient Labyrinth Library.

Chapter Three: Fishing Fool's Determination

After escaping from the Ancient Labyrinth Library, we returned immediately to Kizuna. As we did so, Ethnobalt read more from the materials that we found.

"It seems the content of that vial can remove any illegitimate power placed on the holy weapons or vassal weapons," he informed us.

"Well? Would you say the curse of sloth is illegitimate?" I asked. Rather than having been in the weapon all along, wrath had been more of a problem found inside my own heart. If the overflowing hatred that had boiled out of me and then been absorbed by the shield could be expressed as being "illegitimate," then the content of the vial could probably have removed it. On the other hand, if it was unable to remove the curse of sloth, that would mean curses like wrath and sloth were some form of function that had originally existed within the legendary weapons.

"I'm aware that it is hard to draw a firm line here. We will just have to give it a try," Ethnobalt said.

"Indeed," I responded. As it was so effective, we could probably also use it to cure curses. We were talking about a small vial so dense it couldn't be appraised properly, suggesting we probably wouldn't be able to replicate it. I'd learned quite a lot about potions and medicine myself, but I had no idea what that small vial contained. It could be some kind of drug or some kind of toxin. It looked like blood but also like some kind of condensate. In any case, it was definitely strange stuff. The sheer density of it made Shildina feel like throwing up. I had to wonder if it could possibly have any effect on Kizuna—but it was right there in the texts we had recovered, so we had to give it a try.

We returned to where Itsuki and Filo were holding back the corruption of the curse.

"Welcome back, Naofumi. It looks like you found what you were looking for," Itsuki said.

"Master! Welcome back!" Filo enthused.

"Thanks. We're all back safely. We found some other stuff too, but we need to treat Kizuna first," I said. I still wasn't sure about forcing something upon a patient that we weren't even sure would work, but we had to give it a try.

"Here you go, Glass." Ethnobalt passed the vial to her. "Simply apply it to Kizuna's hunting tool and it should take effect. Please go ahead."

"Very well," said Glass.

"I'll play some music to increase your resistance to curses," Itsuki said.

"And I'll sing too!" said Filo. The two of them both started making music. They complemented each other pretty well. Itsuki was drawing out the power of the musical instrument vassal weapon, making it sound like he was playing multiple instruments at once, and Filo also sounded like she was projecting multiple voices at once—I had no idea how she was doing that.

"I guess Itsuki is using magic to create that effect, but how is Filo producing multiple voices like that?" I asked.

"The higher varieties of humming fairy have multiple vocal cords. So they can produce more than one voice at a time," Glass explained. That sounded absolutely terrifying.

"If she can produce all of those sounds, surely she can use magic without me having to make her fly," Shildina complained.

"Tell me, little Shildina, do you only use your voice for incanting magic?" Sadeena asked. Shildina thought for a moment and then thoughtfully shook her head.

"No. I divide my soul and have each half perform the incantations. I use that to trigger the first magic and then incant some more," she explained. It all sounded a bit complicated to me. Even if she really dumbed it down, I was pretty sure I'd never be able to copy it.

"That's the sum of it, anyway. Even if Filo can do it in this world, it isn't something a filolial could do," I said. She did seem to be able to use the performance magic that she had learned here even when she was back home, but it had a very different quality to it. She could only pull off the easy stuff.

As we were chatting, the support magic was cast on Glass and she gained extra resistance to curses. It looked like Chris was also adding his own strength, providing a bit more protection for Glass.

"Kizuna, I'm coming to save you now," Glass said with determination in her voice. She proceeded to allow a few drops from the vial to fall onto the cursed weapon of the lounging Kizuna. The contents of the vial that fell onto the cursed weapon was immediately absorbed into it as a material. Immediately afterward, the accessory attached to Kizuna's weapon cracked with a loud splitting sound and then scattered into dust.

"Wow," I said. It seemed to have worked.

"Kizuna! Hurry up and change that cursed weapon!" Glass exclaimed to the still lethargic Kizuna.

"What? What a pain . . ." Kizuna said. She sounded completely disinterested and then fell asleep right where she was lying. She was elevating sloth to an art form. Maybe I wasn't one to speak, but if this was the effect of the sloth weapon, then it was terrifying indeed.

"Even allowing her to change weapons hasn't restored her will to act . . . This is serious. Maybe the curse wasn't illegitimate after all," I said. The accessory had been, but the cursed weapon itself was not. That was what it looked like.

"I thought destroying the accessory would bring her back . . ." Raphtalia muttered. The others all nodded their agreement.

"Kizuna! You can't stay like this forever! Come on! Stand up!" Glass started to berate Kizuna, unable to take this situation any longer.

"You can't keep coming to me with every little problem . . ." Kizuna mumbled, descending into snores again. That seemed to freeze Glass in her tracks, but I wasn't sure why. *Does she really rely on Kizuna that much?* From my point of view, Kizuna seemed like she was just having some fun doing whatever she liked.

"If you were put under this curse, Mr. Naofumi, and said the same thing to me . . . I might not be able to reply to it either," Raphtalia admitted.

"I think you'd handle yourself pretty well in this kind of situation," I replied. If I ever did end up like this, corrupted by a curse and out of control, I had faith that Raphtalia would stop me—and that she could do it by force, if she had to. She was pretty muscular, actually.

I might have to take it easier on her going forward.

"Ren once said it, didn't he, Naofumi? You were working as hard as a slave for everyone in the village," Itsuki mentioned.

"Itsuki, no need to bring that up now," I told him. I was no slave! That was one of the nastiest things Ren had ever said to me, something he would need to work to repay for the rest of his life.

"Kizuna! If you think I rely on you too much, at least prove yourself worthy of being relied on first! Like Naofumi!" Glass seemed to have decided that the only way to defeat Kizuna's shaky logic was to drag my name into it. I had to wonder why it always seemed to come back to me.

"Oh my," said Sadeena with a chuckle.

"Oh dear," added Shildina. I didn't need mockery from the killer whale sisters at that juncture either!

"That certainly seemed like the hardest thing for Mr. Naofumi to hear—" Raphtalia started.

"Raphtalia, can we please just stop talking about it? Otherwise, I'm going to spend all of tomorrow stroking Raph-chan," I threatened.

"Raph?" Raph-chan asked. It did the trick, though, because Raphtalia nodded and fell silent. Seriously . . . after all, I could be lazy sometimes too.

"I have doubts myself." Now it was S'yne's familiar who was voicing an opinion about me working too hard. I took breaks— I did—whenever I needed them. In fact, I got annoyed about having to do stuff far more often than not.

Meanwhile, there was no sign of the slumbering Kizuna changing her cursed weapon. In fact, her fishing rod looked even more dark and troubled than it had when I first saw it.

"It looks like she's becoming even lazier . . . like her sloth is intensifying," I said, unsure about the correct terminology in such an instance. It looked like the longer she did nothing, the more intense the condition became. I was starting to feel that, among all of the seven deadly sins, sloth might well be the one that could cause the biggest annoyance to other people once it became a weapon. It was powering up simply by Kizuna doing nothing and spreading its curse all around itself.

"I guess the silver lining here is that she doesn't even have the energy to use a curse skill . . . but if they start to be activated automatically, it's going to be hard to get her back," I pondered. Kizuna's level had already been reduced, so if this curse made her take even longer to recover, we really would be at our wit's end.

"Kizuna! Just change your weapon, please! Otherwise, I really will get mad!" Glass threatened.

"What a pain . . . Ah, napping is such fun . . . Working is for losers! NEET life forever!" Kizuna drawled.

"Why does working mean you lose? Lose what, exactly? What are you fighting?!" Glass asked.

"Different worlds, same crap," I muttered. It seemed Kizuna's own Japan was also overrun with the scourge of the NEET.

"Naofumi, do you know what Kizuna is fighting?" Glass asked me.

"The ones who say that kind of thing back where I'm from mean that they are fighting against society," I told her.

"What is this 'neat'? Someone who is very tidy?" she asked.

"Originally it was used to indicate young people 'not in

education, employment, or training,' but the way Kizuna used it, it just means 'lazy bum,'" I explained, shaking my head at having to do this, here in another world. It didn't help that after graduation I'd been likely to turn into one myself.

"'Sloth life forever.' That's what she said," Glass confirmed.

"She really has slipped into total lethargy. I'm starting to get scared that I might trigger the same curse myself," I replied. This whole "teleported to another world" gig was surely something young people who didn't want to work would dream about. After it had actually happened to me, I found myself with an annoying volume of things to do. Nowadays there were also people exhausted from work who envied the NEET lifestyle.

"You can seem a bit annoyed about having to . . . well, do things, Mr. Naofumi," Raphtalia said.

"I'll do my best not to end up like her," I promised. "Like cooking, stuff like that."

"You can slack off on the cooking if you like," Glass said, once again coming at me with the cooking stuff. What should I do instead, then?

"Ah . . . I can't even be bothered to breathe . . . Can someone breathe for me please?" Kizuna asked. This might be a terminal case. The cursed accessory had been removed and yet she was still lazing around. It didn't look good for saving her from this.

"Ethnobalt, you got any ideas?" I asked. The book we found had information on breaking curses, after all.

"Well . . . it says that a diligent mental attitude is required in order to break the curse of sloth," he reported.

"Diligent, huh?" I replied. In order to break the curse of wrath, I had needed the mercy of Atla, but that didn't sound like what was going on here. I was also well aware that I had no mercy to give anyway. Getting back on track, the issue was that Kizuna didn't show a single shred of diligence at the moment.

"Have you heard of the seven great virtues, intended as the opposites of the seven deadly sins?" Itsuki asked. "There is some debate about their content."

"I've heard of the concept, yeah. But I don't recall them being all that clearly defined," I replied. The seven deadly sins had started out as the eight evil thoughts. There was little evidence that the seven virtues would be able to directly oppose the sins—they weren't even exact opposites. It would just depend on how the weapon perceived what was happening. "That said, we don't have many options on the table. Ethnobalt, is there no other way to cure sloth?"

"It also says that hope and bravery have the power to scatter sloth," he said.

"Oh boy . . . that's a lump of putrid sugar if ever I heard of one," I muttered.

"I don't think you should be dismissing the idea out of hand, Mr. Naofumi," Raphtalia chided me. I knew where she was coming from, but it just sounded so corny.

"So Kizuna's own diligence, combined with hope and bravery . . . it sounds like she just needs some motivation, basically," I surmised.

"I'm not sure that's exactly what it adds up to . . ." Raphtalia responded.

"Sloth—the desire to do nothing—is opposed by motivation, right?" I replied.

"You might be right . . . but that still doesn't tell us what to do," Raphtalia bemoaned. Glass, meanwhile, looked like she was checking something in her status.

"Naofumi," she finally reported, "it seems there's some candy—rainbow candy, it's called—that can be used to boost motivation."

"You want me to make some? Do we have the ingredients?" I asked.

"Hmmm, it looks like it uses some pretty rare stuff," Glass replied. Even if we had the recipe, that still meant another bug hunt for all the ingredients. Even as we did that, Kizuna was clearly going to continue to get worse. Quite aside from anything else, the cursed weapon she was holding was a fishing rod. She was the Hunting Hero and had quite a range of weapons at her disposal, but this one was a fishing rod.

Then it hit me.

"Glass, considering how long you've known Kizuna for, aren't you going about this in a bit of a roundabout fashion?" I asked.

"What should I be doing?" she replied.

"I've got an idea. Let's give it a try. Rather than stand around thinking, we need to start getting Kizuna motivated," I said. Then I turned and looked over at the killer whale sisters.

"Oh my!"

"Oh dear!"

"Is this really going to work?" Glass asked.

"That all depends on Kizuna," I replied. I had carried her on my back from the castle to the port in the adjacent town. Then we had boarded a ship owned by L'Arc and headed out into the offing. "If it doesn't, we'll just think of something else," I said. Kizuna, for her part, was still completely out of it. I had Itsuki, Filo, and Raph-chan boost my curse protection and then took Kizuna by the hand. Then I forced her to swing her arm, sending the fishing hook on the end of her rod out into the ocean, where it splashed down heavily into the water, looking more like an attack than just casting her rod. After a short while, the line dipped low into the water and the reel started to spin at high speed.

"Good! You've got this! Killer whale sisters!" I shouted. This was the entirety of my plan: bring Kizuna out to the ocean and motivate her by getting her to do some of the fishing she so loved. However, I figured some regular old weak fish weren't going to motivate her to do anything. However, I thought, what about a powerful fish . . . well, I mean a sea creature that pulled the line directly toward the seafloor? That was when I had turned to the killer whale sisters, Sadeena and Shildina, for their aid. They were by far the best swimmers we had access to. Itsuki had already cast support magic on them, and they had raised their levels considerably since coming to this world. They could easily play the role of monster fish, pulling harder than any lazy denizen of these waters.

I was staking the entire operation on Kizuna's passion for fishing.

With a whirring sound, Kizuna's slackline was pulled tight as it continued to play out from the reel. I touched the reel and stopped the line for a moment, and the rod pulled so hard our entire ship leaned to the side.

"Kizuna. Do you really love fishing? It doesn't look like it to me," I taunted her, even as she made another listless noise.

"Mr. Naofumi, the ship is going to tip over! Are you sure about this?!" Raphtalia asked.

"Tell me you're sure! This isn't Ethnobalt's ship!" Glass added.

"Fehhh?!" Rishia contributed.

"Don't worry, Rishia. Even if we do sink, I'll play a song to make us float," Itsuki said reassuringly. I wonder where he picked that up from. He was becoming quite the jack-of-all-magic.

"Raph!" exclaimed Raph-chan.

"Shall we sing a sinking song? Mel-chan told me about monsters called sirens that sing songs and sink ships," Filo said. I seemed to recall this topic coming up back at the Cal Mira islands. I needed to warn Filo to pick her spots to start singing, otherwise she might get mistaken for a siren or nereid herself.

"If you want to fish—" S'yne said.

"Lady S'yne is recommending the use of a fishing net," her familiar reported. "She says that using a fishing rod is extremely inefficient." I shook my head. Now was hardly the time for comments like that! However, that very comment also made Kizuna visibly twitch. It might actually be working!

Dragged by the killer whale sisters, the ship started to move along. Kizuna still showed no sign of taking real action. Seriously, it was feeling like the curse was going to jump to me in a moment. Even though my weapon had changed to the mirror, the Shield of Compassion should still be providing some curse protection . . . but I guess I had no choice.

"This is the extent of your fishing spirit? I'm disgusted," I said, increasing the intensity of my taunting. Kizuna twitched a little, as though she was convulsing. But I might just have been imagining it. The fishing rod in her hands bent and quivered unnaturally. It was starting to look like all of this was just serving to power up her sloth. A weapon that got stronger just by doing nothing really was a pain in the ass.

The shape of the fishing rod itself wasn't really changing

much, however. So why was it shaking so hard? The strange aura Kizuna was continuing to give off . . . suddenly started to scatter, starting from around her chest. Then Kizuna's eyes opened wide and she stamped down on the deck.

The next thing from her mouth was an impassioned roar.

She shook off my support, placed one foot up on the lip of the ship's railing, gave a determined grunt, and started to reel like crazy.

"I never felt a pull like this before in my life! This feeling . . . this power! I can't let this one get away!" Kizuna shouted.

"Kizuna! You've got your motivation back!" Glass exclaimed, her expression instantly brightening.

"I can't believe this worked," Raphtalia said, shaking her head.

"Fehhhhh!" Rishia yelled, while Itsuki started playing some up-tempo music to set the mood. It felt like everything was finally working out!

"Raise the fishing flag!" Filo started to sing, mixing some bizarre lyrics with rhythmic noises. "We're the true fishing masters!" I hoped it wasn't one of the sinking songs she had been talking about. As I tilted my head in puzzlement, Filo was able to explain it even as she continued to sing.

"I heard some people singing this in a tavern in Q'ten Lo. I'll also sing something from the village in a moment," she explained. Fishing had been pretty big business in Q'ten Lo. It made sense that there would be some fishermen in the taverns there. Sadeena and Shildina liked fishing too. Lurolona village, which I had restored, was also originally a fishing village, so I guessed they would have some fishing songs.

Itsuki and Filo provided more background music as Kizuna desperately continued her fishing battle. Sadeena and Shildina didn't seem ready to lie down and just get fished out of the sea, however. They started to move left and right at incredible speed. Kizuna's rod bent even further. The light of magic started to glow from under the waves. Glass had told us that Kizuna would sometimes hook a fish-type monster, causing it to counterattack with magic to avoid capture. It looked like Sadeena and Shildina had decided to also recreate that situation. The magic was from an ofuda.

"This rod is so hard to use!" Kizuna complained, groaning and growling. "The reel is so stiff! And my body feels so heavy! Give up? Never! There are fish to be caught beneath those waves!" Her frustration with the situation was reaching its peak . . . and as though she was resisting the very sloth that was infesting her, the smoking rod started to change shape.

"Kizuna!" Glass exclaimed, her expression lighting like a candle as Kizuna finally changed her weapon completely from the sloth rod. Kizuna roared louder than I thought her little body was capable of.

"I'm catching this fish!" With energy flowing from her entire body, she unleashed a skill. The therianthrope forms of Sadeena and Shildina were pulled from the waves and flew up into the air.

"Oh my!"

"Oh dear!" I heard them exclaim. Then they landed on the deck. They had recovered in the air and landed on their feet. There was no doubting their physical abilities.

"What a surreal scene," Raphtalia said, narrowing her eyes and shaking her head.

"Raph," Raph-chan agreed.

"This is pretty much what I'd expect from Kizuna," Ethnobalt said, smiling wryly.

"Great! That was close! I just managed to catch it . . ." Kizuna struck a victory pose and then actually saw the killer whale sisters. "Them? I caught them? And who are they?" Then she looked around at everyone else on the boat. "Huh? Naofumi, what are you doing here?" It looked like she had finally grasped the situation, at least to some degree.

"Nice to see you again . . . I guess I should say. I did talk to you after we turned you back from stone," I told her.

"I remember now . . . that guy who took L'Arc's scythe tricked me and I was captured . . . Then they put some strange accessory on my hunting tool . . ." she murmured. It seemed her memory was still a bit fractured.

"First things first, let's take a rubbing of these fish! Glass! I've landed two big ones today!" Kizuna enthused. Her fishing spirit, which even sloth had been unable to quell, quickly alleviated the tension among everyone on deck. Glass almost immediately changed from happy to joining Raphtalia in disapproval.

"Is everyone who comes from this 'Japan' a bit strange in the head?" Glass wondered.

"Mr. Naofumi definitely is," Raphtalia said. How rude! There was no way I was on the same level as this fishing fool!

"Oh my. She wants to take a rubbing of us," Sadeena said.

"Very well. I've got size to match you, Sadeena," Shildina responded.

"Oh my! You really think you can defeat me, little Shildina?" Sadeena mocked.

"Stop thrusting your breasts out," I told them. "What exactly are you expecting to get rubbed?"

"Hmmm . . . this feels odd. Like I've been tricked into something," Kizuna said. The killer whale sisters' joking around meant Kizuna gave up on taking her rubbing too. Chris, who had been supporting the sisters, popped out from the water with a squeak and struck a pose on the side of the ship, celebrating the successful mission.

"I also remember someone suggesting we use a fishing net! I'm never going to allow that!" Kizuna seethed.

"I bet you wouldn't allow our harpoon fishing either, would you?" Sadeena said.

"Of course not! Fishing is about rod and fish, that's it! A one-on-one battle!" Kizuna stated.

"Sure, sure, whatever." I didn't care about any of that. All that mattered was that Kizuna had escaped from the clutches of the rod of sloth and was back to normal.

Chapter Four: Sisters and Jealousy

After confirming Kizuna's recovery, we docked the boat back in the port and then returned to L'Arc's castle.

L'Arc greeted her. "Oh, Lady Kizuna! You're back with us!" He was back from his big meeting.

"Pretty much. I'm still not sure about a lot of stuff that happened . . . Naofumi is suddenly here, and Ethnobalt's weapon has changed . . . A lot has happened," she said.

"Kizuna!" shouted another voice, one I vaguely thought I'd heard before somewhere. I looked over at the speaker but only saw a couple of the soldiers who guarded L'Arc. I wondered why these grunts were showing such an interest in Kizuna's recovery.

"Huh?" Kizuna was tilting her head in puzzlement too. Even she didn't know them!

"You don't recognize me?" the speaker asked.

"I mean, I kind of do . . ." Kizuna said defensively.

"I have no idea," I said flatly.

"Even the hero from another world doesn't know me? Seriously?" the speaker said. I really didn't have a clue. They also seemed pretty brazen to act like that, being just common soldiers. Then the speaker, as well as the person standing next to her, proceeded to take off her helmet . . . to reveal Yomogi and Tsugumi.

Yomogi had been Kyo's woman, but he had almost disposed of her due to her recklessness, and Tsugumi had been Trash II's woman.

"How are we meant to recognize you with your faces hidden!" I shouted. "We're not friendly enough for me to know you from your muffled helmet voices!"

"He makes a good point," Raphtalia said, siding with me for once.

"Yomogi has been acting as a goodwill ambassador since you left, Naofumi," Glass explained. I looked at Yomogi again. I recalled being told that she'd opened a dojo next to Romina's store and had been heading out to quell the waves in other nations.

"This wild boar of a woman, a goodwill ambassador? If you're going to make a joke, at least make it funny!" I said.

"Who's a wild boar?!" Yomogi raged back. I thought she was going to come right for me. She was lucky I just didn't call her a traitor, to be honest. "With Kizuna captured and Lord L'Arc and the others caught up in the fighting, we've been providing support as reinforcements," Yomogi explained.

"Ah, okay then," I said. Kizuna had been pretty good to them, so they were just repaying that favor.

"Thank you. You've been a big help. My recovery is thanks to you all," Kizuna said.

"All for the sake of the world and the sake of its people. It's no trouble," she replied. Kizuna had a lot of folks like this among her allies—people who had started out as enemies but then became allies. If I fought someone as an enemy, there was generally no coming back—there were exceptions, like Sadeena and Shildina, so it was probably better not to generalize.

"You too, Tsugumi?" I asked. At first she didn't reply, just stared at me silently. She probably hadn't forgiven me for everything that went down with Trash II. I'd never thought I'd see her again, but here we were.

"She's not wrong. I'm doing everything I can to repay Kizuna's kindness," Tsugumi finally said.

"Oh?" That was an unexpected answer. Kizuna was great at making people better versions of themselves, that was for sure. I never had been able to make peace with these two.

"Tsugumi also spends quite a lot of time with Kizuna," Glass said.

"That's right," Kizuna chimed in. "Her name sounds a lot like my big sister's. She's much cuter than my sister too, and so I felt like I wanted to get closer to her." Kizuna circled around Tsugumi, looked her in the face, and then looked at me. Tsugumi looked a bit embarrassed, not sure what to do. She was making Kizuna feel a little homesick, from the sound of it. I was then told that Kizuna's sister's name was Tsumugi. I wasn't sure if they sounded similar or not. Then I was told her younger sister's name was Kanade, but by that point I was receiving more information than I needed. The "fishing sisters," I'd probably call them.

I did wonder about that . . . Should I encounter someone with a name like my own brother, would I give them special treatment? I took a moment to think about what he was doing. His head was probably still just stuffed full of thoughts about food, studying, and his girlfriend.

"Wow, so you've switched to Kizuna? I feel sorry for whoever you liked before," I jibed.

"That's not what this is!" Tsugumi quickly said. Glass seemed to look upon that answer a little coldly. Perhaps feeling Glass's cool gaze, Tsugumi gave a start and then calmed down. It all seemed very suspicious.

"Indeed, that's not what this is," Glass stated firmly. That looked like a flash of jealousy. Was it okay to make that determination? Was it okay to tease her a little?

"Mr. Naofumi, please stop making that face just before you tease someone," Raphtalia said. She had a read on me by now. I really needed to work on my poker face.

"Enough of this, anyway. You are both operating out of that dojo next to Romina's studio, correct?" I asked.

"It was too cramped to stay in Kizuna's place, and we couldn't stay in the castle forever either. So we borrowed that place," Yomogi said.

"We've been traveling a lot recently, but if Kizuna is back, then we'll probably be around more too," Tsugumi added.

"Okay then," I replied, wondering exactly why they were being this cooperative. Was it Kizuna and her charisma? I really couldn't understand why that fishing fool was quite this popular. As I puzzled over the issue, Raphtalia sensed my confusion.

"Another reason Yomogi and Tsugumi are working with us is because there is a traitor among those who gathered with them under the banner of a man they had feelings for," Raphtalia explained, with some exasperation. "They are currently among those we captured during the previous battle."

"Right, I did hear something about that. The one who leaked the information on the heroes' power-up methods, right?" I said. Yomogi wasn't the only one Kizuna saved, after all. There had been quite a few others who Kyo had also been modifying, and now one of those had turned traitor.

"That's right," Raphtalia confirmed. At her explanation, Yomogi and Tsugumi gave uncomfortable coughs and averted their eyes.

"A sad state of affairs. I have already fought more than enough of my former comrades . . ." Yomogi muttered.

"Kyo is gone. I'm not against them finding someone new to love, but I wish they would choose that person with more care," Tsugumi added.

"Old habits die hard," I said. Kizuna showed them a sliver

of compassion, reducing their crimes even though they weren't repentant, and immediately they turned to betrayal. Now these two were practically forced to cooperate in order to clean up this mess. I could hardly imagine how hard that must have been on them.

"We wanted to aid in the defense of the castle, but the allies of the one who stole L'Arc's scythe also attacked our homeland. Then we were helping them prepare for a wave, so it took us longer than expected to get back. My apologies," Yomogi explained.

"We must offer our unvarnished thanks for all you have done, Naofumi," Tsugumi added.

"That's a pretty roundabout way of thanking me . . . but I guess we're never going to be closer than this," I said. Both girls gave nods. The complexity of the situation was clear on their faces.

"One other thing, Naofumi. I heard you encountered someone like Kyo in your world too?" Yomogi asked, looking at me again.

"You mean Takt?" I replied.

"That's right. Kyo maintained a certain distance from us, but there were still those who did whatever he told them to. One wrong step and we could have ended up executed too. Pretty scary, when you think about it," Yomogi said.

"You escaped the axe because you started working with

Kizuna so early in the proceedings," I recalled. Having at least one person like that among Takt's forces would have been great. In his case, anyone showing signs of acting like Yomogi had acted was promptly kicked out or killed off in an "accident." It seemed that Yomogi had heard that too. Kyo had given her a suicide bomb in an attempt to end her recklessness.

"It would have surely been the same result if only those who truly believed in Kyo had tried to take over the world and been defeated. Considering the trouble they would have caused if they had been left alive after Kyo died, I think the punishment was a fitting one. We had a lot of trouble too," Yomogi said. I could tell they had been through a lot. Those events probably caused their fair share of trauma—in those cases I could only say that they got what they deserved. Someone like Eclair would likely have been arrested and disposed of within the group.

"Is it true that Kyo was a vanguard of the waves?" Tsugumi asked me, one eyebrow raised.

"The only answer I can give you is a provisional yes, according to the Shield Spirit or whatever it was I was talking to. We still don't know anything about the one behind him," I replied. The Shield Spirit and Atla had called them the "World Eater." I'd explained all this before, so they had probably heard it too.

"In which case . . . based on the similarity in their behavior . . ." Tsugumi muttered. It sounded like she was recalling

Trash II. No doubt about it. Trash II had been called a genius in his own nation, and there was evidence of him causing some serious trouble. The moment he learned that we had the katana vassal weapon holder amongst us, he had attacked and tried to kill her too. Without even understanding the situation, it would have made more sense for him to discuss things first. But his attitude had been as though obtaining that weapon was his basic right. "Hearing about the power to steal vassal weapons settles it, I think. He probably thought that killing Raphtalia would have allowed him to obtain the katana vassal weapon. That's the only way to explain his major arrogant attitude," Tsugumi said. She'd been paying attention too and had some understanding of the meaning of what she saw—something else that distinguished her from the women surrounding Takt.

"You think the katana vassal weapon has gone to the wrong person?" I asked.

"No . . . looking at the current situation, I definitely can't say that," Tsugumi said, shaking her head in response. "After you left, we joined Kizuna in fighting the waves. I started out underestimating them, but now I could never consider just accepting them, not after all the tragedy I've seen them cause."

Talking with Yomogi and Tsugumi made me wonder if we could have explained things to Takt's harem. *Nope, probably not.* Tsugumi was one thing, but Yomogi was totally different. When someone she liked and common sense were placed on the scales, she was the kind to lean toward common sense. She wouldn't get along with those who just took everything from the one they loved as fact.

Indeed, her attitude was totally different from the one Takt's sister had displayed at her execution. Now that had been one twisted individual—going on about making Melty her slave and saying that Takt had done nothing wrong. Tsugumi had harbored her doubts about Trash II's actions, making her completely different on a basic level.

"I owe a great debt to Kizuna, one I still haven't repaid. I have no qualms about continuing to work with her, even if that includes the ones who killed . . . him," Tsugumi said. There was no sign of anger or a desire for vengeance on her face. No problem then. This meant both Yomogi and Tsugumi were going to help in our ongoing fight. They didn't appear to have any desire to betray us—in fact, they would probably report it themselves if they did discover anyone spying.

"I'm starting to feel a bit embarrassed about all this . . . Think we can blow off this stuffy atmosphere and celebrate a little?" Kizuna asked, looking pretty abashed.

"Great idea! The return of Lady Kizuna is definitely something to be celebrated! Let's go wild—" L'Arc started, and then suddenly his face froze when he looked at me, almost as though there was some reason he didn't want me around.

"Okay! This might sound presumptuous, coming from me,

but I'd like to celebrate this reunion with Naofumi and the others too!" Kizuna said.

"Kizuna! Quiet!" Glass hissed. She was also looking warily at me. I wondered if this was just a new bit they were trying out. It looked like a "don't press this switch! Whatever you do, don't press it!" kind of moment. Very well then, I thought. *I'll press that switch as hard as you want!*

"If you're all so keen to celebrate, I'll cook the best damn meal you've ever tasted!" I shouted.

"Hooray!" said Filo, who had been quiet while the adults talked, and now started rushing around happily.

"Brilliant! Parties are always so much fun!" said Kizuna excitedly.

"Yes, they are," Yomogi said, a little unsure.

"So much fun," Tsugumi added. The two of them didn't really know what was happening, clearly, but were just matching Kizuna's attitude.

"Dammit . . . here we go again!" L'Arc spat, a repulsed look on his face. It had been ages since the last "feeding." Surely, he could cram some more in now.

"L'Arc . . . sometimes you just have to accept things," Glass said.

"All shall be as the Master Craftsman desires," Therese intoned. That was probably going a bit far.

"Glass, Raphtalia, what's going on?" Kizuna asked.

"Well . . . the upshot of it is that we can all get stronger," Glass replied. "You'll see for yourself soon enough. I don't think this is something we can get away from. It's also going to make you pretty passionate about finding more efficient cooking ingredients."

"Whatever do you mean?" Kizuna pondered. I wondered which side she would end up on. Hopefully, it would be the side that ate a lot.

"A celebration sounds like the perfect place for you to help me out with something," Ethnobalt proposed. "A certain ritual that I need to perform."

"Something happening?" asked Yomogi.

"Huh?" said Tsugumi. They both had similar reactions.

"Yes . . . Naofumi. Can you take me to the Ancient Labyrinth Library before the start of the party? There's a meeting taking place with my tribe about that vial," Ethnobalt explained.

"Huh? Sure thing. I'll have the staff in the kitchens start the basic preparations and then take you over there," I replied. We all split up and started preparations for the party tonight.

With Kizuna along, we returned to the Ancient Labyrinth Library. It felt like I'd been going back and forth all day. S'yne had said she wanted to get the party venue ready and so stayed behind in the castle. She'd even played a clown before, so I guessed she enjoyed celebrations. Sadeena and Shildina, meanwhile, had been poised to raid the castle wine cellar.

"It's a bit strange, Naofumi, being told you're using the mirror vassal weapon now. It just looks to me like you're using a shield that looks like a mirror," Kizuna said.

"It feels like that to me too," I admitted. Honestly speaking, that's basically what this was. It even had numerous skills that simply had a different name and could be used almost the same way as with the shield. The changes in movement skills were a bit of a hassle, perhaps, but it was still just a different version of the same thing.

"So there's still a question of what to do with this vial?" Kizuna asked.

"Your weapon absorbed it as a material," I told her. "Did that change anything?"

"Huh? Now that you mention it, I do have something called the 'Hunting Tool 0' here," she realized. Kizuna changed her weapon. It looked like a pretty simple fishing rod, nothing more.

"Any special effects?" I asked.

"It's equip effects are Judge of Reason and World Protector. For unlocking it, you get the skill Hunting Tool 0—same name," she reported. That was pretty odd in and of itself.

"Any useful abilities?" I inquired.

"It's just a '0.' Nothing more," she replied.

"What?" I said, surprised.

"It doesn't seem to increase anything," she explained.

"Okay . . . and it isn't cursed or anything?" I asked, just to make sure.

"I'm not seeing any penalties or anything either," she confirmed.

"Hmmm . . . if possible, I'd like to have some of that liquid for the rest of us to use as materials," I said. I took the vial from Ethnobalt for a moment and checked how much was left. Not much, to be honest, especially for everyone who could use it. It sounded like the bunnies were going to use it in some kind of ritual, so I'd just ask for whatever—if any—was left after that.

"I've been told that's pretty potent stuff," Kizuna said.

"Some kind of toxin, apparently. But it sounds like it can be used effectively under the correct conditions," I told her. It had done us the service of only destroying the accessory that had been attached to Kizuna's hold weapon, after all. But as one well versed in making medicine, I understood how dangerous it could potentially be. Too much of anything could become poison, and this was definitely a case of that—use of the precise volume was surely vital.

"I think I'm going to have to drink it," Ethnobalt said. I made a surprised noise. Drinking poison didn't sound like a good idea.

"Are you suicidal?" I asked.

"No . . . but I am the master librarian. If this is something left by the first master librarian, then I have a duty to test it," he replied.

"That's how things work around here?" I asked.

"That's not all this is, of course. Have you noticed, Nao-fumi, how I'm larger than the other library rabbits?" Ethnobalt inquired.

"I mean, I didn't want to say anything," I said. I'd seen plenty of the other bunnies when we came through here before. Ethnobalt was not only bigger than the others; he could converse with humans too. It didn't seem to be because he had been raised by a hero, which made this something of a mystery. That reminded me of the plan we had discussed to have a hero raise a library rabbit. I asked about it later and was told that the growth type had turned out to be the same as Rishia, but the rabbit hadn't grown as much as Ethnobalt. It was bigger than others, but Ethnobalt was still the biggest.

"My size is because of the potion that the rabbit who will become the next master librarian must drink," Ethnobalt revealed.

"Wow, okay . . . and?" I asked.

"That potion is made from a whole bunch of ingredients . . . in an attempt to recreate this poison here," Ethnobalt continued.

"I see. So what you're saying is this might have been something that a library rabbit used to have to drink in order to become master librarian," I surmised. The death of the first master librarian had meant the way to reach the master librarian's chamber had been lost. In order to recreate the proper method to become master librarian, they had combined a bunch of ingredients to try and copy the toxin we had discovered. That sounded plausible and also meant they hadn't been following the correct procedure.

It still seemed reckless for him to test it now, however.

I wasn't sure why, but I had a feeling that this first master librarian and Fitoria were the same. Maybe Fitoria would know something about this poison too.

"That's right. It is said that this potion, passed down among the library rabbits, must never be consumed by a human," Ethnobalt stated.

"I've heard about this. The secret potion of the library rabbits," Kizuna said.

"It's quite famous, isn't it? The potion that determines the chief of the library rabbits can provide eternal life, but if a human were to drink it, they'd die immediately," Ethnobalt said.

"We don't want you to die, right?" I said.

"If that happens, then it happens," Ethnobalt replied.

"Ethnobalt, if this is going to be dangerous, maybe you shouldn't do it," Kizuna said, trying to bring a stop to the proceedings. I mean, he was about to drink poison. That made it a bit hard to go along with.

"I am the chief of the library rabbits and the master librarian. Tradition states that a second dose is forbidden, but I have a duty to drink this," he stated firmly.

"Even if you are doing this for your tribe, Ethnobalt, I'm not going to be pleased if you just throw your life away," Kizuna stated. Ethnobalt smiled happily to hear this sentiment.

"Thank you for saying that. I am so happy to have met you and all of your friends . . . and yet I also wish to fulfill the role for which I was born. This is what I have spent my life studying for. My determination is firm," he replied.

"I'm still not sure—" Kizuna didn't seem pleased with Ethnobalt's reply.

"If I can become master librarian, I think I will be able to reduce the burden placed on you and your allies. You've protected and saved me so many times in the past. If I don't put my life on the line here, I will be unable to forgive myself," he explained. Kizuna looked like those things didn't really bother her but also like she didn't want to let Ethnobalt's determination go to waste.

In regard to the potion itself, Ethnobalt reported it to the other rabbits in the library and a meeting was held. The library rabbits were sticklers for tradition and so they all quickly agreed that Ethnobalt should drink it. The timing was perfect. It was decided the ritual would take place along with the party at the castle. That meant I had to transport a whole bunch of bunnies over to the castle, which was a bit of a pain. The good news was the mirror didn't have many restrictions, which made it possible to send large parties. Things seemed to be getting pretty serious, but I decided to just watch them unfold in silence. The original point of the party—to celebrate Kizuna's safe recovery—seemed to have become a little buried under all this other stuff. Kizuna herself was starting to look a little worried. Glass gently took her shoulder.

"Kizuna, I hope you can understand this. Everyone faces a test that they have no choice but to accept. Just like when I had to accept my fate, that time has now come for Ethnobalt. L'Arc, you can understand this, right?" Glass asked, seeking some backup.

"That's true. I understand that it's a required step. As part of the royal family, I've had my own share of trials to face too," L'Arc interjected. It wasn't easy being royalty, that was for sure. Raphtalia had been through her own ritual when she was appointed as Heavenly Emperor. It had allowed her to use all sorts of new techniques too.

"Very well then. We shall begin the ceremony," said one of the bunnies.

The speaker was a venerable old library rabbit. He gave a bow to Ethnobalt and took out the small vial that he had been handed prior to the ceremony starting. Then Ethnobalt took a swallow from the contents.

As soon as he did so, he started to moan, as though his throat was in severe pain. Maybe it was just poison. It would be quite disillusioning if he were to simply drop dead right here. I decided to prepare an antidote and have it on hand, just in case.

Even as I had that thought, a red aura began to glow around Ethnobalt. It quickly turned into what looked like a whirling tornado . . . and then scattered apart. I noticed his fringe was now lifted up. Not another cowlick! In the next moment, a shoulder bag appeared, already hanging from his shoulder diagonally across his body. It was some kind of symbol of him becoming their leader, perhaps.

"I can still feel it writhing inside me," Ethnobalt managed to report, breathing heavily, "but I think I've managed to . . . get it under control."

"Which means—" I started.

"Yes. I have become the true master librarian," he stated.

"That's great!" Kizuna said. The other library rabbits were all celebrating too.

"It is quite strange," Ethnobalt marveled. "Now it feels like I know where absolutely everything is inside the Ancient Labyrinth Library, apart from the sealed sections."

"Wow," I replied. Great news, apart from the fact that we already found what we'd been looking for. This ability might come in handy to look for other things though. "Can you search for the recipes for special weapons that can only be obtained via weapon copy?" I asked. We were talking about a vast volume of books, so he could likely find one or two special ones.

"A good question . . . yes, I'm sensing something on the sixty-seventh basement level of the Ancient Labyrinth Library.

It looks like it carries information on Kizuna's weapon. Wow, the precision of my abilities has really increased!" Ethnobalt enthused. Indeed, this looked like a pretty convenient power to have awoken to. Still, something was bothering me.

"Mr. Naofumi, is there something on your mind?" Raphtalia asked.

"No, I was just wondering if maybe the library rabbit who was the original master librarian was something like the Fitoria of this world. If so, they've had things hard too, surely," I mused.

"Indeed . . . Fitoria is very strong, isn't she?" Raphtalia agreed, nodding. Filo, meanwhile, was sniffing at the vial that Ethnobalt had drunk from.

"Do you want a taste too, Filo?" I asked.

"What? This is poison, right? No way!" Filo spat.

"Yeah, maybe better not," I replied. There was no reason to risk drinking poison, even if I was the one who suggested it.

"Why do you want Filo to drink it?" Raphtalia asked.

"I was just thinking that maybe Fitoria has some of that, too, and intends for Filo to ultimately drink it," I replied.

"Oh, that might make sense," Raphtalia responded.

"What? I don't want to drink it!" Filo exclaimed.

"You might have to. You're the next queen, right?" I reminded her. She'd received her tiara (cowlick), and if she was the same type of race as the library rabbits, then this was completely within the realm of possibility. I was still a bit concerned about the whole "one drop means eternal pain" side of things, but in any case, that was all up to Ethnobalt now. I really hoped he would do a better job of things than that selfish and threatening bird queen.

"Kizuna, shall we go looking for these materials that Ethnobalt found?" I asked her.

"If we can find the time, I guess we should. My level has taken a real hit," Kizuna replied. She had been using the curse weapon to protect Glass and the others. Just like using Bloody Sacrifice had lowered my own abilities, she had suffered the negative effect of her level being lowered.

"The killer whale sisters from my party can handle leveling," I told her.

"Oh my? You have a job for us?" Sadeena said, her ears pricking up.

"Yeah. While healing Kizuna, can you also help raise her level? Things are quickly going to get pretty busy around here," I told them.

"Of course! Leave it to us. One thing, though, little Naofumi. I would really love to be able to use magic too," Sadeena complained.

". . . It does look like the Way of the Dragon Vein can elicit the same effects as the magic Therese uses," I pondered. "Maybe I can make an accessory to help you out."

"It is similar, but not the same," Therese interjected, choosing that moment to join the conversation. "The gemstones are cooperating thanks to your power, Master Craftsman, but it isn't easy for them. That means both power and effects are reduced. I wouldn't recommend abusing that potential." I hadn't been aware of all that. It would mean Sadeena couldn't fire off magic left and right . . . but it would still be better than nothing. I had thought ofuda magic might be a good alternative for her, but she hadn't been able to pick it up as quickly as Shildina had.

"I've been meaning to ask, actually. Most of you guys don't really use magic, do you?" I said. Apart from Therese and Ethnobalt, I hadn't seen any of Kizuna's other allies using magic at all. If there was a reason for that, I thought I should ask about it.

"I can't play any instruments, and ofuda interfere with my weapon restrictions," Kizuna said. "That's not to say I don't have any magic." That was it for her, then—just the standard stuff. There were so many types of magic in this world though. It all felt a bit . . . convoluted. Our world had a much simpler approach to magic—just making use of the elements—and that seemed a lot easier to me. "There's also an element of me relying on my allies, I admit," Kizuna continued.

"There might be some hero-exclusive magic available to you, so it might be better to learn some," I told her.

"It sounds like you can use crystalian magic, Naofumi," Kizuna said.

"According to Therese, I can use it only kind of artificially, and it puts a strain on the gemstones," I said. It was also still prohibited in this world, and while interference with casting was possible, Way of the Dragon Vein itself would not activate. I guess it was imitating the crystalian magic that allowed it to work.

"That still seems pretty impressive to me," Kizuna responded. "How do you do it?"

"There's a method in our world called the Way of the Dragon Vein. It's magic that you can use with the blessing of monsters, such as dragons, and this is an application of that. You also need the special protection from a Spirit Tortoise class monster," I explained. I'd actually applied it to Ethnobalt as an experiment. There was a chance he could use it, if he tried.

"A dragon and a guardian beast, huh?" Kizuna said with a catch in her voice. Whatever I had said, it was clearly resonating with her. Here in Kizuna's world, however, the guardian beasts had pretty much been wiped out, so she probably didn't have an opening.

"We can't pine after things we can't get. We need to be as ready as possible to face the enemy, that's all," Glass stated.

"True enough . . . but considering how enhanced our enemies are, we also can't afford to make any rash moves," I replied. The power-up methods for the mirror and book probably hadn't been leaked to the enemy, but they had all the info on the four holy weapons and the remaining power-up methods. From our perspective, we didn't know three of the four holies or the harpoon power-up methods. That was a dangerous situation to be in.

I mean, if they showed up and used higher-level versions of skills or enhanced magic that we already knew about from our own holy or seven star weapons, maybe we could read the situation in the instant they unleashed it, enhance ourselves, and respond. But surely that wouldn't cover everything. First things first, we couldn't use a power-up method if we didn't know which weapon it was coming from. That part really hurt us.

"S'yne's sister taunted us pretty harshly on that front. If we made some poor attempt at magic buffs or skills, she would just nullify them. So I guess they didn't need any other preventative steps," I recalled. Even if I could use Aura X, it would be pointless if it was nullified. Could we hope to win if they started using it against us?

These were the problems arrayed against us. Now that Kizuna was back, we had to start thinking seriously about them.

"One thing we could definitely do is search for a way to counter their nullification of our support," I said.

"That does sound like a good idea. I'll help," Kizuna offered.

"Well now! Enough of the shop talk. This is a party to celebrate Lady Kizuna coming back to us, so let's have some fun!" L'Arc declared, even louder than normal. That brought an end to all serious discussion. Kizuna's allies really did love to throw a party. They had a lot of positive energy.

"Here, Lady Kizuna! Eat some more! More!" L'Arc laughed.

"Wah! L'Arc, that's probably too much for me!" Kizuna replied. L'Arc was clearly attempting to bring her over to his side, piling her plate with so much food I thought it might topple over.

"What is all this? I thought you were a good cook before, but you've really upped your game, Naofumi!" Kizuna said.

"I mean, I've got a few tricks up my sleeve, that's all," I replied. I was making use of all sorts of things I had learned, including adding life force to my cooking to increase its quality. Of course, I had already confirmed that depending on how much someone ate, it provided a big chunk of experience to the food level.

"What's going on here? I can't stop eating! Tell me, what's going on?" Kizuna exclaimed. As she continued to stuff her face with the parade of food, she was paling considerably. L'Arc and Glass looked at each other with confident smiles, thinking they had another member on their side.

"This is starting to feel a bit like torture to me," Raphtalia said, eating her way through her own plate with a practiced hand.

"Raph," said Raph-chan.

"Master, can I have some more?" Filo chirped.

"Sure thing. I can't fault your stomach, Filo," I said.

"Thanks!" she replied. Filo was eating so much I wasn't even sure where she was putting it. She had the highest food level by a kitchen mile—if such a thing were to exist. "Being able to eat a whole bunch makes me feel so happy!" she said.

"That's great, glad to hear it," I told her.

"Can I eat like this again tomorrow?" she asked.

"You certainly can. Eat as much as you can and grow up big and fat," I told her.

"Yay!" Filo celebrated.

"Filo, if you eat too much, you'll definitely regret it!" Raphtalia warned, but Filo didn't seem all that bothered.

Still . . . I had no idea how high this food level could go, so it was hard to settle on a point at which it could be considered high enough. It was really beneficial to a lot of the party and felt similar in application to the growth adjustment found inside weapons for allies. I decided we'd just keep feeding them until it became untenable to raise it any higher. I wanted those allies I could trust to have the best possible abilities prior to the final battle.

L'Arc and Glass were feeding Kizuna, so I decided to go and serve some to Yomogi and her table. They were just sitting, watching the party unfold, without eating anything. I needed them to get some of my cooking inside them too, but seeing what was happening to Kizuna had probably scared them off a bit.

"Do you have any requests?" I asked them.

"No, we're fine . . . thanks," Yomogi said.

"I'm not going to eat anything that can turn Kizuna into . . . that," Tsugumi added. They seemed so scared! A full belly wasn't going to kill them. That said, even if I ordered them to eat, they would probably just shrug it off.

"Yomogi, the wild boar, has finally found something that makes her back down, huh?" I teased.

"Say whatever you like!" she replied. "I admit I already ate a light meal before coming here, so I doubt I could fit much more in!" That might explain it, then. She had already eaten.

"I'm sure you've still got some room for dessert?" I offered, pointing over to the dessert corner. I'd gone continental the previous day, so now I'd rebounded to Japanese and Chinese. That looked like just the kind of stuff Yomogi and Tsugumi would go for.

"Kusamochi? I could go for some of that," Yomogi said. I knew it—I hooked her! She reached over, took some of the mochi I had carefully prepared, placed it on her plate, sat back down . . . and then her eyes popped open when she actually ate it.

"This is delicious . . . What's going on? I can't stop eating!

Is there something addictive added to this?" she asked.

Tsugumi exclaimed, "Naofumi, your food trap extends even to the desserts! Everyone, be careful!"

"Laying such a trap for us at Kizuna's return party!" Yomogi spluttered, still stuffing her face.

"Taking advantage of the fact you knew we would come!" Tsugumi accused.

"You make me sound like some kind of monster! If you don't like it, don't eat it!" I told them. What was with these two, honestly? The mochi Yomogi was eating used nothing but normal medicinal herbs. It promoted digestion and absorption without causing any tummy troubles. The bean jam inside was only lightly sweetened, creating the kind of subtle and refined dish that was like catnip to anyone hailing from a Japan-like nation. I also had some bean buns laid out as well.

In that moment, Kizuna wandered unsteadily over to Tsugumi and placed a plate of sashimi on the table.

"Come now . . . join me on a trip into a world of pleasure, Tsugumi," Kizuna said.

"Kizuna, dear, you're scaring everyone," Raphtalia chimed in.

"Why are you so keen to make it seem like you're about to eat something terrifying?" I asked. I wasn't keen to have all my effort to make this food toyed with in this way. "Shall I stop cooking completely?" I suggested.

"No . . . more . . ." Kizuna managed with a look on her face like she might throw up at any moment. Glass was quick to contain her.

"Let's get you over to the Musical Instrument Hero and have some support magic applied at once!" Glass said. The area close to the stage where Itsuki was playing was currently functioning as a rest space for those taking a break from eating. That said, listening to the music for too long just made them get hungry again. It was, upon reflection, like an infinite loop—at least while the food lasted.

"That's not what this is, kiddo!" L'Arc said.

"Master Craftsman! I need another serving of jelly!" Therese said.

"It isn't that we don't like your cooking, Naofumi. Quite the opposite, it's so delicious we're scared of eating too much," Ethnobalt explained with a wry laugh, even as he offered some food to Tsugumi. "It's the same as eating confectionery. You just need to control yourself. In either case, it will definitely make you stronger, so think of it as an experiment and eat your fill."

"Okay . . . it's just . . . this whole scene is a little terrifying," Tsugumi said. She gingerly raised some sashimi to her mouth, and then her eyes popped open too and she started to eat with enthusiasm. "This is delicious! Bring me more!" She groaned, "Having tasted this, my regrets are . . . Ah, I am such a sinner! Someone, please punish me for how far I have fallen!"

I shook my head, deciding to just warn them to try and not eat too much.

"It's terrifyingly tasty. I can still do some more!" Yomogi exclaimed.

"These flavors . . . are making me want to eat more even when I'm full . . . It's like physical violence! Make it stop!" Tsugumi exclaimed.

"Oh my, how about joining us in some drinking while you eat?" Sadeena suggested.

"No! Thank you, no!" Yomogi replied.

"No way!" Tsugumi added. Even with the differences in language, the two girls had clearly understood that a hardcore drinker was propositioning them.

"Oh my," Sadeena lamented.

"Oh . . . my stomach . . ." Kizuna was moaning and groaning over by Itsuki and his music.

"All this talk of food reminds me of this place I heard about, in a town somewhere, that serves the most delicious food possible," Tsugumi muttered, also looking like she might hurl any moment. "Maybe if we got the chef there to cook for us, we wouldn't have to pack it in like this?"

"Indeed . . . that sounds like something worth considering," Glass said.

"Once you get used to it, I think Mr. Naofumi's cooking is more than up to the task," Raphtalia said.

"If it tastes that good, won't the results just be the same?" I suggested. This kind of conversation made me consider whether or not I actually was a good cook. People praised me enough for it, but maybe the reactions of Kizuna and the others were coming from the pain of having to eat so much of it. Even if this place was as delicious as it was rumored to be, I couldn't see it being any more effective than what I was serving here. Unless the food from this fabled chef would allow for vast volumes of food level experience without having to cram so much in.

"Sounds like it's worth a try, if it could cut down on how much we needed to eat," L'Arc agreed. "Let's track the place down and dine out." And so it was decided that we would consider the food issue again after we had tried the dishes from this special chef. I still felt a little offended about the whole thing, to be honest. It wasn't like I was force-feeding them or anything! They ate more than enough of their own accord.

I was left with no choice, anyway. It sounded like it was going to take a lot of time and trouble, two things I preferred to spend in as small doses as possible. But we were going to have to try and find food that would optimize the food level experience.

The rest of the party passed in fun and games.

Chapter Five: Ultimate Soup Stock

It was afternoon on the following day.

Glass and some of the others had taken Kizuna out hunting to boost her level a bit prior to our departure for the special chef's place, and they had just returned. I was starting to feel like I'd only really been doing three things recently: fight, train, or cook. I really wanted to add someone to the party who could cook instead of me. Prior to our departure, I was in the kitchen, handing over my cooking duties to one of the other staff. That was when Kizuna, Raphtalia, and the others came to find me.

I greeted them with a big yawn. I'd been up all night, but even I wasn't entirely sure how—or why—things had come to that.

"Mr. Naofumi, are you okay?" Raphtalia asked.

"I'm fine, although I'd like to get some sleep while we travel," I said. I hadn't had a wink since yesterday. It had felt like a waste of time to do so.

"Master, you smell nice," Filo said.

"I've been cooking some really difficult and long-winded dishes," I explained.

"Raph!" added Raph-chan.

"Of course, Raph-chan has been helping out. S'yne's

familiar too," I said. They had turned up in the night and helped out in all sorts of useful ways. Being covered in fur meant there were some tasks I'd been worried about leaving to her, but Raph-chan had been one step ahead of me. She had put on what was basically a sack and hood from which only her little paws protruded, protecting the food from her fur.

S'yne ordered her familiar to help and had donned the same kind of outfit. S'yne herself had freaked me out by staying in the kitchen and sleeping with her eyes open.

"I see . . . I'll help out next time, okay?" Raphtalia said. S'yne didn't say anything but gave a taunting victory sign, at which Raphtalia puffed up her cheeks belligerently.

"What's this, Raphtalia? Feeling like S'yne and Raph-chan have got one over on you?" I taunted.

"No! Nothing like that!" she shot back at once. Hah, she was so easy to understand. Raph-chan was more attentive to my needs, that was true, but Raphtalia still did a lot to help out. She would periodically help out with cooking, and always lend a hand when things needed washing up.

"There is some unique fantasy-world technology that helps out with things, like controlling the temperature too," I said. Sometimes I did have to use firewood or charcoal to make adjustments, but they had a device here that was almost like a gas stove and operated on ofuda and made it pretty easy to control the heat when cooking. It was probably quite expensive to use, but this was L'Arc's castle, and no one had bothered me about it yet.

Whenever I was cooking, anyway—and it had been the same in Siltvelt and Q'ten Lo—any other chefs in the vicinity would come over, eyes sparkling, to look at what I was doing. Some of them did kind of give me dirty looks, but that was likely a case of trying to save face. I could see my presence impinging on the pride of those in the top-chef positions.

After a little while, though, those types either just went away again or changed their tune and started taking notes.

"I can't wait to start eating!" Filo said.

"I'm going to be trying all sorts of new things, so you've got plenty to look forward to," I told her.

"Great!" she replied.

"Raph!" said Raph-chan. This scene, prior to our departure, was observed with slightly puzzled expressions from Kizuna and her allies, including Glass and L'Arc. Ethnobalt was back at the Ancient Labyrinth Library, performing some further searches with the intent of providing us with more information. He had practiced the use of life force and had developed skills much like Rishia, so he could fight well enough even on his own. He was the master librarian, after all.

Itsuki and Rishia, meanwhile, were going to focus on reading ancient texts with Ethnobalt and aid the preparations in fighting the waves in the castle town and other countries.

"Whatever are you making, kiddo?" L'Arc asked.

"Just experimenting, really. I hope you'll give me your thoughts after you've tasted it," I said. I had my own culinary failures—of course I did. I was always experimenting and verifying things. "For example—and Raphtalia probably already gets this—I'm looking at the difference created in the final quality by the timing of imbuing life force into the dish. Stuff like that."

"I do have some idea what you mean," Raphtalia said.

"That's why I can only let you taste it once I've made the very best I can. Otherwise, all this time will have been wasted," I told them. What I really wanted to compare was how big a gap could be created between two versions of the same dish, one easy to make and the other more difficult.

"So this is the stuff you are putting your all into, kiddo . . ." L'Arc, Kizuna, and all her other allies seemed to swallow in unison. I almost asked them if having to eat so much of my cooking really was such a problem. At the moment, they looked like they couldn't wait to tuck in.

"You say 'putting my all into,' but that's the issue. After learning how to add life force, I performed some simple verifications of the technique, and since then I have been slacking off. So I'm trying to find a comfortable point between the two," I explained.

"I see," Raphtalia said.

"I'd really like you and Kizuna to both help me out and polish your own skills," I told them. "Especially you, Kizuna. You might need this once we've gone back to our world."

"No way! I can't hope to become as good at this as you, Naofumi!" Kizuna wailed.

"I also doubt I can match your skills, Mr. Naofumi. Remember that time you recreated that dish for Fohl based just on his testimony?" Raphtalia said, striking at me unexpectedly from behind. There had been a time when Fohl had wanted to make a dish for Atla that their parents used to make. He hadn't been pleased with his own attempts, but I had recreated it based on his description of the flavor. It sounded like that was weighing on Raphtalia's mind a little, but . . . I wouldn't know about that.

"It's not that hard. You'll have to rely on Ethnobalt otherwise," I told her. He was likely the only one among Kizuna's allies who could consciously imbue things with life force. Glass and some of the others could apply it in battle, but they couldn't use it when making things.

"You're good at taking things apart, Kizuna, so you should at least master its applications to sashimi and hot pots," I said. Because Kizuna loved fishing, she also loved fish recipes and often made sashimi and fish stews. If she took the time to learn the skills, I was pretty sure she could make something very similar to me. It didn't have to be anything too flashy.

"Raphtalia, we have someone in the village who loves to

cook, right? They managed to do this, with proper teaching," I told her. I was talking about the person who handled all the cooking in the village. I mean, you would have to pretty much devote yourself to cooking in order to recreate what I was doing here, that much was true. I'd make the judgment in terms of them having reached a point that was good enough, but from which further progress would be difficult.

"I'll do my best," Raphtalia said.

"Good to hear," I said. The chefs in L'Arc's castle had also made similar dishes in the past. They were able to overcome certain differences in the recipes because they were specialist chefs. I'd imbued everything with plenty of life force, so the castle staff should be able to handle the rest of this.

"Wow . . . there's a whole row of big pots over there. Did they all have the same thing in them?" Kizuna asked.

"No. I'm making bouillon, fond, and consommé. All using local ingredients, of course, so it's a little different from the official recipe," I reported.

"They all look the same to me. How are they different?" Kizuna asked. I shook my head, appalled that Kizuna didn't know the difference.

"They all look like scalp to me," L'Arc muttered. That was the name for something close to consommé in L'Arc's nation.

"You're a king and you can't tell the difference between some simple dishes?" I accused.

"Shut it! Let me eat them and I'll tell you the difference, but I don't know what they look like when they are being made," he retorted. I had to admit, bouillon, fond, and consommé did all look very similar.

"That brown was already finished beforehand, wasn't it?" Kizuna asked.

"No, that's fond de veau. The original recipe uses calf bones and sinews, fried until brown and then boiled. The Maillard reaction creates the color. This time I used parts from a similar kind of monster and browned them in the oven," I explained.

"So it's a meat soup?" Kizuna asked.

"That's right. There are all sorts of varieties of it. Those using fish or other fowl can still be a 'fond' but have a different name," I said, pointing to a white fish fumet de poisson and chicken fond de volaille. "There's a boar monster that has a similar quality to the meat, so it might be closer to a fond de gibier? The flavor is more like a fond de veau, however, so that's what I'm calling it." After this, I was also planning on further simmering the fond de veau and creating a glace de viande to check what that did to the experience rate.

"You're getting far too specialized for me," Raphtalia said, seemingly giving up already. I'd only said all this because they asked about it!

"The next step is to turn them into things like stews. You'll find they taste completely different from the more easily created ones," I said. These things were a pain to create even back in Japan, but the extra effort paid off in flavor. Stew had been one of my brother's favorite dishes. I'd rarely bothered to make one of the fancy ones, though, due to all the extra work they took.

"You've been cooking instead of sleeping, huh?" Kizuna said.

"Pretty much. There are some things you can overlook when cooking and some things that you absolutely have to do. These elements here are the stuff you can't slack off on, but that also seems to really increase the experience they offer, so it's definitely not wasted effort," I stated.

"Kiddo . . . look at you, doing all this for us . . ." L'Arc said. I did a double take. L'Arc, Glass, and Kizuna were all looking at me quite intently. I wondered if I'd said anything out of place.

"Anyway, the one that takes the most work—and is the most important—is the bouillon. You can't get anywhere without that. Raphtalia, Kizuna, I need you both to learn it. Everyone back home can make it!" I said. It was made with careful preparation of the chicken bones and beef sinew, which were then stewed along with the vegetables. You had to start on a high heat, turn it down low as soon as it boiled, and make sure to scrape off the scum and fat that floated to the top. Once the stewing was finished, a careful straining completed the dish. It could then be used as the base for all sorts of dishes, so it was worth learning—a soup stock that could be used in lots of different recipes. Of course, once you got into things like the ratio of ingredients, there was no end to it, so it also tended to reflect my personal tastes quite strongly, but I had tried to arrange this one to suit the tastes of L'Arc and the others.

"It looks so clear and beautiful," Filo said, her eyes glittering as she looked at the bouillon. "Like you could just drink it like this."

"It's a stock, not a finished dish," I warned her.

"Okay," she said.

"You start here and then proceed to making the fond de veau and consommé," I said. Making these was mainly a fight against scum and turbidity. "Bouillon is like the ultimate soup stock."

"If you say so," Kizuna said, a little cowed by my proclamation. She was going to be making this soon, in any case.

"Kizuna, Raphtalia, you both still just lack experience. I'll teach you some recipes that use bouillon for a small number of people, so make sure you learn them later," I told them. Just making ten liters of bouillon used a considerable volume of ingredients—sometimes an equal volume of beef sinew and chicken bones.

"What! I'm the Hunting Hero! I don't handle the cooking part!" Kizuna complained.

"And I'm the Shield Hero!" I retorted. Not the Stewpot Hero! If anyone called me that, I would kill them with cookery!

"Seeing how the sausage actually gets made, I can understand why your food is so deadly delicious," Glass murmured, her eyes distant.

"I just need you to learn this stuff. You too, Glass," I replied.

Then we started out toward the town with the famous chef. It wasn't a nation we could reach using Return Dragon Vein. In order to make getting around easier once we were there, we were taking a big mirror with us to place there once we arrived. The mirror vassal weapon had skills that allowed me to move via mirrors. However, I couldn't help but feel—instinctually, almost—that this cluster of skills had another purpose too. The only way to work that out would be with some repeated experimentation.

In any case, taking a mirror with us meant we'd be able to move around in a similar way to S'yne's needles.

That night, Kizuna and the others ate too much again. It felt like less of a burden than overeating, however. I had been careful to select foods that offered a bit more of a compromise.

Chapter Six: Seya's Restaurant

Based on Tsugumi's testimony and other rumors, we had set out toward the town with the chef who made the most delicious meals possible.

"Is this the place?" I asked.

"It looks like it," Raphtalia replied. We had a mirror with us so that we could easily go back and forth after arriving here. We also had a mirror for movement placed back in the castle, so a fairly large party came along. At that point there was me, Raphtalia, Raph-chan, Filo, Kizuna, Glass, L'Arc, Therese, and Tsugumi. Tsugumi was the one who had brought all this up in the first place, after all.

Itsuki, Rishia, and Ethnobalt had stayed behind to work on deciphering the old texts. Chris had turned into an ofuda and was sleeping. S'yne seemed to have no interest in joining us and said she'd stay in the castle and eat the food I left behind. Sadeena was searching for Shildina, who had got herself lost. The younger sister's complete lack of a sense of direction was an ongoing concern. She had last been seen in the castle town, according to Sadeena.

The permits we had needed to reach this town, anyway, had been provided under the authority of L'Arc and Kizuna, which had been a big help. Culturally speaking, we were looking at buildings with a medieval feel. That said, something felt off about the place. It seemed quiet and yet pretty developed. It had an atmosphere that was perhaps a bit difficult for a Japanese person to understand—urban but shabby, maybe. The streets were paved with stone, but those stones were cracked in many places, suggesting it had been developed, but someone had failed to finish the process. This was more than just a failure to keep things clean. It was like the external appearance was there, but there was nothing inside.

What the place looked like didn't matter, anyway. We just needed to confirm the rumors of this wonder chef. We'd heard more gossip in the adjacent neighborhood, where there was an imitation restaurant. We'd talked to some of the people who had eaten there, and they said it wasn't as good as the original, but better than nothing.

Maybe I was overthinking things, but something looked off about the expressions of the people here too. Their eyes looked a bit vacant and yet they seemed so healthy. It was unsettling. They were working in the fields, caring for livestock, and transporting carefully prepared monster meat and vegetables, and they were all heading in the same direction.

All of a sudden, a muddy little kid fell over in front of me.

"What are you doing?! You won't get blessed with deliciousness like that! Work as though your life depends on it!" someone said, scolding the kid—most likely their parent.

"I don't want it! I don't want deliciousness!" the kid said.

"Hah! More for me then!" the parent replied. The parent, with their hardened gaze, and the child with their dull and lifeless one . . . I couldn't take my eyes off this bizarre scene.

"Hey, hey! Welcome to our town! You must be here to taste the cooking of the greatest chef in the world, Master Seya!" A soldier at a town checkpoint greeted us in a seemingly overexcited fashion, and so I looked away from the kid.

"Yeah, that's right. We've heard the rumors," L'Arc said, nodding as he spoke for the party.

"I bet you have!" the guard enthused.

"So where do we need to go?" L'Arc asked.

"You can see what the neighborhood looks like, right?" the man replied. L'Arc nodded again. The man proceeded to point at a structure that looked like the tallest building in town. There was something odd about it, though, like it was floating. There were monsters flying around it, but I presumed they were subservient to the owner of the building.

"Master Seya's cooking is all laid out in the square in front of that building all the way up inside! The people of the town work hard every day, fed by Master Seya's cooking. That's how our town continues to grow!" the guard continued.

"Okay, understood," L'Arc said, a little awkwardly. "We'll go and check it out." Ending the conversation there, we all headed together into the neighborhood. I fell in alongside L'Arc.

"That wasn't like you," I muttered to him. L'Arc would normally chat happily with anyone and everyone he met. Yet with the guard, he had clearly been holding back.

"I'm not good at talking to someone who isn't even really seeing the person he's talking to like that," L'Arc admitted. He was a king, after all. He spotted these things. He was right, too. The guard hadn't seemed like he was actually seeing anything around him. It had been like he was looking into another world completely.

"I know what you mean. But this place does look pretty prosperous," I commented, turning an eye to the monsters being carried in. One was a fairly powerful-looking medium-sized dragon, and another was a bull-like monster. The people of the town were looking on with happiness in their eyes. I'd never seen anything like this in Melromarc. Even the farmers had a strange aura around them, like each of them was a powerful adventurer, warrior, or magic user—a feeling of raw power. Kizuna was looking at them too, and then she furrowed her brow.

"What's up?" I asked.

"I mean . . . everyone here looks so strong, don't they?" she said.

"Yeah. I was just thinking the same thing," I replied. I still wasn't really sure how to phrase it. They felt similar to a cultivated village, perhaps. But it would be out of place to call them anything close to "full of life." The reason I couldn't put my finger on it was why they felt so strange.

"Almost feeding time!" one of them said. Others proceeded to chime in.

"Yes . . . the time we've all been waiting for."

"The moment we live for, basically!"

"Even if I only get to eat one mouthful . . . that is the fuel that will keep me alive!"

"I'll never eat anything but his cooking ever again!"

"I think the schweiz is the best! It has to be!"

"No! The stietz!"

"Hey! No fighting! We've been warned about fighting!"

"That's right! What if fighting means no food?" With crazy looks in their eyes, they discussed the meal that lay ahead. Everyone seemed like they were looking forward to eating this food more than anything else at all. That said . . . I hadn't seen any normal-looking restaurants anywhere in the town. Even if the place this wonder chef opened had sucked up all the possible diners, I expected to see a few other places trying to hold on. There didn't even seem to be anywhere selling ingredients, which was very strange. Maybe people could buy those in the fields, if they wanted them . . . but it was odd to not even have a market selling things. Meanwhile, there were plenty of general stores, weapon stores, and ofuda stores on display.

It was definitely weird.

"It looks pretty prosperous around here," I commented.

"Everyone here eats at the place this super chef opened—and works for it too. That's why there's nowhere else selling food. The big place even sells portable rations," someone in the crowd explained to me. If that was the culture here, then I just had to accept it, and I couldn't judge things by Japanese standards . . . but this was a pretty strange place.

In any case, that big building definitely looked like the one being run by the chef we were here to see. We finally arrived in front of it to find what looked like a beer garden. There were all sorts of stalls placed out front with the people of the town all sitting around eating—or, more accurately, stuffing their faces in what looked like a stupor. That was the most striking impression. They were really packing it away.

"Wow, they all look like people do when they're eating your food, Master!" Filo enthused.

"Filo! Shhh! You'll upset Mr. Naofumi!" Raphtalia said. It had been a while since I'd heard Filo's malicious side. She'd been a lot calmer since meeting Melty, but she could be a straight shooter when she wanted to. I glanced over at Kizuna and the others and got some stiff smiles in return.

"But they don't look like they're enjoying it as much as when they eat your food," Filo added.

"What's the difference?" I queried.

"I mean . . . they just don't have that joy around them.

More like they are worried about someone taking the food from them. Eating with everyone together makes food so much more delicious . . . What a waste!" Filo bemoaned. She was right too. Even when I was forcing folks to chow down, they didn't have the rage in their eyes that these guys had. Filo was a keen observer, I'd give her that.

"This is what we're here for. Let's try some," L'Arc said.

"Good idea," I replied. We lined up to get into the strangely divided beer garden.

"Dear diners, is this your first time eating with us?" a hostess asked us. She was a grass person, a species with elf-like ears. She projected a nice neat-and-clean image. I wondered if these grass elves in Kizuna's world had typical elvish characteristics, like being very proud. Your standard fantasy elves definitely had an arrogance about them. They avoided contact with other races because while the elves protected nature, other races destroyed it. I had no idea if the grass people in this world were the same.

"Yeah, we've heard the rumors and are here to try it for ourselves," L'Arc responded.

"I see," she replied. "Then I should probably explain how our system works. First you will be given a special card. You can accrue points on your card by supplying us with quality ingredients, supporting us with cash donations, or visiting us often." It sounded like a fairly standard rewards scheme. "The points you have earned will decide which menu you can order from. If you want to eat our most delicious offerings, you will need to make a suitable contribution to our well-being." Okay, now it was sounding more like some kind of members-only club . . . or perhaps a religion. In any case, they clearly wanted to project an image of luxury. It was just another strange element of the culture of the other world. "That said," the grass girl continued, "we are aware that you cannot suddenly jump right up the rankings. So as a bonus for your first visit, you can sit over here and order from a special first-timers' menu. Please see what you think." Having finished her explanation, the girl passed us some menus and then moved on to the next party.

Kizuna and the others checked the menus out.

"Huh? There are no prices . . . Ah, there at the bottom it says that it's free," Kizuna said.

"Nothing is more expensive than a free meal," I warned her. Speaking as a merchant, I knew there was no way to know what truly lurked in the depths of anything that was "free."

"I guess it's just for the first time. After that, you use that card thing she was talking about to pay, right?" Kizuna guessed.

"That sounds about right," I agreed. That sounded like a pretty honorable approach too . . . but there had to be something behind it. My instincts as a merchant were tingling. The most important thing, first and foremost, was to taste what they were peddling. They were clearly confident that, after you tasted their wares once, they could have their way with you however they pleased.

"I've seen this approach before somewhere," Kizuna muttered, looking at me. She was remembering the time I went around selling soul-healing water at ridiculous prices. We couldn't do anything until we found out what kind of product they were pushing. It was quite a cunning approach, when considered from that angle.

"First you will eat outside the building," said the girl, returning to our party and leading us toward our seats in the beer garden. "As you rise through the customer ranks, you will be able to eat on the first floor inside, and then the second, and so on, with an enhanced menu on each floor. Our first-time diners get to order from a menu equivalent to the third floor. Please see what you think." It looked like we started out eating outside this massive restaurant.

"Let's order," L'Arc said eagerly.

"I can't read it," I replied. It was inconvenient that neither the shield nor the mirror could handle this kind of translation task.

"I'll order for us," Tsugumi said. She glared at me for a moment and then turned her attention to the menu. I wondered why she was so interested in my face . . . and then I worked it out.

"I'm not some gourmet diner. I'll eat anything that won't kill me. Just pick whatever you like," I said. Anyone who ate my cooking seemed to get the impression that I was some kind of freaking food critic. The one who did the cooking in the village had been worried about that to start with too, unable to relax in my presence. In actual fact—while not on the same level as Filo—I'd eat pretty much anything that was put in front of me.

"It's true," Raphtalia confirmed, choosing to provide some mysterious support. "I've never heard Mr. Naofumi complain once about food."

"Hey, I'll complain if they serve up some dollops of mud, trust me. But this is a famous restaurant, right? So anything should be fine," I replied.

"Okay," Tsugumi said. "I'll take a look." Her face looked pretty ghastly as she turned back to the menu, however. I wondered if this was really the best idea.

"I understand how you feel. I'll discuss what each dish is with her and decide together," Kizuna said thoughtfully. But behind her, Glass was trembling with an aura of jealousy, and Tsugumi had noticed it.

". . . Once we get back, I'd better prepare some indigestion medicine and some food soothing on the stomach," I said.

"Shut it!" Tsugumi shouted.

"I'm with you . . ." Raphtalia said.

In the end, Tsugumi and L'Arc were the two who ordered for all of us.

"Your food will be right with you!" The hostess gave a

bow of her head and then went off inside to place our order. I had nothing better to do while we were waiting for the food to arrive, so I took to doodling my plans for my next accessory. Therese peered over, interested in what I was doing. I had already made the accessories that would allow Sadeena and me to use simple magic. The issue with those was the number of times they could be used, the types of magic they could unleash, and their firepower . . . That last point wasn't too bad, actually, but they still couldn't match the real deal. Sadeena had decided to just learn how to use ofuda magic from Shildina.

When I was working on accessories like this, L'Arc always started to glare at me a bit. I wished he'd just accept the situation, ask me to teach him some more, or anything at all.

As this tug of war continued, the food was finally delivered.

"Sorry to keep you waiting! Here is our most excellent Seya Third Floor Curry!" Curry, huh? I wondered if the "third floor" part was some kind of taste or spiciness rating.

"That smells . . . good!" Filo said. I wondered why she phrased it as a question. It did smell like the curry I knew from back home . . . but I'd already recreated that myself. It was a while back, but I'd make a curry-like dish in the old guy's weapon shop in Melromarc. That really took me back. I'd been kicked out in the end because the smell kept on bringing in diners rather than weapon customers. After that, I'd perfected my curry and fed it to everyone in the village. Keel actually hadn't liked it much.

"Let's give it a try," I suggested. The others agreed. They all seemed to know how to eat it. I used the spoon to mix some curry in with the rice and prepared to tuck in.

Warning!

That single word floated up into my field of vision. My toxin appraisal had been triggered . . . by what looked like something similar to tobacco. So it had addictive properties. I mean, I'd heard that all food contained some kind of trace toxin. Simply packing in carbs like rice and wheat was considered toxic by some people. My weapon was sometimes triggered just by using the wrong spices or herbs, so I wasn't going to throw down the spoon and scream poison. It had been a while since I saw a reaction this severe, however.

Raphtalia, L'Arc, and Kizuna were all already chowing down without any trouble, anyway, so it couldn't be a serious problem. It should be fine, I told myself. I was just . . . imagining things. My toxin appraisal had become too finely honed after I learned all those compounding skills. I took a moment to alter my checked items . . .

Silence. It was almost spooky how quietly everyone was eating. Even L'Arc, the hyperactive life of the party, was quietly chomping away. That definitely freaked me out. He was still glancing over at me as well. I felt like screaming, *I'm not a food critic! I'm not about to ask to see the head chef!*

"Raph. . ." muttered Raph-chan, also eating quietly. Even Filo wasn't getting excited. There was definitely something out of place here.

"Filo, how is it? Does it taste good?" I asked her.

"Hmmm? Well, it's not as good as yours, Master," she said.

"What?" I replied. It was rare for Filo to downplay the deliciousness of anything. You could roast up a whole monster out in the wilds and she'd still tuck in, saying it was the best thing ever.

"Filo! Shhh! Naofumi won't like comparisons like that!" Kizuna said.

"Huh?" said Filo.

"I mean, I'm not bothered," I said.

"So what's that face for?" she asked.

"Oh, I was just surprised at Filo saying something like that. Recently, she's been so enthused about anything she eats," I explained. She was the greedy-guts of the group, the one who would eat absolutely anything and enjoy it.

"I'm not sure about that. Filo actually has quite a discerning tongue," Raphtalia said. "She always says things like this for pretty much anything you didn't make, Mr. Naofumi." I thought back and realized when she was stuffing herself at the castle, she had been so excited and said it tasted so good that I hadn't really asked for her detailed opinion on the flavor. She'd said something similar when she stole an evening meal from the old guy.

"After you and Ruft were trampled by the filolials, Mr. Naofumi, the Spear Hero tried to make himself welcome by cooking for the village while you were incapacitated. He eventually managed to convince Filo to try some of his cooking, but she said pretty much the same thing as she said here," Raphtalia reported. Just at the mention of Motoyasu, Filo's face twisted in pain. She really didn't like that guy.

"It isn't bad," Filo said. "It just isn't as nice as yours, Master."

"Well, okay . . ." I replied.

"All of the heroes have cooked in the village, Mr. Naofumi, but Filo and everyone else all feel the same way," Raphtalia told me.

"I really feel the pain of a hero who gets compared to you," Kizuna said, offering sympathy that I didn't really understand. Still, it was odd to see Glass, Tsugumi, and L'Arc so quiet. Kizuna seemed to be feeling that too, as she kept glancing over at Glass. Had they gotten hooked on the addictive ingredient already?

"Dear diners, how is everything for you? Are you enjoying your repast?" The hostess girl was back, probing a little suspiciously, and so I started eating again. To be quite honest, the flavor was no better than a boil-in-the-bag curry from back home in Japan. If I had to choose between being delicious or disastrous, it was the former, but even then, it wasn't anything special. Considering this flavor to be incredible sounded like nothing so much as subjective taste to me.

"Well . . . how can I put this," Raphtalia replied.

"It's not as nice as my master's," Filo stated point-blank.

"Raph," Raph-chan added. At that point, simple personal preference was still on the table.

"Looks like we wasted our time. Let's go home and get some real food," L'Arc stated, now making the food itself sound terrible.

"Then you wish to settle the bill," she replied. *I thought it was free.* As my suspicions intensified, the girl spread both of her hands and continued. "How was the food at Seya's restaurant? It was so delicious, wasn't it? If you wish to become a member, please leave all of your assets or hand over anything that can be turned into money. If you leave some personal items as collateral, you can have some time to go and fetch some offerings." I wondered what she was even talking about. Maybe she had recently hit her head.

"Sorry, but we won't be back. We're leaving," L'Arc told her.

"Excuse me?" Her face stiffened at L'Arc's words. Then she quickly recovered herself, smiled again, and carried on. "No, no, that cannot be. Or are you dissatisfied with the food at Seya's restaurant?" she asked.

"I mean, I don't have any complaints. Just let us leave. And no more talk about 'all our assets' or anything like that," L'Arc said, obviously getting a bit upset with the pushy girl. The confidence of this place was crazy, given that this was the flavor they were peddling. It wasn't terrible, and I wouldn't put down anyone for liking it, but it also wasn't worth all of your assets. In Japanese terms, I'd pay 300 yen for this. Boil-in-the-bag prices.

"Just what do you think Master Seya's cooking is?! This is the flavor of the third floor, I'll have you know!" the girl exclaimed. *So? So what?* That was the only response that came to mind.

"Oh boy . . . you're very pushy, little miss. I'm going to have to speak plainly now, aren't I?" L'Arc looked at Glass and Tsugumi, and both of them nodded in return.

"To be quite honest, it doesn't taste very nice at all," Glass said.

"Yeah, it stinks!" L'Arc added.

". . . I can't disagree," Tsugumi concluded. All three of them had disgruntled looks on their faces.

"Hold . . . hold on . . ." I said.

"Glass?" Kizuna queried. The hostess was still off in a world of her own, however.

"I'm sorry . . . You have more to say after that, I presume?" she said.

"Like what?" Raphtalia asked. They had already said it

tasted bad. I wondered what more she could want to hear.

"Like, 'It stinks. Now I have to stay in this town and become a regular diner!' Something like that, perhaps?" she asked. Was that what people who ate this food normally said? They seemed far too confident in their product here. I mean, I had tasted it as well. Maybe the addictive quality was just making people eat it. In either case, L'Arc and the others didn't seem to have been affected by it at all.

Maybe she thought we wanted to leave so we could bring some money back. He had clearly stated we weren't going to return, however. Maybe she thought L'Arc and the others were planning some kind of surprise. That sounded far too optimistic though.

"We have nothing more to say, especially nothing like that. Our honest opinion is that it doesn't taste any good," Glass said.

"Right on. We wasted our time coming here. We're leaving, missy, that's what we're telling you. Goodbye," L'Arc added.

"I agree completely with my friends. It seems the rumors were nothing more than that—rumors," Tsugumi finished. It was as though the three of them were actually looking for a fight. Therese, at least, kept her mouth shut, but the look on her face was not promising.

With a stiff smile on her face, the hostess turned toward me and Kizuna.

"Just average," I said.

"Average," Kizuna agreed. "I mean, some people might like it." Kizuna and I landed the final blows. Even the experience we received was only about half of what could be expected from the same food I made. Just as Kizuna had said, it was just average.

"Let's go." I stood up to leave, and the temperature in the vicinity suddenly plummeted with murderous intent. A gaggle of other girls that also worked the restaurant all came over and started to berate us.

"You're saying that the food at Seya's restaurant tastes bad?"

"You need to learn your place!"

"Your jokes aren't funny!"

"How are you unable to recognize pure facts?"

"You are so small-minded!"

"Do you even have taste buds?"

"You need to change your tune or we're going to have a problem!"

Not only those in the beer garden but everyone around us all clattered to their feet, grabbing whatever was at hand that could be used as a weapon and looking ready to jump on us at any moment.

I couldn't believe this place. They'd asked what we thought, and we replied honestly. They might not like what they heard, but there was no need to mob us! If they didn't like it, they should just let it slide. These restaurant people were way too quick to anger.

"I see it now! You're assassins from some other restaurant!" one of the girls shouted. I was almost willing to accept that assessment if they would just let us leave.

"That's not right! I'm just honestly saying that it doesn't taste good. That it isn't worthy of consideration!" Glass said.

"That's right, what she said!" Tsugumi added.

"I've wasted the space for a decent meal by eating this!" L'Arc shouted. I wondered why he had eaten it all, then—some sense of obligation?

"Hey! Glass! L'Arc, Tsugumi, can you all just calm down? What's gotten into you?" Kizuna asked them.

"Don't you see, Kizuna? We eat such delicious food every day, and now we're told that *this* food has the ultimate flavor! So how would we feel?" Glass replied.

"Maybe our tongues have become so pampered there's no turning back. But even so . . . this just isn't it. What kind of racket are you running here, trying to get us to give up all our stuff when we just want to leave peacefully?" L'Arc said.

"When I was eating, I just kind of spaced out . . . but also felt pretty uncomfortable. This taught me just how happy, how blessed, I have been by the flavors I've enjoyed recently! So what if it makes me fat? It's far worse to be unable to say stuff tastes bad!" Tsugumi ranted. I was starting to have a real bad feeling about where this was headed.

"Sorry, but . . . I'm starting to get a real bad feeling about this," Raphtalia said, placing her hand on the hilt of her katana, ready to fight at any moment. From my varied experiences so far, I could tell this was heading for trouble.

Was this my fault? No, it was L'Arc kicking things off. However, the restaurant staff pressing us for money was definitely wrong. Still, my group wasn't normally like this, really.

"I don't need any trouble. Can we just pay what seems like a reasonable amount and leave?" I suggested.

"Yes, not a bad idea. Glass, everyone, just keep your mouths closed. Naofumi doesn't want you to make things worse," Kizuna said.

"That might be for the best," L'Arc admitted.

"In respect to Kizuna and Naofumi, let's just do that," Glass agreed. They were still being a bit stubborn about it, but L'Arc and the others were at least backing down. It was too late, however.

"Unforgivable! Badmouthing Seya's restaurant means one thing . . . death!" One of the other customers shouted and leapt at us. But Tsugumi moved faster than the eye could see, intercepting the attack and pinning the attacker.

"Stop the violence. If we have offended you, we apologize. We just want to leave," Tsugumi said.

"Everyone! Punish these assassins from a rival restaurant!" the hostess girl suddenly shouted, riling up the crowd. Talk about terrible customer service! If we didn't leave all our assets behind, would that be the equivalent of a dine and dash? But they had said it was free, so I took that to mean we could run if we wanted.

As I was thinking this over—*bang*! The doors to the restaurant flew open and out came someone beating a frying pan. All of the customers and staff looked in that direction.

"Everyone, stop fighting!" The speaker was a man, around seventeen, holding a frying pan and ladle. He was more handsome than average, but not on Motoyasu's level. His hair was kind of reddish. He was wearing a rough outfit, like a T-shirt, and had a handkerchief wrapped around his arm. He didn't look much like a cook and didn't have that special craftsman kind of feeling about him. He looked more like Motoyasu might have if he had set up to do some cooking prior to going crazy. The words he said, though, calmed the hubbub down.

"Master Seya?!" said a girl.

"What's all this noise about?" Seya asked. These women had been about to lead the customers in an all-out attack; that was what the noise was about.

"These assassins from a rival restaurant said that Master Seya's Third Floor Curry tastes bad! We were about to teach them the error of their ways!" one of the girls shouted.

"Seriously . . . I've told you not to give such diners the time of day. Unless they start causing trouble, just ignore them," he replied. I was surprised by how legit his response was. Maybe we were going to avoid trouble and just get out of here after all.

"But, Master Seya! They claim to have tasted food better than yours!" At that line from the hostess, Seya's eyes narrowed and glared sharply at us. *Oh no . . .*

"Some part of this excitement has to have been caused by you and your party," he said, addressing us for the first time. "If you have food that's more delicious . . . maybe we should play by the rules in our town and have a cooking battle," he said.

"Huh?" I replied.

"Allow me to explain, assassins from a rival restaurant! Not just here in town, but in the neighboring towns too, we compete to see which of two establishments has the most delicious food, staking the restaurant's sign, rights, and assets on the table! If you lose, you have to hand over everything to us. Of course, at the mercy of Master Seya, we will feed you every day," one of the girls explained.

"Nope. Sounds like a pain," I said, shooting back a response with almost reactionary speed. It was starting to sound like I was going to end up taking part in some kind of bizarre contest.

"In which case, take back what you said about Master Seya's food tasting bad!" the girl shouted.

"No, we won't," Glass immediately responded. I just wished they would back down!

"No way we're taking anything back! You think the country is going to allow your stupid rules?" L'Arc bit back. In that same moment, an old man emerged from behind Seya.

"Hoh-hoh-hoh-hoh! I assure you, peasants, my presence here makes this quite official—" the rotund little fellow started, and then L'Arc and Tsugumi gave him a withering glare. He immediately paled and fled back inside. I felt like shouting after him. *Yes? You were saying something about peasants?* He was likely some bigwig from somewhere, but we had the bigger wigs with us. This Seya fellow seemed to grasp the situation and raised an eyebrow.

"I'm going to remember your face. You need to learn that your supposed authority isn't going to work on everyone," L'Arc said. Seya responded immediately.

"Gah! We're not going to bend to you! If you say our food tastes bad, prove that yours tastes better! Otherwise, we can say your food tastes worse, and you can't stop us!" one of the girls shouted.

"We're going to spread all sorts of nasty rumors about you!" said another. It felt like being back in kindergarten; it really did.

"Kiddo! Can you really back down after they've said all that?" L'Arc asked me.

"Let them say what they like. This is all too much of a pain for me to handle," I replied.

"Hoh-hoh-hoh-hoh! I wonder what the other nations would think about the trouble these people are causing?" It was the rotund guy again, coming back to taunt us. "I'll turn this into an international incident." So now politics was getting involved, and over nothing but dinner. This was really getting out of hand. I couldn't stand either of them.

"Gah! Kiddo, why aren't you getting more worked up about this?" L'Arc asked.

"I think it's more like you are getting too worked up! You aren't normally like this," I told him.

"I'm not sure why everyone is getting so angry about this stuff," Kizuna said. "This whole place feels ready to explode."

"Can't we just take things down a notch?" Raphtalia muttered. I strongly agreed with that sentiment. Then I looked over at Filo . . .

"Do we get to eat your cooking, Master?" Filo asked.

"Raph?" said Raph-chan hopefully. The two of them had sparkling little eyes looking up at me. They got to eat it every day, and they still wanted more. I didn't know what to do with them.

L'Arc proceeded to take both of my shoulders and bow his head.

"Kiddo! Naofumi! This is a battle of pride! What does 'deliciousness' really mean? That's what we need to show them! Please, lend me your cooking skills!" he begged me.

"I don't want to lend you anything for this pointless charade!" I replied.

"Hah! All I see is some third-rate chef without a delicious dish to his name, trying to wriggle out of being exposed! You can't even bring yourself to face me, coward!" Seya turned on me, sounding like he thought he had won already. I had no intention of fighting this food battle, but his attitude really did piss me off. Part of the reason was how much he looked like Takt. Should I just subdue him physically? That might shut him up, but it wouldn't answer L'Arc's issues about pride.

". . . You're going to owe me big time for this," I said.

"Kiddo!" L'Arc said, his eyes opening wide. I pointed at Seya and delivered my reply.

"Very well. This will be a massive pain, but I'll take you on," I said. It was true: everyone always said my food was so good, and so maybe I was getting a bit carried away. But backing down was only going to piss me off even more, so I seemed to have no choice but to fight him.

"Victory," Therese muttered, her arms crossed.

"You said it," L'Arc agreed. I thought that was putting the cart before the horse a little!

"We're quickly becoming problem customers here! How has this happened?" Raphtalia said. I really was on her side in this. "I have to say, though, this also reminds me of when I had just met you, Mr. Naofumi. Ah, that takes me back." I wasn't that concerned with her remembering that piece of history! It might be an important memory for Raphtalia, but I wish she'd consider the location a little more!

In the end, I was forced to take part in this mysterious cooking battle.

Chapter Seven: Contentious Cooking Battle

A massive kitchen was quickly prepared in the beer garden of Seya's restaurant. I shook my head at the facilities on display; it seemed like they did this a lot. Then a mysterious group of cooks gathered around Seya and faced us down. While this crazy drama was unfolding, the hostess girl, who looked like she was going to act as MC, snaffled some ingredients to snack on and glared us down. Was this an intentional parody?

The cooks lined up against the wall of the restaurant.

She began, "This is it, folks! The fight begins! Seya's restaurant versus the cooking assassins from who-cares-where!" They didn't seem bothered about getting the facts right or even learning our names. "I'll now explain the rules for everyone who has never taken part before. The time limit is one hour and a half! You need to bring the judges your dishes within that time! Then it will be strictly but fairly judged. And which dish is more delicious will be ultimately decided." The girl pointed toward the judges. The rotund guy was there, along with numerous others, all raising their hands. "Strictly but fairly judged," she said. I didn't expect any of those words to apply to judges who were looking at us like we were trash off the street.

"We raise these markers, do we?" one of the judges asked.

"That's right," the girl confirmed. All the judges immediately gripped a stick with what looked to be a logo for Seya's restaurant attached and ignored the stick that presumably represented us. They had completely been bought off, for sure, and the result seemed to be in the bag already.

I'd rushed into this, foolishly. Nothing was as subjective as food.

"How did it come to this?" Kizuna was shaking her head. I was right there with her.

"I have no idea. Glass and the others got riled up for some reason," Raphtalia said.

"Raph," Raph-chan agreed, puzzlement on their faces as they stood in the spectators' seats for our side.

"Master's food!" Filo said.

"They'll get a surprise when they taste what you're cooking, kiddo," L'Arc said.

"Indeed. Your victory is assured, if that's the best they can do," Glass agreed. I was still concerned about how aggressive they were being. Were they hopped up on endorphins or something? They weren't acting in character at all.

"Ingredients have been prepared in each seating area. You are not permitted to use ingredients belonging to your opponent. You may also bring in any ingredients you like . . . if you are capable of doing so." Her attitude was already getting on my nerves. "What genre of cooking will be the topic this time,

Master Seya?" *Oh God, he gets to choose?!* There was nothing fair about this at all, I could tell that already. It reminded me of my second day after I was summoned. This girl really was shaping up to be Trash III.

"Hmmm, an excellent question." Seya looked me up and down, mocking me completely. That very attitude made it far more likely that we were looking at another vanguard of the waves. Then he chatted a little with Trash III before looking at me again and laughing.

"The genre can be whatever you like. I have to teach these cooking thugs the sheer degree of difference between us," Seya said. *Whatever!* He was really going to make this a pain, wasn't he?

"I can use people to help me, correct? And I need to make food for each of the judges?" That was about all I needed to ask.

"Correct," she said. Then the ingredients Seya's restaurant provided were brought out. I needed to cook whatever I could with these ingredients or whatever I could get my hands on in an hour and a half. Normally there would be some time to prepare a bit first—

"Start cooking!" Trash III shouted, and a gong rang out. Seya rushed over to where his ingredients had been placed and started to select what to use. From what I could see, he had the choice of all sorts of different produce from various regions, and it all looked to be good quality. I moved over to the table where my ingredients were laid out and checked the vegetables.

> **Grassear carrot**
> **quality: close to rotten**
> **Biped radish**
> **quality: hard**
> **Boom-boom potato**
> **quality: about to explode**

I swore. Then I looked over at the judges' seats and Trash III to see them looking back with mockery in their eyes. I wondered for a moment if winning like this would damage their pride at all—but of course it wouldn't. Without really wanting to know what was in it, I looked at a barrel of water.

> **Trauma tiger pufferfish**
> **quality: excellent—danger! warning! deadly toxin!**

Appraisal indicated it was poisonous. I couldn't help but give a sigh.

"You expect me to use these?" I accused.

"You have a problem, do you? Look more carefully!" Even before I had finished complaining, Trash III was already pointing at the handful of ingredients on the table that looked almost edible.

Grassear carrot
quality: normal
Biped radish
quality: normal
Boom-boom potato
quality: normal

One of each. And I had to make enough for all the judges using these?

"Are you really a chef?" Trash III taunted. "You can't even spot the good ingredients!"

"This is a setup!" L'Arc raged.

"You cowards!" Tsugumi shouted. No one was really paying any attention, however; they were all watching Seya cook.

"You poor fools. Everyone who has battled us before has always brought their own ingredients with them. It's just common sense," Trash III said. Like we knew anything about the silly rules to this thing. If you didn't like what you were given, you could go get your own . . . but what could we manage in an hour or less? There was no market selling produce in the town. It was just the fields, perhaps. There would be monsters outside the town, but we didn't have the time to go hunting, let alone drain and prepare the meat. There might be fish in the river . . . but it would require some pretty hardcore hunting.

Cowards, indeed. This was all shaping up to be a royal pain, but losing would be an even bigger one.

"Kizuna, Kizuna," I called, beckoning her over.

"What?" she replied. I proceeded to fish a trauma tiger puffer from the barrel and slapped it down on the slab.

"Do your thing," I told her.

"Huh?" she responded, startled.

"Cut out the poisonous parts and make some puffer fish sashimi or something. You're good at dressing things, right?" I said. In the moment I told her what to do, the faces of the judges all turned pale. They knew the fish was poisonous, clearly.

"Daring to even try and feed us such a fish is like throwing the battle away already," the rotund noble spat. He was a noisy little ball. I'd have L'Arc strip him of his authority and pack him off into exile once we were done here.

"But hold on . . ." Kizuna said.

"It's not to feed to them. Just for you to practice. If you make it work, let Filo eat it for all I care," I told her. It was the one excellent-quality ingredient we had been given, and a rare one too. It would be wasted on the judges. We'd just keep that one to ourselves.

"What about you, Naofumi?" Kizuna asked.

"I've got some moves. Don't worry," I told her. I selected whatever looked like I might be able to use from the mountain of ingredients. "It looks like there are actually some usable ingredients among the rotten stuff they have provided. They probably didn't have the capacity to spot them." A lot of the meat was rotten, for example, but it also included some that had been treated in order to let it age. They had carried it all out seemingly without understanding that fact, so they must have thought it was just rotten. Many amateurs thought that fresh meat meant it was the most delicious, but that simply wasn't the case. It looked like Seya and his underlings were among those who didn't understand this.

I noticed a few of the cooks against the wall were looking at me, and looking shocked, perhaps realizing their mistake.

"I'll leave cutting all this up to you too. There's less edible stuff here than I thought," I told Kizuna.

"Okay," she replied. Even as I quickly sorted through my own mountain of ingredients, Seya placed a large cooking pot onto a kitchen range, filled it with water, and then lit the flame beneath it. Once it started bubbling and boiling, he touched an accessory on his right wrist, which seemed to just be a recreation of the vassal weapon drop function, and started to fiddle with something. A mysterious bag suddenly popped into existence in the air, and Seya grabbed it and turned it upside down. A brown powder spilled out and filled the pot that Seya had prepared.

From where I was standing, it looked like he'd created ingredients using the auto cooking function found in the holy, seven star, and vassal weapons. I wondered if this was an advancement of accessory modification or perhaps customization technology. If he had achieved that through his own personal modifications alone, then he wasn't so much a chef as he was a master accessory craftsman.

The smell of consommé started to waft over from Seya's pot. What a neat trick. Maybe I should try copying it, but I wasn't sure if it would work. It must have been a pain to prepare that powered consommé, and yet the final quality probably wouldn't be anything special.

"There it is!" Trash III and a second MC were now passionately describing everything that Seya was doing. "Master Seya's magical power!" That made it sound like something you definitely didn't want mixed into your food.

"Drown in the rich flavors of my food!" Seya taunted, even as he stirred the pot. It looked to me like he was stirring a bit too hard.

"What was that powder? Looks suspect to me!" Raphtalia said.

"You're really going to call mixing some powder into water 'cooking,' are you?" Tsugumi added.

"You look like you're just screwing around to me!" Glass finished off, all three of them not missing their chance to get a hit in. I had to agree that it was a bit much to call what he was doing "cooking."

"Right! Time for the next dish!" With that, Seya touched his accessory again and took out . . . something in silver packaging, it looked like. Then he put the entire thing, bag and all, into a pot of hot water and started to boil it. He looked like nothing but someone . . . making boil-in-the-bag curry. Seriously.

"That's the best dish Seya's restaurant has to offer! Seya's curry bag! And it's Fifth Floor too!" one of the MCs shouted. I barely stopped myself from tipping over onto the ground. He really was just reheating a premade curry in a bag! So he was allowed to heat and serve already finished dishes? I mean, that might give me some ideas myself . . .

"The flavors that are normally lost in reheating have been sealed in the bag using proprietary technology! Now you get the maximized flavor from the moment you open the bag! This truly is the ultimate culinary technique! Everyone, watch this kitchen miracle closely as it unfolds before your astounded eyes!" The MCs continued their diatribe, but it just made it harder for me to keep a straight face. It was all a matter of perspective. Capturing the flavor in a bag was certainly a worse approach than making it on the spot.

"Naofumi . . . am I imagining things? It looks to me like he's just adding or warming up instant ingredients using hot water," Kizuna said.

"What a coincidence. It looks like that to me too," I said. I mean, that was one way to prepare some food. I hadn't seen it done like this before, so I hadn't given it much thought, but if we could make use of it ourselves, then it might be worth checking out.

"I remember eating powdered soup as a portable meal, but I don't recall it being all that tasty," L'Arc muttered to Therese.

"Edible, but no better than that," Therese agreed. Drying it out, turning it into powder, and then turning it back into a soup was possible, and it could certainly be eaten. I wasn't going to deny that form of cooking. However, Seya continued to just produce bags and warm them up. He really was a one-trick pony.

"This is the one, folks! You are about to witness Master Seya's very own legendary noodle dish, which he perfected all on his own!" Spurred on by the MCs, he took something out of a bag, revealing instant noodles. So he was recreating things that four holy heroes from the past had talked about. All of this cooking would be commonplace back home, and there were already numerous dishes in these worlds that originated with tales from the heroes.

Still, being able to complete his meal so quickly would mean he could quickly get it out in front of the judges. That was what he was clearly thinking when he looked over at me, a grin on his face.

"Cooking is all about speed. How long are you going to be standing around for?" he taunted.

"Come now! Challenger! Master Seya is waiting! Finish your dish at once and prepare to learn the superior flavor of his cooking!" the MC squawked.

"I'll let you go first. Just do your best," Seya said. It sounded like he wanted to go second. Just a moment ago he'd been saying that cooking was "all about speed," so this seemed like a bit of a contradiction. He hadn't put the instant noodles into the pot yet, clearly worried about them going soggy if left in for too long.

I wasn't enjoying this. I'd just started to feel like I really was in some kind of cooking-manga battle, and then my opponent started wheeling out nothing but instant stuff, completely ruining the atmosphere. I wondered if he was even taking this seriously.

Seya continued his cooking, anyway, proceeding to dessert. He took out some fruit from what looked like a refrigerator— a simple ice box recreated using magic—and chopped it up. Then he put some water in a bowl, added more powder, and mixed it up. So this time he was just putting frozen fruit in instant gelatin.

"Just what is cooking, anyway?" I mumbled. It wasn't like I'd reached some great truth or wanted to have some deep philosophical discussion. But all the energy was just draining out of me as I looked at this menu from my opponent that made all my cookery efforts look outlandish and ridiculous. Why did he even have that mountain of ingredients anyway? It wasn't like he was using them!

Even as I thought that, Seya proceeded to use his accessory

to suck up some of those very ingredients. He was using some kind of special compounding. It amazed me that no one was asking any questions about how he was "cooking."

"Stop watching him and start cooking!" Kizuna said, snapping me back to myself.

"Okay, okay," I replied. Ah, but perhaps thinking that it was too much to rely on just instant stuff alone, Seya now took out some fish and meat and started to do something with them. I put aside the fact that it looked like he was just frying up some readymade wieners or something. He cut the meat, did no further preparation . . . and cooked it like steaks. That would bring out the flavor, but nothing else.

"Right . . ." I took a moment to think about the curry we had eaten here before the battle started. We were going to get to serve our food first. In either case, we didn't have enough ingredients.

"I'm going to go collect some ingredients. Kizuna and . . . Raphtalia! You do the basic prep while I'm gone," I told them.

"Huh?! Hold on, Naofumi!" Kizuna shouted.

"Mr. Naofumi?" Raphtalia said. I left her with preparing the ingredients we already had and headed over to the MCs.

"Hey, MC. I can go and get more ingredients, right? Including finished dishes?" I asked.

"Yes, if you can make it in time," she replied, with an attitude that barked, *Why are you even asking me something so obvious!*

"Okay then. I'll be right back." I quickly hurried out of the beer garden and away from the restaurant. Scroll of Return would have worked too, but using a movement skill would allow for a more advantageous use of cool-down time. And it would be quicker too. I headed for the wagon with the mirror on it. Along the way—

"Hey, you're the chef challenging that restaurant," someone said. I turned around. Normally, I wouldn't expect anyone to be talking to me, but in this case, it seemed pretty clear. I was almost expecting an assassin sent by Seya.

Instead, I was faced with the muddy kid we had seen working in the fields on the way here. He was a young boy, with a basket on his back.

"What is it, kid?" I asked. "I'm kind of in the middle of something." There was a clock on this, so I could do without any interruptions. Then the kid pushed his basket into my hands.

"You don't have any ingredients, right?" he said. "I'll share ours with you." I couldn't help but be suspicious of a stranger suddenly showing up like this and offering aid.

"What do you get out of this?" I asked. I checked out the basket. It was loaded with wild plants and herbs. Even politely, it would be hard to call them good quality, but I could tell it must have taken him a long time to pick them all.

"There are guards in the fields and storerooms, so you won't get anything from there. If you can't bring in any of your own ingredients, you'll have to use that rotten pile they provided you with," the kid said. I'd worked that much out myself. Not that I had been expecting much help from the other side. "You don't have much time to get anything, right? This is about all we can offer," he went on. Some kind of peace offering, then. "I saw what happened before the battle started. You're actually a good chef, right? And you've got allies who are more important than the guy on Seya's side. So please . . . defeat Seya for us!" This was unexpected. I'd thought almost everyone in the town was supporting Seya, but this kid seemed to want to support me.

"Why are you coming to me with this? I need to hear your reasons or I can't take you up on anything," I said.

"I didn't suspect anything from Seya's cooking at first," the kid said, glaring at the building back in the town. "It was super delicious and filled me with energy, and everyone in town was eating it. It felt like it was making the place so much better," he said. It was strange. It almost felt like I was talking to Keel. "But then, one day, my grandma and mother suddenly collapsed. They had seemed so full of energy, but then they just fell down, like puppets with their strings cut," he said. *Cut strings, huh?* There were tears of frustration in the boy's eyes as he went on. "We tried to help them, but they died . . . and then my dad too. I was so shocked. I remembered how much we had all enjoyed eating at Seya's restaurant, and I just didn't want to go anymore . . . so I started cooking for myself." The boy suppressed his shaking hands and looked at me with hate-filled eyes. "It reached the point where I could only think about the food from Seya's restaurant. Then my body had this terrible spasm, and I was laid up in bed! There's definitely something up with that food!" Then he looked at the basket he had handed me. "Now I only have to smell his food and I start to feel sick. There's definitely something strange in it."

Then suddenly some other voice interjected, "I helped collect them too!" This came from another child, a little girl looking at the boy with worry in her eyes . . . his sister, probably. She grabbed onto the boy and the two of them looked at me. They had innocent faces, but they also looked kind of thin. They reminded me of Raphtalia when she was small—or Fohl and Atla, who were also brother and sister—and I let down my guard. I'd seen kids this age lie, and lie convincingly, but I couldn't see any merit in tricking me like this. If they were trying to trick me, that might involve mixing some poisonous plants in with the medicinal herbs. But I could appraise them easily enough. I'd only taken a quick look, but poison didn't seem to be the case.

"Seya loved to cook for others ever since he was small, but after opening that restaurant, he started to take out all the competition and make it the only place in town!" the boy continued. "Everyone living here said they just wanted to eat

Seya's cooking and stopped cooking at home. That's how we got here!" It had smelled a bit like a dictatorship from the start . . . and then I realized that maybe my village was in a similar situation. But no, in my village everyone cooked together, so it was different. The idea was that everyone ate together. The adjacent neighborhood had been pretty normal too. But here . . . there was definitely something going on here.

"There's been a big increase in people suddenly dropping dead or being defeated by monsters and dying!" the boy said. "But no one thinks it's odd! It definitely is! But when I say that, everyone just gives me weird looks . . . Please! The only people who are going to believe me are outsiders like you!" It sounded like the boy had tried to act on his suspicions, but no one had believed him. Considering the permanent state of addiction coming from that toxin, it certainly wasn't impossible. This was one of those situations in which it seemed to be making the people healthy but actually wasn't. Food might even be mixed in that extracted life energy in exchange for immediate strength. There were such status-boosting drugs among the drops of the monsters in this world, but I hadn't heard anything about side effects directly making you weaker even when you looked strong and healthy.

Then there was Seya's attitude, which could be considered an affront to cookery. I mean, I was using cooking to dope up my allies as well, so I could hardly take a holier-than-thou attitude here, but I was confident I could get a result that would please this kid.

I looked over the vegetables and herbs in the basket again.

"Sure, I can use this stuff," I said. *Why not?* "Okay. I'll use these ingredients to make your wish come true. Just you wait and see." There were some things mixed in that I'd been planning on getting from the castle anyway. I could make this work.

"Really? You promise?" the boy exclaimed.

"I promise. You just be good and wait here," I said. I continued over to the carriage and set up the mirror we had onboard. The kid watched me, clearly puzzled about what was going on. "I'll be right back. You watch that basket," I said.

"Sure thing!" he said, still a little unsure about what was happening.

"See you soon. Transport Mirror." After making sure I had a good lock on the mirror, I incanted the skill and returned to L'Arc's castle.

"Huh?! What the—" The boy's voice was cut off mid-sentence, and I emerged from the castle mirror right into the killer whale sisters.

"Oh my, little Naofumi!" said Sadeena.

"Oh dear! Just you, sweet Naofumi?" Shildina said. It looked like Sadeena had managed to track down the lost Shildina after all.

"Great timing, girls. I need you to carry some stuff for me," I told them.

"Oh my," Sadeena said. I proceeded to fill some sacks with whatever we had on hand in the castle and then had the killer whale sisters carry those sacks. Then I headed to the kitchen and picked up with both hands one of the pots I had left in the care of the castle chefs. Of course, for a normal person it would have been too heavy to carry, but in addition to the other-world concept of levels, I also had the protection of the mirror. It wasn't heavy or hot for me at all.

"Good luck—" S'yne started, sitting in the food hall and eating all the food I had left behind.

"You are doing a good thing," her familiar relayed. "Please make that boy's wish come true." S'yne was waving, and her eyes looked assured that she understood the situation and was sure I would win anyway. From her attitude, it seemed like things were fine here.

"Let's go," I said. "Movement Mirror." I used another movement skill to return to where I had just come from. On the way out, I had used Transport Mirror, a skill that connected two mirrors together. On the way back, I had used Movement Mirror, which allowed me to jump to any mirror I had been to before. They were both pretty similar skills, but the difference was the cool down. Transport Mirror took a lot longer. Spending some points on Portal Shield could really reduce the cool down, but I couldn't use that right now and so had used a combination of these two skills.

Now I was back to cooking and had more ingredients.

"You came out of the mirror!" the boy exclaimed.

"Awesome!" His sister's eyes sparkled as she looked on.

"Right, back to the battle. Pass me the basket," I said. He did so, and I returned toward the battle venue.

"You have to win!" the boy said.

"I will," I replied to the two kids supporting me, continuing to walk as I did so.

When I arrived, the hostess girls and MCs at Seya's restaurant were looking at my dishes and ingredients, obviously wondering where I had got all them from.

"Sadeena and Shildina?" Raphtalia said, looking at the sisters and then at me. She had finished cutting the meat.

"Yeah, I wanted to bring all the basics, so I brought those two along as pack mules," I said. Levels and enhancements and whatever might let me carry a lot, but I still only had two hands. Bringing volume was the problem.

"Little Naofumi, where should we put this?" Sadeena asked.

"Right on the table there," I said.

"Okay!" Sadeena replied.

"Let's get cooking," I said. I put some pots on the stove and then got started. It had taken a bit of time to reach this point, but I still had plenty left. I let life force flow around my body, as though I was about to go into battle. I grated the herbs and compounded them. Then I took up the knife. I was pretty sure I didn't have to make a full-course dinner, which for a continental course would have been an appetizer, soup, fish, meat, sherbet, roast meat, salad, dessert, fruit, and then coffee. I'd cooked similar meals back at L'Arc's castle. I'd used roasted beans similar to coffee beans and medicinal herbs to make a tea. I didn't have time for all that in this cooking battle, though. Just something quick, something I was accustomed to making, would be fine.

The order I served the dishes in would be important, of course.

I appraised the aged meat that Raphtalia had pared out and trimmed it down to the part that definitely wouldn't cause any food poisoning. Imbuing it with life force further activated the aged meat, filling it with power, and by the time I finished cutting, the quality had been raised to excellent.

That was definitely something we could work with.

As for Kizuna . . . I handed her some of the fish we had brought in and had her cut it up. She'd finished with the poisonous fish already. Her life as a fishing fool was paying off now. She knew her way around a fish. The blood had been skillfully drained, and overall, she was a step ahead when it came to gutting and cleaning.

"Kizuna, give me that," I said.

"Huh? Ah, okay," she replied. I used the herbs I had

brought back with me and arranged the cut pieces of fish on a plate. Then I added a dressing made from those same medicinal herbs and some cooking oil. Finish off with plenty of life energy . . .

"There we go, one finished. That's a fish carpaccio—almost," I said. Next, I melted the fatty part of the meat in the frying pan, then added the rest of the meat and lightly seared it to seal in the flavor. All the while I continued to provide a suitable volume of life force in order to keep the quality from falling.

"What are you doing?" Seya was looking over, a mocking tone in his voice. "You need to cut meat up before you cook it! You can't cook a lump like that." It made me wonder what kind of chefs he had fought against so far. Not very good ones, from the sound of it.

Adding some life force allowed the heat to pass through more easily. It was the perfect temperature before I knew it, and then I arranged it on a skillet with the remainder of the vegetables I had selected and put it in the oven that Raphtalia had carefully adjusted. I then moved on to reheating the soup I had brought in with me. I transferred some over to a separate pot, added some chopped vegetables and meat, and started stewing.

All my cooking experience so far was really coming to bear now. I was even able to cover for the Japanese vegetables we couldn't get here. Then I added some of the milk and cheese I had got from the castle, and the stew was complete.

"Just a few more things . . ." With the remaining time, I made an original sauce from a combination of the medicinal herbs and a simple appetizer.

That appetizer was sliced chicken and medicinal herbs with a side of gelatin. The soup was consommé, made from the bouillon I had carried back with me. Then there was the stew that my brother had so liked—it was rapidly becoming a favorite among Kizuna's allies—and the "almost" carpaccio. The main dish was roast beef. For the dessert, I had gone with a kind of faux fruit punch, mixing subtle fruit flavors with sweet herb juice.

I could have tried for something flashier, but in the time allotted, this was the best I could do. I'd never taken part in a battle like this before, after all. I'd been thinking of a full-course meal but hadn't been able to turn out that many dishes.

I mean, in the cooking manga I had seen, they normally won with a single dish. So I thought I'd made a pretty good account of it myself. The gong to signal the end of the cooking time rang out pretty much right at the point everything was finished.

Chapter Eight: Medicinal Cooking

"Phew . . ." My experience with cooking for a large number of people all the time had really helped too. At the village, I normally just plunked down a couple of things, but this had been fun too. I would have liked to have polished each one a little more.

"Kiddo, you were looking really good out there," L'Arc said.

"Indeed . . . a real craftsman. You pulled your weight too, Kizuna," Glass said.

"All I did was pick out the ingredients and cut the fish . . ." Kizuna replied. All of her allies were quick to praise me. Kizuna was downplaying her role in things too. That side of preparation was very important, especially when it came to fish.

"You have a unique timing when applying your life force. I think it would be pretty hard to emulate," Glass said.

"Master's food! Huh? We're not allowed to eat it?" Filo asked.

"He had Kizuna prepare something just for you. Look, Filo, Mr. Naofumi is bringing it over now," Raphtalia said.

"Yay! Oh boy, it smells delicious!" Filo said happily.

"It might be kind of poisonous, so watch out for that," I told her.

"Oh my . . . can someone finally explain to us exactly what you are doing?" Sadeena asked.

"Explain!" Shildina added.

"It turns out we got involved in this cooking battle . . ." Raphtalia proceeded to explain to the sisters what was going on, with everyone else sticking their oar in whenever it suited them.

"Will both chefs please bring their food forward? I'm sure Master Seya will win, but we will be eating the challenger's food first," the MC said, her biased flag still firmly flying. The judges started to carry my dishes toward their mouths.

First the appetizer.

"Hah, the food of this challenger surely can't hope to compare to Master Seya's—" the rotund noble started. After a single mouthful, his eyes opened wide and he started to scoff the food down. "This can't be?! What is this? It's delicious! Too delicious! And it feels like some kind of poison is draining from my body as I eat! So refreshing! This is the best!" The noble quickly accelerated into top gear, stuffing his face with every-thing in reach. The other judges were doing the same. They weren't especially clean eaters, to be honest.

"That meat looked practically rotten, and look at it now! The flavor, the texture, it's stunning!" the noble exclaimed.

"Because it wasn't rotten at all. It may have looked that way at a glance, but really it was just aged meat that had become more delicious. And it was mixed in with the meat supplied to the restaurant. Someone went to all that trouble, but some other moron thought it was rotten and gave it to us," I explained pointedly, looking at Seya, Trash III, and the other MC. Trash III responded by flipping me off. I could taunt with the best of them, and I mouthed some swear words back.

"What's this tingling in my nose I feel? It harmonizes so well with the texture. What condiments have you added?" the noble asked.

"It's a mixture of medicinal and fragrant herbs. Slightly spicy herbs that are good for your health and promote your appetite have been formed into a jelly with an awareness of medicinal cooking," I explained. I signaled at the kid who was watching in the gathered crowd, knowing he would like this.

"I see. That's why as soon as I had one mouthful, I just felt like eating more. The more you eat, the more you want, and yet it makes your body feel strong and purified! What mysterious cooking!" the noble exclaimed. All of the judges were reaching for one dish after another.

"This is like the soup that Master Seya always serves . . . but it's far more delicious! It's like swimming in a sea of concentrated flavor! Compared to this soup, Master Seya's tastes like ditchwater . . . but what am I saying?!" the noble exclaimed. I had trouble understanding exactly why he would go so far too. He was the closest to a character from a cooking manga out of anyone here! Consommé wasn't like being in the sea, not really . . . but maybe that's what it felt like to him when he tasted it. His imagination was a little too flowery for me.

"I would think it goes without saying that a carefully prepared soup is going to taste better than a simple powdered one," I said. "Some third-rate chefs think serving something quickly makes it delicious." I'd happily admit that being quick was convenient, but being delicious came from somewhere else. Of course, I was also fine with anything, so long as it was edible.

"If you insult Master Seya any further, you will be disqualified!" the MC stated.

"This is a cooking battle, and yet what I say will change the results. Is that what you are suggesting? Your Master Seya is more narrow-minded than I thought," I said.

"Hah. Let him have his moment," Seya said, still looking pretty confident as he quieted down the MC. That said, there was an "I'll never forgive you for this" look buried in his eyes that I couldn't help but pick up on. The MC calmed down a bit, anyway.

"This is a simplified version that I made in the time I had. If you give it more time to cook, it becomes what is called a double consommé," I explained.

"It can go a level higher than this?" the noble said, his eyes wide. All the judges were looking at me with their mouths practically hanging open. Talk about a lack of culinary education.

"And this . . . am I to presume this is no ordinary stew? After everything you've cooked so far, I admit I've started to have certain expectations!" the rotund noble said. He and the other judges tried the stew.

"What's this now?!" one of them exclaimed.

"Hoh-hoh-hoh-hoh! It feels like I can only laugh! There's no time for talk when eating something so truly delicious!" the rotund noble said—a clear contradiction—as he continued to chatter on while stuffing his smiling face. He said there was no time for talk, even as he babbled on. "This fish is a pure delight! The sauce really brings out the flavor . . . It's got a similar flavor to the gelatin in the appetizer, but it doesn't get old, does it?"

"I was conscious of resetting the tongue and bringing out a different experience through the combination of foods. Just by changing the order you eat things in will change the flavors you experience," I said.

"What?! You've even arranged that kind of surprise for us! But I've almost eaten all of it . . ." The noble looked over at the dishes the other judges were eating, longing in his eyes, but they had all almost finished as well. L'Arc and Glass looked on, practically puffing up their chests in pride, even though they didn't exactly make much of a contribution.

"Just what are we even doing?" Kizuna said, shaking her head.

"Please, don't ask me," Raphtalia responded, also feeling

how dumb this all was. Hey, don't look at me! I had as much a clue as either of them.

"Next, then . . . now this looks like something I've eaten before," the noble said.

"It's roast beef, so I guess you have. I thought the main dish could get away with being simple," I explained.

"Good golly!" the man managed to exclaim around his mouthful. "This matured meat practically melts in the mouth! I know it's meat, it should be meat, and yet it simply melts away . . . This is a realm of flavor normally reserved for the highest-quality marbled meat! This looked like red meat, nothing more, and yet it melted in the mouth! Ah, I can see it! I see it so clearly! The monster, aged, becoming an ingredient far more enhanced than it ever was in life . . . and now it is evolving, evolving in my mouth! Ah, the very soul of that monster is trembling with joy! The joy of being relegated to the rotten pile . . . and having been transformed into this! Having been saved!" The rotund noble spoke so quickly I was worried he might bite his tongue.

Another one of the judges gave a wild shout. I looked over . . . and it seemed that horns had sprouted from his head. I wasn't going to get involved with whatever that was. Raphtalia looked at me in surprise, but I just ignored her too. This was a crazy fantasy world, after all. Maybe a monster could be revived inside someone who ate it. The meat I used might have had some kind of parasitic attributes.

"Kiddo, hey . . . that's not going to happen to us, is it?" L'Arc asked, genuinely concerned.

"No idea. I would keep your parasitic resistance up," I told them.

"And finally, the dessert . . . such a shame the meal is over already . . . oh my. Very simple. I feel refreshed and still just a little puckish," the rotund noble said.

"I know you've got another meal to eat after this, so I wanted to give you room to judge him too. That's a medicinal dessert. It prompts digestion and builds strength," I explained.

"So thoughtful, giving such consideration to Master Seya! You must be the greatest rival he has faced so far!" the rotund noble proclaimed. All of the judges seemed pleased with the outcome . . . if not left wanting a little more. "My own regret is that there wasn't more of it!" The rotund one was quick to voice that very thought.

"I've seen what you are normally eating, after all. One of the fun things about meals is being left wanting more, no?" I said. At my reply, an expression of acceptance spread across the noble's face, even if he wasn't listening to everything I was saying.

"Hoh-hoh-hoh-hoh! A cunning strategy, seeming to give consideration to your opponent while actually undermining him. Very clever. I tip my hat to you," the noble acquiesced. Seya and his goons seemed pretty unimpressed with the reception we had received from the judges. They clearly didn't want to see or hear their opponents getting any kind of praise. If they just paid some attention, they might have learned something from me, but they only had ears for praise for themselves. There was no hint at all of them learning anything from their battles. The judges certainly weren't on their side at the moment.

"If you want to give up, now is the time," I told Seya.

"That's my line," he retorted. He'd let us go first, and look where it had got him . . . I was willing to give him the room to step down, but he still didn't have a clue.

"Why all the herbs in the cooking?" Kizuna asked.

"Someone asked me to," I said.

"Asked you?" she replied.

"Yeah. It was to free everyone from the pollution of Seya's cooking," I told her.

"Pollution?" Kizuna asked, looking puzzled.

"You didn't notice that?" I replied. "Well, just watch." She wasn't the brightest bulb, that was for sure.

"Hmmm, I think I need to go wash up," the rotund noble said. "I'll be right back." The judges proceeded to take turns visiting the washroom. Once they had all returned, it was time to eat Seya's food.

"Huh?" Kizuna, L'Arc, and Therese were looking puzzled. The other diners around us too. I guess there was cause for a little suspicion.

"Well then, let's enjoy Master Seya's cooking," the rotund noble said. He and the other judges proceeded to tuck eagerly into the dishes Seya made. In the moment the noble ate his first mouthful, a smile filled with confidence spread across Seya's face.

"This is the skill of a true chef!" Seya proclaimed.

"You're getting full of yourselves now because the judges have been so nice to you, but this is where you feel Master Seya's awesome might!" the MC crowed, quickly joining in. The results hadn't even been given yet and they were already claiming victory. There was only one side getting full of themselves here.

Things weren't going to go their way this time.

"What the hell is this soup?!" the noble exclaimed, literally spitting it out of his mouth. "This is nothing like the normal delicious soup you serve! What's going on?" He glared at Seya, unwanted soup dribbling back out from his lips.

"What? What are you rambling about?! I made my normal, incredible soup!" Seya exclaimed. That powdered soup—incredible? He had added some things, some meat and whatever, but basically it was just powdered soup. That was only going to get you so far! Not to mention, it was cloudy and looked horrible. But that was the point—he'd been tricking them. The MC reached for the soup the noble had tasted and tried some herself.

"There's nothing wrong with it at all! This is Master Seya's incredible soup, just like normal!" At her testimony that it was the same as normal, the noble's eyes opened wide in surprise. This time he reached gingerly for the curry and tried a mouthful.

"What's this now? It tastes like nothing more than spicy mud! No, in fact . . . not that I've ever tasted it . . . but it looks more like, well . . . something else brown! It's bitter and disgusting! I can't even stomach the smell! What's going on here?! Hmmm . . . the flavor has come back a bit, but it's just . . . a regular curry. It doesn't have any of that usual Seya curry taste!"

"Impossible! This is the Seya Curry at the highest possible floor! Ah, it's delicious enough to make my tongue melt!" There was just too large a gap between the evaluation of the judges and that of the MC. Voices of protest were starting to rise from the spectators too. The noble went on to try the other dishes, but he had a sickened look on his face and spat most of them out, holding his nose the entire time.

"Master Seya, just what is going on here? Are you serving us this disgusting slop on purpose?" he asked. He had a look in his eyes like he just couldn't believe what was happening. His trust in Seya seemed to only be enhancing the impact of this betrayal.

"Impossible! How is my ultimate cooking being evaluated so poorly?" Seya shouted. Then suddenly his gaze snapped angrily onto me, accompanied by an accusing point. "You cheated! That's the only way to explain this!"

"I'd expect no less from someone like you, running to that as an excuse. I'll say this, then. You're actually right," I replied. No matter how fair I tried to play things, we were dealing with the kind of people who always found fault as soon as they were defeated. So I'd just put a plan into action. Nothing that could really be called "cheating."

"Kiddo!" L'Arc exclaimed.

"Mr. Naofumi!?" Raphtalia joined him.

"Naofumi . . . I can't believe you'd stoop so low!" Kizuna added. Everyone who was supposed to be on my side was now looking at me with suspicion in their eyes. I mean, sure, I had pulled a bit of a fast one, but they could have had a little more trust in me!

Even the kid who'd asked me to help was looking suspicious. I wished they would all hear me out first.

"Hey, don't get me wrong. I didn't do anything that would change their evaluation if the food actually did taste great. Seya had already cheated to enhance his own flavor, and all I did was reset that," I explained.

"What? You coward! What trickery is this!" Seya exclaimed. He wasn't listening.

"The proof is in the pudding. If you eat some of my cooking, the appetizer, the soup, or the dessert perhaps, and then eat some of your own food, you might experience the same thing the judges are going through now. This is the kind of thing you opened yourself up to by letting me go first," I said, with a casual air. Kizuna jumped on that real quick.

"I've seen this in an old anime! You cooked something with richer flavors, which made the opponent's flavors taste washed out!" she exclaimed.

"No! Nothing like that!" I shot back. *Which side are you on!* I had read a similar trick in a cooking manga myself, but I hadn't used anything like that this time. I pointed at Seya's cooking and continued my explanation. "When I first tried your cooking, I realized that it contained something addictive. Something likely far more addictive than tobacco, alcohol . . . even narcotics. That's the true special ingredient in this delicious, captivating cooking."

"You've got to be kidding!" Kizuna shouted in surprise. *Some hero she was!* Even L'Arc, Raphtalia, and Glass looked surprised by this news. I wondered how they couldn't possibly have noticed.

"What is this now? You're saying I've been fed something addictive?" the noble asked, also unable to hide his surprise.

"And there's nothing like that in your cooking, kiddo?" L'Arc asked. I almost wanted to slap him! *Enough with the attacks from my allies! As if I'd ever add anything like that!*

"You want me to try it? If I did, you'd be unable to think of anything but eating . . . You'd be even worse than the people here in this town. Is that what you want?" I asked. Hearing this threat, L'Arc shook his head vigorously from side to side. L'Arc and the others were heroes, anyway, so they would have some resistance.

"So what the hell did you do?" Seya raged.

"Ah!" Kizuna finally cottoned on. "So that's why you used so many medicinal herbs in your dishes!"

"Exactly. The reason they all wanted to go to the washroom after eating was to expel the toxins. I also used other herbs to bolster the lethargic feeling that would bring on," I explained. They had been eating the stuff habitually for a while, so they wouldn't have been able to get rid of it all. But this should have at least a temporary effect. As proof of that, all the judges looked in far better health now than when I had first seen them. Those in the audience could easily tell the difference too.

"Remember what the judges said when they were eating?" I continued, rounding on Seya. "That it felt purifying. Well, that's exactly what it was. I drew out the toxins from your cooking with my herbs, recovered their vitality, and gave them some resistance. That's all. That allowed them to give a more rational evaluation of your cooking while highlighting how disgusting the toxins in it taste." It was basically cooking that made alcohol or tobacco taste really bad.

The explanation was dragging on too. I could feel that myself. Explaining stuff seemed to take forever sometimes.

"You must be joking! You should be ashamed to have

cooked such filth!" Seya accused. I wasn't ashamed of anything. In fact, I wanted to ask him if he wasn't ashamed of making food full of addictive toxins.

"You're one to talk!" I shot back. "You've been putting toxins in your own food, gave me a pile of rotten ingredients, and made a load of nothing but instant food while crowing about how I'd 'drown in your flavor' or whatever! You're the one who must be joking." There had been less edible material in that pile than nonedible. He had given me that crap-pile to work with while also cowardly mixing highly addictive toxins into his own food. Not to mention the already bought-and-paid-for panel of judges! He couldn't possibly expect me to take this farce of a cooking battle seriously!

I really hated people who tried to rig the results of anything prior to it even taking place.

"Ah, there's one other thing I have to do," I mentioned. I pointed at the noble and beckoned for him to come to me. Of course, he didn't comply. Left without a choice, I moved quickly over to him. Seya's allies, the restaurant staff, tried to stop me, but I just pushed them out of the way.

"What is it? What do you want?" the rotund one asked.

"Choose. Do you want to keep on being used like this, in a stupor of addictive toxins until you die, or do you want to try the food I make when I really get serious?" I asked him. He grunted at the question, and I pressed on. "My allies will probably tell you that my food is also delicious and highly addictive, so on that score, both might seem the same. But you do want to eat food that is just powder thrown into water, just reheated in a bag, or do you want to eat food made from proper ingredients, cooked and prepared with all due care to your eating experience?" This noble in particular had a kind of gourmet air to him, and I was sure I was making a better offer than continuing to eat this instant stuff. If he had thought my medicinal herb cooking tasted so good, I was confident the real deal would knock his socks off. I'd seen what our enemies were feeding him, after all.

"Don't let him trick you! My cooking tastes better for sure! There are no toxins in it! They're making all this up!" Seya ranted.

"That's right!" Seya's MC quickly backed him up. "You are one of Master Seya's top-ranking customers!" The rotund noble in question looked in befuddlement between Seya and me. If he already wasn't sure, that meant I had him.

"They're lying! My family ate at this place and now they're all dead!" The kid picked this moment to speak up, in a nicely timed move.

"Quiet! We don't know why your family died," someone in the crowd said.

"You can't blame Master Seya for all the bad stuff that happens!" said another as everyone nearby started to lecture the poor kid.

"We won't allow anyone to insult Master Seya!" The MC got in on the action too. "I'll strip all your points if you do!" This threat caused quite the commotion in the crowd.

"No, not that!"

"You have to apologize, right away!" someone said.

But the boy didn't back down.

"Don't you think this is strange? You all used to cook at home before Seya opened this place! Now you eat here for every meal! Getting hooked on something and enjoying eating are two totally different things!" the boy shouted.

"Shut up! We can't live without Master Seya's restaurant!" someone replied.

"That's right!" said someone else. Cooking really was ruling the whole town, that much was for sure.

"I'm not sure . . . I like this . . ." The noble was further shaken by seeing all of this. It looked like he did have some good left in him. Now I needed to pry my fingers into the opening. I leaned toward him and whispered into his ear.

"Once I win and claim all of his assets, I'll take that accessory apart and give the recipes to you. Then you won't even need him to make the cooking for you anymore, will you? You know who we are as well, don't you?" I said to him. All his recipes were simple ones that could be made using tools. It was highly likely that if we could just get our hands on the recipes, anyone would be able to make them. The noble seemed to be having the same thought, because a change came over his eyes.

"Challenger, return to your starting position! Master Seya, you calm down too!" the noble said.

"Yes, yes, of course! The judges have seen which of us is loyally, faithfully doing his best! You've lost, giving away your tricks before the results have even been revealed!" Seya spat.

We would see about that. As for "loyally, faithfully doing his best," I didn't have words to reply to that. Even speaking objectively, he couldn't really be said to have been putting much effort in.

I quickly moved back and returned to where I had done my cooking.

"What is this feeling? Like something bad is about to happen," Raphtalia said.

"What a coincidence. I have the same feeling," Glass quipped.

"Hmmm. This is quickly becoming a pretty personal problem," Tsugumi said. For her, she'd been in a similar position before in her own past. She looked pretty cool about things, given how that had gone.

"That said . . . from what that boy claimed back there, it sounds like Mr. Naofumi did the right thing," Raphtalia said.

"The kiddo normally does," L'Arc agreed.

"The skills of the Master Craftsman," Therese marveled.

"Therese, hey . . . do you think you could stop becoming a

totally different person when you talk about kiddo?" L'Arc said. He had his own stuff to deal with, that was for sure. He wasn't any different from her anyway, going crazy over a single dish.

"Master, is this all the food you have?" Filo asked. She was starting to bug me, but leaving her dissatisfied would only cause more trouble later. I put some soup in front of Filo.

"Just make do with that a little longer. I'll make you some more once we get back," I told her.

"Okay!" she said. Then I noticed the killer whale sisters, who had now been brought up to speed by Raphtalia and the others, looking at Seya with suspicion in their eyes. I wondered what was up with that. The judges had started whispering among themselves too. Seya and his goons were still glaring at me with some dissatisfaction.

"Do you think we're in the clear, Naofumi?" Kizuna asked.

"No idea. In either case, I really messed up their cooking," I said. That did make me feel a bit better. When I put aside the whole cooking battle thing, their bad attitude and lack of respect for cooking had been pushing me close to the edge.

"I'm just not sure about your methods," Kizuna said.

"There's nothing fair about this battle. The winner was always going to be the one who was more cunning, more conniving than the other," I said.

"Hmmm, it's a shame you couldn't just win because your food tasted the best," Kizuna said.

"Hey . . . you've been reading too many cooking manga. It's an illusion that delicious and good things will be evaluated highly. What you need is popularity and demand," I said. Of course, it had to taste good, but putting the emphasis on that as a bare requirement was also a problem. If you were planning on selling food in a restaurant, of course it had to taste good. Customers came because of other elements, because of popularity. If Seya's restaurant collapsed here, it would cause trouble for all the judges. That was why I'd created an escape for them. In order to realize the future that boy wanted. Itsuki's talk of justice? I didn't care about that. If I didn't fend off the dangerous sparks raining down on us, I'd get burned myself.

Take this restaurant, for example, which was practically a crazy religion. Leave this place running and it could trigger all sorts of other problems.

"That's really how it works?" Kizuna asked. "Sounds more like being a merchant than being a chef."

"You're not wrong. The most delicious food should be the winner. But Seya's food doesn't taste good at all. You guys wanted this, right?" I said. When I looked over at L'Arc and the others, they didn't look entirely impressed.

"This doesn't really feel quite like what we expected . . ." L'Arc said.

"If Seya had kept to the rules—the best taste wins—and fought fair and square, I wouldn't have taken things this far.

But think about what they did. They had no plans to give us a fair battle," I reminded them. If they had given out equal ingredients and we simply had to cook something within the time limit, the results might have been different. But not with the way they had handled things. They had maximized their home advantage, giving us rotten goods and toxic fish. They'd even bought off the judges. They were cowards and had been rewarded accordingly.

"I'd expect no less from you, Naofumi. The means still bother me a little . . ." Kizuna said.

"It feels like I've seen the nastier side of this world," Raphtalia added.

"We need to be tough, or we won't survive the enemies that lie ahead," I warned them. Bitch was bad enough, but S'yne's sworn enemies were the very picture of cunning. Something like this would just be the warmup for them.

"I mean, you're probably not wrong . . ." Kizuna said.

"I reckon you've learned a lot from this experience. Even so, things seem a lot better here in your world, Kizuna," I told her. That kid turning up with his big old basket and helping out wasn't something I really expected to happen in our world. The best example I could think of was the kid who helped us when fighting the second wave.

One good deed definitely deserved another, anyway.

If the rotund one didn't go the way I wanted, we'd use

L'Arc's authority to bend things our way. I was the Mirror Hero, after all, and heroes also had certain rights.

The rotund noble and the rest of the judges all stood up, with faces looking more determined than before, their discussions finished. Some tension-creating music started to play. Itsuki wasn't with us, but I looked around anyway, almost expecting to see him.

"Duh . . . duh . . . duuum!" It was Filo, singing to herself. I both wondered who taught her that and wished she would stop it at the same time. She was only ratcheting up the tension!

The noble and the others all held up their indicators. The one with Seya's insignia was crossed out (they had already thrown away the ones to indicate us before the match even began).

"The winner is the traveling cook!" they proclaimed. It looked like this skullduggery-filled cooking battle had ended with my victory.

Chapter Nine: Resolution via Violence

The guy who had been about to ring the victory gong stopped mid-stroke, looked at the judges, and then did a double take. The gathered crowd of diners did one better. They immediately started shouting and screaming at the judges.

"What are you talking about?!"

"You've been paid off, clearly! Traitors!"

"That's right! Traitors!" As the tension rose, they started to throw things at the judges. The scene started slipping toward what looked like a riot.

The boy was smiling at me though. He looked happy that I'd defeated his hated enemy.

"Hey! Explain this!" Seya shouted, casting a look filled with vitriol at the rotund one and the other judges.

"We conducted a fair evaluation after the removal of your addicting toxin. I've had numerous suspicions about your cooking for a while now, Master Seya. You explained it as magical cooking, combined with the power of an accessory you modified yourself, but still—" the noble said and was then cut off.

"I'm not going to feed you anymore! What do you think that means for your strength? The strength that my food has been giving you!" Seya demanded. Just as I'd suspected, he'd been doping the people using means similar to the mirror power-up method. In regard to the fact that some of his test subjects seemed to have been dying . . . he didn't seem bothered in the slightest. This was a world with drugs that had similar doping effects, but in this case the enhancement he was performing definitely didn't seem to be healthy.

"You seem to be making one big mistake, Master Seya," the noble replied. His expression was one of victory, not concern or defeat. "We are not on your side. We are on the side of delicious cooking!" He just came right out with it. I stood there, shaking my head. He was clearly just ignoring everything that had happened between them so far, but he had acted as the ally of delicious cooking, I would give him that much. Even if Seya never cooked for him again, we now had a chance to break down that cooking method for ourselves.

"Liars! How can that disgusting-looking food possibly beat ours?!" Trash III pointed at one of my plates of food. "They used some cunning trickery to get in Master Seya's way, that's for sure!" I was amazed that they could still try to push that narrative, after everything they had done. The rules did allow us to bring our own food in, but that was no reason for what they gave us to begin with, rotten food. In fact, even if people did bring in their own dishes, they could probably force them to lose by indicating a genre that didn't allow the use of those dishes. Those kinds of tricks wouldn't work on me, of course.

"Regardless of how we got here, it looks like I'm the winner, right?" I said.

"Shut up! A trickster like you could never defeat my cooking! This battle doesn't count!" Seya retorted.

"If I'd lost, do you think that would have worked if I'd said it?" I asked him. Of course, it wouldn't, and it wasn't going to work now.

"I said shut up! My cooking could never be defeated by the likes of you!" he raged.

"You need to go back to the basics and learn cooking all over again," I said. All he was making was instant dishes. That was it. If you could call that cooking, then you could call yourself a chef just by boiling some water. Then there was the fact he had been mixing that addictive toxin into his food.

"You dare to lecture me? I can't take any more of this! Everyone! Chase them out of town!" Seya shouted. So this was what things came down to. He didn't like the way things were going, so he turned to the mob for aid. I barely had the words. The assembled diners were definitely glaring at us, armed with hoes, swords, and various other weapons. It looked like they might attack at any moment.

"The loser gives everything over to the winner, no complaints! Those are the words you have always used against your opponents, Master Seya!" the rotund noble said.

"You can shut up too! Traitor!" Seya fired back. Then the kid jumped up on a table and shouted.

"Everyone! Calm down! It's a fact that Seya has lost the cooking battle! There's no reason to be doing all this!" he pleaded.

"We've heard enough from a child!" someone shouted.

"Shut up!" another one said more succinctly.

"I won't!" the kid shouted back. "I've been suspicious of Seya's cooking for a while now! But I'm the only one! You all used to cook for yourselves, didn't you? So why do you rely on Seya for all your meals now? Isn't that strange?!" His words seemed to have reached some people in the crowd, because they started to look away from him.

"Learn your place, child!" shouted the MC. "We're punishing him because he only defeated Master Seya with nasty tricks."

"Seya is the one using all the tricks! Picking a theme and then giving his opponent all the wrong ingredients. Or just giving his opponent rotten ingredients! Like now! Look how he's 'won' so far! And then, when he loses, look how he acts!" The kid wasn't giving up yet.

"Silence! Just shut up! Your insults have earned you death!" Trash III threw a knife at the boy. He cried out.

"That's going too far," I shouted. And I was ready for this. "Formation One: Glass Shield!" The knife bounced off my shield. Luckily, I deployed it as the knife flew through the air, and it hit my shield before it could hit the boy.

"What's this?!" Seya looked at me.

"It looks like you're planning on getting violent with us," L'Arc said, swinging his scythe. Glass, Raphtalia, Filo, and Tsugumi all followed suit, preparing for battle. Then he beckoned tauntingly to the surrounding crowd. "If you want a fight, we'll give you a thorough but nonlethal beating. If that's how you want things to go."

"Cooking is similar to craftsmanship. If you are going to get violent over the results of a battle to determine who is superior, we'll respond with violence of our own," Therese added. The villagers backed off from the waves of violence emanating from everyone involved but then—

"Master Seya's cooking is the best! We won't let you take him down!" one of them shouted.

"Huh? They seem a bit more skilled than regular villagers. Kiddo, did you say they've been pumped up with drugs?" L'Arc asked me. Backed by Therese's support magic, L'Arc chopped down the attackers. They screamed and collapsed, but he was holding back sufficiently. No one had been killed, at least from the look of it.

"Just who are you? It can't be!?" Seya exclaimed.

"Of course, I forgot to make the introductions," the rotund noble said. "Here we have King L'Arc Berg, accompanied by one of the four holy heroes who protect the world, the Hunting Hero, Kizuna Kazayama, and the rest of her party. Some of the strongest in the world, I assure you." He sounded pretty gleeful and had obviously been waiting for just the right moment.

"Hah! Like I care about a bunch of so-called heroes!" Seya scoffed, but with some uncertainty.

"That's right! That's right, Master Seya!" his cheering section crowed.

"Right! The holy weapons and vassal weapons are no match for my cooking! Check this out!" he shouted. Standing in the kitchen, he unleashed a torrent of powder from his accessory into a bubbling pot of water. Trash III, the other MC, and the girls who worked the restaurant all lifted the large pot and chugged it down together. I was impressed by the capacity of their stomachs, if nothing else.

With various shouts, the women all dropped to the ground, then rose back up with glowing auras crackling around them. Not to mention, rippling muscles now covered their bodies. Their voices had changed to little more than guttural growls.

"Well? This is the power-up effect that only my cooking can provide!" Seya gloated. The girls, all now looking really macho, stood up to protect Seya, ready to crush us into pulp. This was getting pretty crazy. Power-up consommé soup? Was that a thing now?

"Hahaha! I'd planned to allure the leaders with my cooking and create my own nation, but it seems you leave me with little choice! You fools! You're going to regret having forced me into this corner!" he shouted.

"Seriously, you're like one of those third-rate bad guys who reveals his plan the moment he's defeated," I said.

"What? You're the bad guys here! Making that disgusting cooking! This is all your fault!" he shouted back. He really couldn't take responsibility for anything, could he? I was so sick of dealing with these morons who just wouldn't listen. "The power of my cooking has exceeded even that of the heroes! Girls! Wipe these losers out!"

"Of course! Master Seya!" All the girls were really getting into it too.

"Uwah! This stinks so bad I want to plug up my nose! What's going on? Ugh!" Filo got a whiff of the soup and grabbed her nose, almost passing out. It definitely was nasty. I wondered why no one else in the town seemed to have a problem, after seeing them getting all pumped-up from drinking it.

"Dammit! I can't believe these guys," L'Arc said.

"Neither can I," Glass sympathized. They both clicked their tongues while pointing their weapons at the women.

"You all looked ready to jump on them before they did any of this," Kizuna quipped.

"Kizuna, you just stay back please," Tsugumi said, stepping in front of her.

"Say, sweet Naofumi?" Shildina said, getting my attention.

"We still don't really understand the whole situation here," Sadeena continued for her sister, "but there's something we need to tell you." They both pointed at Seya. "Takt," said Sadeena.

"Hidemasa," said Shildina.

"He feels the same as both of them," Sadeena confirmed. Shildina nodded. I'd been feeling it a little, but now the sisters made it plain.

"I was thinking pretty much the same thing," I responded. His attitude and the things he said were loaded with confidence, which lined up pretty closely with what I had experienced with those others. That meant he was another vanguard of the waves.

"There's something else though. I can see something . . . coming off him," Sadeena said.

"He's not like Sadeena, exactly, but his soul is . . . off, some-how," Shildina said.

"What do you mean?" I asked. Sadeena tilted her head, seemingly struggling to find an answer. They had only spent a short time in Seya's presence, after all, and he was hardly receptive to discussion. The two sisters had been glaring at him pretty intensely since the start, however.

"I've not mastered it yet, but I'm starting to be able to tell at a glance," Sadeena said.

"You can see souls too?" I asked her.

"I'm not sure if that's what you'd call this. I just feel a kind of tingle," she said.

"I'm not sure how far I can trust your vague instincts . . ."

I said, but it seemed pretty certain that Seya was a vanguard of the waves.

"Die!" someone shouted. Then the townsfolk and the staff of Seya's restaurant all flew at us from every direction.

"We've got this," Sadeena said.

"Let us suppress them," Shildina added.

"Okay," I replied. I quickly grabbed the boy and sent him an invite to my party.

"Huh?" He looked puzzled.

"Just accept it. I can't protect you otherwise," I said.

"Okay then," he said. I confirmed he had joined the party, and then—

"Stardust Mirror!" I threw up a barrier and looked at the attacking townsfolk. They looked like nothing less than demons. They were like slaves, even, chained to the cooking of Seya's restaurant, right down to the bottom of their hearts.

"What are you doing?!" the rotund noble exclaimed.

"Death to the traitors!" someone on Seya's restaurant staff roared, attempting to kill the panel of judges with their newly formed muscular arms.

"I won't allow it! Stardust Blade!" Raphtalia unleashed an attack to protect the judges.

"Gah! Stay out of our way!" the girls screamed. The entire beer garden was quickly turning into a battlefield. The townsfolk, some soldiers who had also showed up, and the massive muscle-freak women were all coming right for us. Rather than hang around and fight them all, I wondered if retreating might be the better option. They weren't all that strong, but there were plenty of them.

"Everyone! Don't kill them!" Kizuna shouted, as naive as ever. She wanted us to hold back against enemies who were definitely trying to kill us.

"Of course not!" Glass replied at once.

"Kiddo, Lady Raphtalia, and Lady Filo . . . you understand too, right?" L'Arc checked with us.

"I really don't want to," I sniped back, still clinging to the kid. "Hey, what about your sister?" I asked him. He looked over to an alleyway some distance from Seya's restaurant, from which his sister could be seen looking out. Away from the fighting, but also a bit closer than I would have liked.

Perhaps realizing that we had something else to protect, Seya was also pointing at the sister.

"You monsters! Greedy scum! You're always gobbling my food, so now put yourselves to work! Get her!" Seya shouted. The monsters circling above Seya's restaurant quickly obeyed his orders and set their sights on the kid's sister. I wasn't about to allow that. Still holding the boy, and keeping the barrier up, I set off.

"Filo! Are you with me? Stop those monsters getting close to the girl!" I shouted.

"Gotcha!" Filo replied. She changed into her monster form and flew up into the sky, attacking the monsters above Seya's restaurant.

"We'll help too!" Sadeena shouted, swinging her harpoon to aid Filo while Shildina deployed some magic using her ofuda.

"This is our power!" Seya retorted, still laughing to himself. "The townsfolk won't accept cunning cowards like you! Die!" I shook my head again. He thought the people completely trusted him and that he could get away with anything as a result. I had no words to reply.

"Now! For the sake of Master Seya, just come over here and join us!" Trash III said. The little sister looked pretty shaken by all this as unwanted advances reached toward her. She gave a scream.

"Formation Two: Glass Shield! Mirror Cage!" I shouted.

"What? It's stopping our attacks! It's so hard!" someone responded. I'd managed to protect the girl, somehow. I rushed over and repelled more enemies with my barrier.

"Mirror Bash!" I shouted, using a shield skill that had now been adapted by the mirror. The townsfolk fell back, groaning. It was originally called Shield Bash and could cause a brief moment of unconsciousness. It was not much use against monsters, but it could certainly slow down the greedy townsfolk. The problem was I just wasn't getting enough hits in to drive them all back!

"Raph-chan! To me! C'mon, Raph!" I shouted.

"Raph!" Raph-chan replied. I summoned her to me and she started using her illusions to confuse the townsfolk. It appeared to be working—

"Hah! You'll have to do better than that!" Okay, so it wasn't working on the muscle-bound girls. The cooks were also attacking with knives, and there were too many of both groups to handle them easily.

"Hah—" That was when S'yne appeared, unleashing countless threads that bound up the townsfolk. But even that wasn't enough, as more people continued to pour in toward us. We were reaching a point that could really be considered open warfare.

"We're going to get overwhelmed if we try not to kill anyone! Kizuna! L'Arc!" I shouted.

"Kiddo!" L'Arc shouted back. "Dammit . . . Therese! Don't you have some magic you can use?"

"I thought of using some status effect magic on them, but I'm not sure it would take hold. What's going on, exactly?" Therese asked. It looked like even heroes had trouble with crowd control. If we could kill them, of course, we could just wipe them all out. But it seemed that magic had a weakened effect against those brainwashed by . . . food.

"I'll incant some wide-scale suppression magic, so just hold on a moment," Therese said.

"Me too," Shildina chimed in, and they both started incanting.

"Naofumi, one thing," Kizuna said. She chose this moment to approach me.

"What's up?" I replied.

"I'm not sure if it's just an aftereffect of being cured from that curse, but since we arrived here in this town, I've been sensing a strange presence," she explained.

"And?" I asked. If she was sensing something, she should have brought it up sooner. At my question—and while Tsugumi was protecting her—Kizuna changed her weapon into the one that had appeared when the curse was broken. It looked a bit like a dressing knife.

"Tsugumi, thank you. I should be okay now," Kizuna said.

"Kizuna?" I asked. Then she set her waist low and gave a shout. She proceeded to dash at high speed through the crowd of people, then sheathed her dressing knife at her hip.

"Hunting Tool 0: Blood Flower Strike!" she shouted. There was a sound of something popping. Trash III, who was locked in combat with Raphtalia, had something cut out of her.

"All who resist the glorious light of Master Seya must die—" she had been ranting. But when Kizuna slashed her, she spluttered and stopped. "What? What is this? My strength . . . is fading . . ." Others in the crowd also started complaining of the same problem. Those who had been slashed collapsed to the ground, still alive but simply unable to stand.

Seya and his women looked shocked at Kizuna's ability to defeat his massive number of minions with a single strike.

"Impossible! You can't have dealt with my powered-up warriors so easily!" Seya scoffed. Then Kizuna pointed her dressing knife at Seya and made a declaration.

"I can cut out the illegitimate power that you've been using. As one of the four heroes, the Hunting Hero, I make this declaration. Give up and surrender at once!" she said. Kizuna normally couldn't attack other people, but it looked like that didn't apply to this crowd! Maybe the power-up had pushed them into the monster category. Or maybe something special about her weapon was cutting something illegitimate out of them. In any case, it was great news for us.

Then Kizuna turned her hunting tool into a bow and fired off countless arrows. Each time an arrow found a target, another villager collapsed to the ground, and then another, easily taking care of the townsfolk S'yne was restraining. Some of them just grunted or groaned, while others voiced their complaints.

"What's going on here? My power is fading away!"

"It hurts! Ah, this is so strange . . . We should be able to put up more of a fight than this."

They weren't dead, of course, but seemed unable to move now that the effects of the power-up had been stripped away. The kid had been telling the truth.

"Wow! Lady Kizuna, you kicked ass!" L'Arc shouted.

"I'm impressed, Kizuna!" Glass added.

"Like when you saved me, you just removed the malignant power," Tsugumi said, sounding as impressed as if she had just been saved again.

"Heh, this is all power that you've lent me," Kizuna said humbly. Now things were going well. Seya had thought he could swing things his way with violence, but now, even that tide was turning against him. Seya, however, was discussing something with the remaining powered-up woman. Then with the woman in tow, he charged at Raphtalia with a knife. Behind her was the noble and the other judges. He screamed in rage.

"I won't hold back," Raphtalia said, adopting a fighting stance with her katana. She then drew her second weapon from its scabbard and slashed into the woman in a haikuikku state. With a single attack, she caused a blizzard of sakura petals to whirl through the air. It was captivating.

"Sakura: Powder Snow!" Raphtalia shouted, swiftly chopping the bulked-up woman down. Then Seya emerged from hiding behind her and chopped at Raphtalia with his knife. With a grunt, Raphtalia took the knife on her katana. A loud noise rang out.

"Haha! I win!" Seya crowed.

"Unfortunately . . . not!" Raphtalia replied.

"We'll see about that!" Seya said.

"I've seen that face before," Raphtalia responded.

"Hah!" Kizuna took that moment to fire an arrow between Raphtalia and Seya. Seya acted as though he had avoided it, but Kizuna hadn't been aiming for him to start with. Then Seya looked around in puzzlement.

"Huh? No, impossible! What's going on?!" he exclaimed.

"Something wrong? You were expecting to steal her weapon, weren't you?" I taunted him.

"How do you know about—" Quickly realizing he was saying too much, Seya pressed his hands over his own mouth. It was too late though; he'd given the game away.

Kizuna's new Hunting Tool 0 had the ability to repel the connections formed by illegitimate power. That had surely been what she just shot through.

"I'm finished incanting. It was a pain to make the adjustments," Shildina said.

"Me too," Therese added. Both of them proceeded to activate their magic.

Shildina incanted first.

"I now command you. Ofuda! Respond to my words! Lull these foes into dreamless sleep! Rain of Sleep!"

Next up, it was Therese's turn.

"Permeating power of gemstones! Respond to my call, and make your power felt. My name is Therese Alexanderite. My companions. Become the power to put these people to sleep! Shining Stones! Slumber Smoke!"

The rain Shildina unleashed and the magical smoke Therese let loose filled our surroundings, causing almost all of the townsfolk to drop to the ground and start sleeping. In the same moment, Filo crashed down from the sky, stamping down on the neck of one of the monsters, and struck a victory pose.

"I win! Master's cooking will be mine!" she shouted gleefully. She was practically dancing for victory on top of the monster.

"Looks like things have taken a turn," I said to Seya.

"Damn you! This isn't over yet! I'm not going to lose to cowards like you! Get them!" he shouted.

"Anything for you, Master Seya!" one of the last macho women yelled and flew toward us.

"Sorry to say, but we can't lose to you!" Kizuna shouted, then circled around quickly and slashed into a woman. There was the sound of something being cut, and the power-up applied to the macho woman faded away. Her exaggerated muscles followed, and now thin as a rake, she slumped to the ground.

"Anything . . . for Master Seya," she whispered, still trying to stand back up. She had some guts, I'd give her that.

"Checkmate, ladies," L'Arc said, placing the blade of his scythe against Seya's neck.

"Cowards!" Seya said, falling back to that lame insult again.

"What has Master Seya ever done to you?!" one of his women exclaimed.

"What has he done?! He killed my family with his cooking!" the kid in my arms shouted back angrily.

"Whatever are you rambling about?" one of the women asked back.

"Master Seya's cooking could never kill anyone," another said.

"Enough with the jokes!" said a third. Even with the doping removed and unable to move, they were so brainwashed that they were still coming at us.

"That's not especially convincing, coming from you! Look at yourselves, emaciated and unable to move due to the removal of Seya's illegitimate power," Kizuna said.

"It means that power-up is definitely the type that shortens your life. Look at the ones you cut, Kizuna," I said. Their groans could be heard all around us. We hadn't killed them, but the kickback from the removal of the power-up Seya provided—his doping—was clearly hitting them hard. This was something different from getting your level reset with a dragon hourglass. With the way they were struggling to breathe, even I was getting worried about them. Therese started casting magic on each of them, just as an emergency measure. That's how bad it was for some of them.

"This is how you burned through the lives of this kid's family," I said. As soon as they were confronted with these words, a number of the women from around Seya's restaurant took a knee, put their hands together, and lowered their heads.

"Seya tricked us! We'll provide all the testimony you need! Seya is an evil chef who has been using illegitimate ingredients to agitate the people!" one of them said. I almost fell over at this swift change of heart, but I willed myself to stand in place and quietly stare them down.

"Whatever are you talking about?" Kizuna demanded.

"Pathetic," Glass spat.

"This reminds me of my own worst day," Tsugumi said, all three of them shaking their heads as they looked at the women. Tsugumi was clearly seeing shades of her own allies here.

"Girls?!" Seya exclaimed, quite rightly surprised by this turn of events. The women turned their frigid gazes to him and spat back insults.

"I'd rather you never talk to me again, you evil chef!" said one.

"The best cooking won, plain and simple, and in the name of justice!" crowed another. I was really starting to flashback to Takt's execution. Raphtalia looked like she was struggling with it too.

"Do you think there are people like this everywhere?" she asked me.

"Everywhere we go," I replied.

"Now! All of the assets of the chef of evil shall be transferred to the ultimate chef!" another woman shouted.

"Now!" agreed another.

"Fair enough . . . but you know that all of you are on the hook for this too," I told them.

"No! We had nothing to do with this!" the same woman pleaded.

"Nothing at all!" said another. The speed at which they had flipped on him reminded me immediately of Bitch.

"I really hate women like you. Let's resolve this quickly . . . L'Arc, dispose of them," I said.

"That's a pretty sick order to give so casually!" L'Arc fired back. He could have at least played along for a little while.

"No! We are your allies, ultimate chef!" they pleaded, dashing toward me. They probably wanted to grab onto me or something, but I wasn't having any of it. I used Stardust Mirror to bounce them away.

"You scabby vultures!" Tsugumi shouted. She couldn't take any more of it and whacked at them with a stick she was holding. After some cries and grunts of pain, the women finally fell silent.

"Good, well done, Tsugumi. I'll treat you to some special food later," I said. Tsugumi staggered in place, putting her hands on her forehead.

"That's not why I did that. That's not why I did it! We must not forgive them! Never forgive!" she rambled.

"Tsugumi?! Get a grip! Naofumi, can you please learn to

read the room?" Kizuna said. Tsugumi looked like she was completely closing herself off mentally, even as she continued to mutter to herself. She certainly wasn't an easy person to handle.

"Screw this!" Seya shouted, attempting to use a Scroll of Return.

"Not with me around!" Raphtalia retorted, quickly smashing him down. No way he was going to escape now.

"I so hate to say it," I said, laying it on nice and thick, "but you losers have lost. Never underestimate a bunch of heroes."

"What is your problem?" Seya raged back. "You call yourselves heroes, but then you show up and mess with me! I was just peacefully cooking for everyone!"

"Peacefully? You mean like how you extorted all of the assets from your customers? Like how you took over control of the entire town? Like how you resorted to violence as soon as you were defeated at your own game? You've got a pretty crazy definition of 'peaceful,' I'll give you that," I said. Just those acts I'd mentioned made him plenty guilty. "There's more too. You said yourself that you were planning to allure the leaders with your cooking and take over! That's a treasonous plot of the highest order, at least from where I'm sitting. You've been stripped of your happiness because of all these brutal acts," I continued. He was doing whatever the hell he liked and then playing the victim, I'd seen this so much and it made me want to vomit. "All you needed to do was accept the defeat, reflect upon it, and leave with your women." Fanning the sparks into a full-blown riot had not been the move to make. I hardly knew what to say. It went without saying that his suspicious cooking cult was going to get crushed too. "Your selfish happiness has also served to twist the poor townsfolk beyond recognition." I looked at the collapsed and moaning crowd. There were a lot of them. Almost too many. "Now then, Seya. After winning this cooking battle and putting down the violent riot you started, we're going to be taking all of your assets. Thank you."

"I'm not giving up anything!" he raged.

"Oh really. Rules are rules. You even turned to violence and you still couldn't win. Give up," I told him. I proceeded to take the accessory from Seya's arm. I checked inside it . . .

"Hey, butterball," I said. The rotund one was looking around, perhaps wondering who I was talking to. *You, of course.*

"I think he means you," Raphtalia said, giving him a nudge.

"Me?" the man asked.

"Yeah, you. Sorry to say it, but it doesn't look like Seya has been using this accessory for his cooking after all," I said. I tossed it over to the noble.

"What? That can't be. It must have some kind of verification system so only Master Seya can use it," the noble replied.

"Nope, nothing like that. I know a bit about accessory making, and there's no such gimmick to that one. If you still don't believe me, take it to a Jewel you trust and get it checked out for yourself," I told him.

"That can't be . . ." the noble said.

"Haha! My cooking is my own unique power! You won't be able to copy it so easily!" Seya taunted.

"Interesting. So you have other abilities as well as stealing vassal weapons?" I asked. Just what were these vanguards of the waves, anyway? I thought they were focused just on stealing weapons. Now it sounded like they had other strange powers too. I'd have to ask Itsuki about it later.

I recalled that Miyaji had been able to speak the language of this world prior to obtaining the musical instrument vassal weapon. Maybe that had been some kind of extra ability too. There had to be other vanguards of the waves out there, so we needed to be careful of these additional abilities.

"Kizuna, L'Arc, everyone," I said. When they all looked over, I proceeded to whisper my plan to them as quietly as possible.

"Not really something I'm keen on doing," Kizuna said, trying to red-light it already.

"And yet this guy isn't going to listen to reason. If we simply take him captive, he's definitely going to cause more trouble later," I told her.

"Lady Kizuna, the one who stole my scythe was also one of these vanguard people. I think we should listen to kiddo when it comes to this stuff," L'Arc said. Kizuna still seemed unsure, but Raphtalia and Glass raised no objections. They had quietly accepted what had to happen.

"Right then, Seya. If you follow our conditions, we will be on our way. We also won't take your assets, so long as you leave town. Leave town, and we'll let you go. However, I don't know if you'll have much luck opening a restaurant in another town," I told him.

"What?!" The kid and his sister both glared at me, but I signaled with my eyes that it would be okay. Tsugumi spotted the problem and started to gently pat the boy's head and talk to him softly.

"What, then? What do you want?" Seya asked.

"There's someone behind all of this, correct? Someone pulling the strings. If you tell us all about that, we'll let you go. Hey, I have an idea. Write it down on this piece of paper here. I want a record of this." I said and passed a piece of paper to him. Seya's expression immediately brightened.

"That's all you want? Fine, I can—" But the rest of that sentence vanished into an awful grunt. The moment Seya tried to write a single word, his head simply crumpled in on itself. He managed a brief scream, and then his entire melon exploded. I didn't want to traumatize my allies, so I quickly threw up a cage and blocked out the grisly scene. Then I gave a sigh.

"Just as I expected," I said. These vanguards of the waves

were set up to get shredded, soul and all, if they tried to share any of the information they knew. Erased in order to keep that information secret. Even writing it down wasn't allowed. That was a pretty strict NDA.

I'd asked Kizuna to watch and see if her hunting tool could stop the meat explosion from taking place, but she hadn't been able to.

"Not that I didn't believe what you've been telling us, Naofumi, but it's impossible to doubt it after seeing that," Glass said.

"Just what are the waves?" Kizuna pondered.

"Don't ask me," I replied. There were still far too many mysteries swirling around this "World Eater," the one seemingly behind the waves.

"So he was a vanguard of the waves, and trying to answer your question caused him to die," Tsugumi said. She had shielded the boy from Seya's messy death but watched it herself.

"Looks like it. But some of them seem to be aware that talking out of school, as it were, is going to get them imploded," I said. Takt had known. Maybe he had been some kind of experiment to see how he would act while possessed of that knowledge.

In any case, now we were fully aware that there were these vanguards of the waves scattered around everywhere.

"Victory is yours," said the rotund noble.

"We'll get back to you soon enough," I said to him. He was going to find out just how nasty authority could be. Betrayal always carried a high price. The man grunted in surprise, likely sensing the rippling waves of anger radiating from me, and proceeded to hide—along with the rest of the judges—behind L'Arc. "Right, what else?" I said. "Kid. This is the end of Seya's restaurant. You okay with that?" I asked him and his sister.

"I mean, you won, but . . ." He looked, with some understandable concern in his eyes, at the collapsed villagers.

"We'll give them a proper detox, don't worry. It will depend on the individual in question, whether they can pull through completely or not. We're taking out the source though, so they won't really have a choice but to try," I told him. Overcoming something like an addiction to tobacco was difficult because it was so easy to get your hands on. Harder drugs might be more difficult to obtain, but once someone got hooked, they had ways of working that out. In this case, however, the source of the problem—Seya—had been removed in spectacular fashion, meaning no one was getting more of that food no matter how hard they tried. The only choices left were to overcome it naturally or give in to the addiction and die.

"I see . . . so I've finally avenged everyone who died," the kid said. He looked at me with a relieved expression on his face. "Thank you, ah . . . Tray Hero?" There was a sound like the very air splitting.

"Don't say that, kid! That's not a tray!" Tsugumi quickly said, shielding the boy from me at once.

"That's right!" L'Arc backed her up. "Kiddo's weapon here is a mirror that can also become a shield. It's not a tray! Certainly not!"

"Huh? But hold on . . ." the kid started to reply.

"Listen here, you little brat! If you're going to keep this up, then I'll teach you that there's far more terrifying food in this world than anything Seya could cook up!" I snapped.

"Mr. Naofumi, calm yourself!" Raphtalia grabbed me from behind and stopped me from jumping at the kid. *You've got to be kidding! My weapon is not a tray!* It had already been called a pot lid in the past, and now it had another silly nickname!

"Oh my!" said Sadeena.

"Oh dear!" said Shildina.

"Raph?" said Raph-chan. S'yne was drinking the leftovers of the soup I made, without permission. Seriously, what an unruly bunch. I wished they would sort themselves out.

"Raph, raph!" Even Raph-chan was shaking her head.

After our intervention, the townsfolk were apparently pretty displeased with me for the first few days. With a little time, however—about a week—the symptoms of addiction to Seya's cooking started to appear, and the people came to see the extent of the damage his toxins had done to their bodies. Then

I ended up being dispatched to prepare a mountain of food for them.

I worked with the cooks who Seya had defeated and were forced to work for him. Also, I worked with those who had been imprisoned after managing to resist Seya's cooking. Together we cooked up a feast for the entire town. There were a whole bunch of ingredients in Seya's restaurant, after all. The eating enhancement it provided worked wonders as rehabilitation for those who couldn't even walk, but I was careful to do nothing more than let them move.

As it turned out, Seya had been using his own abilities to do all the cooking himself, and the other cooks had never gotten to do any real cooking. Instead, they had been little more than kitchenhands, working like slaves at managing ingredients, cleaning up trash, and tidying things.

Still, after our actions, the fortunes of the town seemed to have taken a downturn. And at first, some of the townsfolk tried to blame us for that. It wasn't long before they could imagine what would have happened if Seya had remained in control. However, if all of the original residents died, fresh visitors would have been forced to take their place and experience the same living hell. After eating the food I and the other cooks carefully prepared, the majority of them also came to accept that it was more delicious than the food Seya made.

It wasn't that long before people of the town were back

to normal, cooking for themselves in their own homes. Eating something delicious and wanting to copy it for themselves was definitely a far healthier reaction. Realizing their mistake in just relying on someone else to keep making it for them was definitely progress. The town would eventually go on to become known as the "Cooking Town," but that's another story.

"I can't believe how things turn out sometimes. We went to hire a famous chef to get away from the overpowering meals kiddo makes, and look at the mess we ended up in," L'Arc lamented, leaning back on his chair in the castle's dining hall.

"Is that really your place to say, L'Arc?" I asked him. He had been the one who got into things with the restaurant and kicked the whole thing off . . . but, it was largely the enemy's fault.

"It seems you have quite a lot of unexpected trouble," Itsuki said, looking on from the sidelines.

"Fehhhhh," Rishia added. I'd chatted a little with Itsuki about our encounter, and he said that while there were instant transmission-style abilities in his world, there was nothing that could multiply the volume of materials. It might have been similar to a duplication ability, but not quite the same.

"How can we avoid chewing ourselves to death on this killer cooking?" Tsugumi said, even as she finished a suitably sized meal and placed down her chopsticks. Kizuna, Glass,

L'Arc, and the others looked at her in puzzlement.

"Hold on? It looks like we've found a suitable point to stop eating," L'Arc said.

"That's because I'm making sure not to overfeed you," I responded after placing more food at Filo, S'yne, Sadeena, and Shildina's table. They always asked for seconds after finishing the first helping.

"What do you mean, kiddo?" L'Arc asked.

"Like Raphtalia said, you just have to get used to my cooking," I replied.

"I mean, I guess that could be all this is . . ." L'Arc said. He didn't seem all that convinced.

"Don't tell me it's even enhanced our stomachs?! I need to go do some exercise!" Yomogi looked practically terrified as she made this declaration. So I stood in her way and stopped her before she ran out.

"That's not the case at all, so just calm down. I wanted to avoid doing this, but you keep on getting into such a fuss over it. So I've put some controls in place," I told them.

"Couldn't you have done this from the start?" Kizuna asked, looking annoyed. "What did you do?"

"No matter how delicious the food is, if you eat the same thing every time, you'll start to get sick of it. Once you get sick of it, you won't overeat simply because you won't want to. I've been applying that concept to my food," I told them. It didn't matter how great something tasted; if you ate it again and again you would get tired of the taste. I had originally been changing my methods and dishes in order to prevent this, but that allowed me to bring in some control to the process too.

"You definitely could have done that to start with!" Kizuna exclaimed.

"I wanted to enhance you as much as possible, that's all. I hoped I could scout out someone who could make delicious food," I replied. I hadn't expected that to turn into such a mess, of course.

"So . . . I'm glad it turned out how I suggested it would, but I'm still not satisfied with this explanation," Raphtalia said.

"Raph!" Raph-chan added.

"Our villagers don't count. Those guys eat so much they'll starve before they ever get fat. Add the mass-produced filolials into the mix and however much I make still won't be enough," I said. There was no point in comparing those with bottomless pits for stomachs to Kizuna and the others here. The focus was completely different. For them, it was purely about nutrition to raise them up, while here we were seeking enhancement and level increases by eating. The very meaning of the act of consumption was totally different. "Please understand that this isn't the best method, but it's what we have to work with," I told them. Sensing my intent, L'Arc and the others nodded without further comment. "Included in the stuff we brought back from

Seya's restaurant, there are some pretty good ingredients. I can make efficient meals for a while using that stuff. We won't have to worry again just yet."

"That sounds fine, but . . . are you sure about leaving things like this?" Kizuna said.

"I can't help but feel it's a 'first-to-flinch' situation. For now, let's just push the food problem into the future a little," Raphtalia suggested.

"If the holy weapon and vassal weapon holders can learn to imbue life energy into their cooking, it would make things a bit easier for me," I said, picking what felt like the perfect moment to bring this issue up again. I at least wanted Kizuna to get this skill sorted. It could be anything she liked, even just sashimi, or just something she could learn and use. There was the potential for some excellent status adjustment on the table, things like a permanent plus three to defense for eating the entire dish, but you couldn't bring them out without putting the time into the cooking itself. "Still, this has all made you a bit stronger," I concluded. And so the food-related issues that Kizuna and her allies had been worrying about headed toward a form of resolution.

Chapter Ten: Dragon of Ultimate Magic

It was a few more days after the trouble at Seya's restaurant. Now that a solid baseline of enhancements had been achieved, we had decided to put our next strategy into action. That said, there was little chance of success if we just charged recklessly in. So we were discussing the best way to do it.

"You said that so long as we had Lady Kizuna back, we'd be able to take the harpoon guy down, right, kiddo?" L'Arc asked me.

"That was before we paid such a pleasant visit to Miyaji. Now that we know that S'yne's sister and her forces are involved in this, just having Kizuna back might not be enough. Even if she revokes his authority, if the weapon itself has been bound to him, then it might not work at all." They also had seven star weapons from our world, after all. Thinking that simply revoking their authority to wield the weapons would be enough was naive at this point.

Then there was the fact that S'yne's sister had enough power to quite easily send us all flying in an instant. If we went in without a plan, as we currently stood, it was highly unlikely we could win. Another issue was that S'yne's sister was one of their key leaders, but not the actual boss. If they had someone even stronger waiting in the wings, we really would struggle to win. That meant in this time during which they hadn't showed themselves, we had to increase our own firepower.

"I really wanted to try revoking his authority," Kizuna said.

"I'm not saying not to try it. There's nothing wrong with giving it a try," I told her. We had Kizuna back now, so it was definitely worth trying. "What's more important, though, is dealing with whatever it is they are using that blocks Itsuki's and my weapons and magic," I said.

"Easy enough to say, but how do we do that?" Kizuna asked.

"Based on what S'yne's sister said about everything, they sealed off the weapons and magic from other worlds by capturing three of the four holies from this world. In other words, if we can release them, then maybe our weapons and magic will be released too," I reasoned. Everyone nodded at my suggestion. "To be honest, I was kind of hoping that bringing Kizuna back would be enough. Any word on that?" I looked hopefully at her.

"Hmmm . . . not likely. I'm not sure how to put this . . . From what I'm feeling from the hunting tool, it's outnumbered and so can't make the change over," she explained.

"It sounds like we need to release at least one more of the holy weapons, then, before Itsuki and I will be able to use our weapons and magic," I concluded. It seemed like an accessory could cancel the effects out, but I had no idea how to make it. If I could get a sample, then I might be able to do something about it . . . It really was an inconvenience. I hoped we could do something about it soon.

"Fehhh!" Then Rishia raised her hand with a troubled look on her face. That stupid noise was completely unnecessary, especially in this instance. It actually made me want to shout at her.

"Is there nothing that can be done using support buffs via the skills inside the seven star weapons?" she asked. It normally fell to magic to handle buffing abilities, but if weapons also had that kind of support ability, then Rishia in particular would be able to apply some pretty powerful effects.

"If you think you can do something like that, I'd love it if you gave it a try," I said. There were a lot of skills that still remained tantalizingly out of reach. I didn't have many buffing skills. Of course, this approach would mean we had to lean heavily on Rishia.

"I'm sorry. I don't actually have any skills like that . . . but I'll search for some and help you out, I promise!" Rishia replied.

"Sure, but the problem we're always going to run into is the use of magic that cancels the buffs. It just turns into tit-for-tat," I commented. This was another issue that S'yne's sister had annoyingly raised.

"How about going into the Ancient Labyrinth Library and

searching for some clues? Ethnobalt, can you help us find what we are after?" Kizuna asked.

"That is another idea . . . but that presumes the information we want exists in book format. Information relating to technology from other worlds might be a high hurdle," Ethnobalt replied.

"To put it more simply, then, we want passages about nullifying magic that removes buffs," I broke it down.

"I'll take a look. Please don't expect too much," he said.

"I won't," I replied to him. We just didn't have many moves we could make right now. "We also can't just stand around wringing our hands. We can at least level up a little and try to turn this difficult situation around. The one thing we do have going for us is that Kizuna's weapon seems to be able to deal with this so-called illegitimate power we have been facing." The best thing we could do right then was increase our levels and try to supplement our lack of enhancement in other areas. "We might—and I mean might—get an advantage if we can thoroughly raise the levels of everyone other than the vassal weapon and holy weapon holders, in a kind of limit break fashion. But if the enemy takes advantage of that to create a powerful force, that would be pretty terrifying." In fact, that was the issue I was the most scared of. Perhaps the biggest piece of luck when we fought Miyaji had been that Bitch and Armor didn't have levels as high as I had been expecting. "This would be a lot easier if the holy weapon and vassal weapon holders could just fight it out alone, but we would be naive to believe that will be the case. L'Arc, you and your other allies are moving on this by considering it will escalate into a full-blown war, correct?"

"That's right," L'Arc confirmed.

"In your world, Naofumi, people other than holy weapon or vassal weapon holders can also break the level cap, can't they?" Kizuna asked.

"That's right," I replied. "Sadeena, you must be getting close to the cap in this world. Well?" Whenever they could find time, everyone had been working on raising their levels pretty much every day. Training had been particularly focused on Kizuna, so it was probably about time she overtook us. Raising levels in this world was pretty quick too.

"Oh my. You're right. Our levels have already crossed the cap," Sadeena confirmed.

"Which means having performed the ritual in another world allows you to break the cap here," I commented. "That said . . ." We couldn't exactly take everyone to our world, get Gaelion to perform it, and then come back. We'd be stuck waiting for a wave. Once the limit break was performed, we didn't have many options in terms of getting back. Maybe using the transmission of a wave was the best we could hope for. While we were messing about with all that, the enemy wouldn't be sitting around waiting for us to return.

"Raph-chan," I called.

"Raph?" she responded.

"Can you perform the same limit break ritual that Gaelion performed for us?" I asked her. When we crossed over to this world, Gaelion had been looking at Raph-chan with resentment in his eyes. I'd been thinking Raph-chan could probably perform the ritual too, so it was worth asking and actually finding out.

"Raph, raph, raph!" said Raph-chan excitedly, making a circle with her paws to indicate that she could do it but then pointing at the ground and shaking her head. There was a moment of silence.

"She says she can do it, but not here in this world," Filo translated.

"Raph!" Raph-chan confirmed. Maybe there were some subtle differences in what was needed for the ritual in this world. It felt so close and yet just out of reach, like an itch between my shoulder blades.

"Sorry, but I have to ask . . . how is Raph-chan able to do such a thing?" Raphtalia asked, but I chose to ignore her question. One of the best things about Raph-chan was how multitalented she was.

Then Therese raised her hand.

"Kizuna, do you remember that one enemy? The one who gave us a lecture on the means of dispelling buff-based magic?

If we could talk to him, we might be able to find a way forward," Therese said.

"Huh? I'm not sure I do . . ." Kizuna said. I personally had no idea who she was talking about. It had to be a foe from back before we met or during the period we were back in our world.

"Therese, who are you talking about?" L'Arc asked, furrowing his own brow in thought. I wanted her to drop the guessing games and get to the point.

"It was the reason Kizuna was summoned to this world in the first place, L'Arc. When we fought him, he kept on nullifying our magic buffs, remember? I think he knows a lot about that side of things," Therese said.

"You don't mean . . ." L'Arc said, voice quivering.

"I do. It sounds like the Master Craftsman has also fought him, and I also know how to revive him. This could be a lot faster than having Ethnobalt investigate," she suggested. A deeply disturbed expression proceeded to appear on the faces of Kizuna, Glass, and L'Arc. It sounded like they were talking about someone very dangerous. I had my own idea on who it might be, and I didn't like it. The things she was saying were starting to sound familiar to me too.

"No way!" Filo knew who they were talking about. She had been a victim at his hands, after all. Still, this wasn't such a bad idea, at least in terms of expediency, but I really wasn't keen on it.

"If there's a problem, we can just have Kizuna mop him up again. It's highly likely he won't listen to what we have to say though," I commented. Still, it was important to give things a go.

We were talking about the primary reason why Kizuna was summoned here in the first place. To put it simply, the idea was to revive the Demon Dragon. If he talked about taking me over again, I'd simply kick his ass. That much was for sure.

"Are you sure about this?" Raphtalia asked, a concerned look on her face.

"We don't exactly have many options open to us . . . and even if we take care of this problem and deal with Bitch and the others, taking Kizuna and her allies across to our world and breaking the level cap for all of them will be such a pain," I said. It would be better to find someone who could handle that at the local level, and that led us straight to the Demon Dragon. If the setup was similar to our world, then we should at least get some intelligence from this move. And in the worst-case scenario, we could raise a dragon into a Dragon Emperor and then have it extract the information we needed from the Demon Dragon fragments.

The fact that the method for breaking the level cap in this world remained unknown was actually to our advantage. It would make it easier to fight those that S'yne's sister wasn't involved with, such as the harpoon vassal weapon holder and his allies. And if we could apply it just to those we trusted, then we would be able to physically overpower these vanguards of the waves. Experimenting with that was all part of this.

"We don't have time to search for other methods, do we, kiddo?" L'Arc asked.

"That's right. Kizuna loves talking things out so much we'll let her try that first. But after that, it just depends on the Demon Dragon," I said. Betrayal would not be permitted, but we had to start from a place of negotiation. Of course, the dragon hated Kizuna and her allies pretty intensely, so he might not listen to anything they had to say at all. Kizuna gave a sigh.

"Very well. I didn't expect to have to revive the Demon Dragon myself . . ." she muttered sadly. Glass looked like she felt much the same way.

L'Arc therefore ordered us a dragon's egg from a monster stable within his nation. In this world they didn't use a monster seal to make monsters subservient, but rather a sealing ofuda. In Filo's case, she already had a monster seal and so the sealing ofuda didn't work on her. I recalled the tragic incident when she had been captured alive and put on show.

Then Kizuna came in with the Demon Dragon core that Romina had returned to me in her store. We made all the necessary preparations. The egg was going to be hatched in the garden of L'Arc's castle. In our world, I had been forced to carry the egg around for a while, but things seemed different here.

"Who will become the owner?" Kizuna asked.

"You do it," I told her. "That will be the most humiliating for him."

I thought we should let him experience the humiliation of becoming the property of his most hated enemy. "When the dragon hatches, we get to choose the gender too, right?" I asked Ethnobalt, who happened to glance in my direction. As the holder of the knowledge about this world, he was preparing the ritual. So I decided to confirm this point with him.

"You've clearly conducted research in your world too," he remarked.

"What about over here?" I pressed him.

"It depends on the type of dragon," he replied.

"Aren't they all pretty similar? I thought dragons were creatures that caused the pollution of a region?" I confirmed.

"That's right . . . That side of things is probably the same," Ethnobalt replied. That side of things sounded the same, certainly.

"Kizuna, if we can choose the gender of the Demon Dragon, which would you prefer?" I asked her.

"Huh? Well . . . what do you think, Naofumi?" she asked. "A girl, right?"

"Why do you think I would want a girl? And call it 'female,' please!" I retorted.

"Your response tells me everything," she replied.

"Gaelion is male. Apparently, that is what Naofumi selected," Itsuki said to Kizuna, stepping in.

"We already had one super-noisy creature. I was worried about further troubles it might cause if I select the opposite gender from me again, so I made sure to pick male," I explained.

"Who are you talking about?" Filo asked. *You*, I almost told her. *I'm talking about you!* She had caused all sorts of issues for us, including the ping-pong dash and the whole Demon Dragon fiasco. But on the flip side of that, in the end we had been able to teach the Way of the Dragon Vein to Ren, Itsuki, and Motoyasu and achieved class-ups that broke the level cap, so all was well that ended well. Maybe.

Filo herself was standing a little way apart, ready to run for it if required. She could hold her own against Gaelion but obviously wasn't keen on the Demon Dragon.

"Indeed . . . in case the negotiations do go well, it might be better to choose the same gender as the owner in order to avoid any annoying issues," Glass proposed to Kizuna, based on my information.

"What does that mean, Glass?" Kizuna asked.

"Annoying issues, huh? You don't have it easy either, do you, Glass?" I said.

"I have a lot of questions about that comment!" Glass replied.

"Nothing to it. Leave me out of this," I replied. I'd seen the jealousy in Glass's eyes when Tsugumi was playing around with Kizuna.

"Fehhh . . ." Rishia made another highly useful contribution.

"Mr. Naofumi, please don't rile Glass up too much. You are upsetting Rishia," Raphtalia said.

"Sure, whatever," I replied. In this case, I decided to accept Raphtalia's warning and ignore the issue for now. Tsugumi herself was off helping clean up the town where Seya's restaurant had been. I'd told her to call us for help if she needed it. Yomogi was back in her home nation, preparing for the next wave.

"It seems a little late to bring this up, but monsters don't really like me," Kizuna said.

"Pen?" said Chris. She used the hunting tool, after all; it would have been pretty crazy if monsters did take a liking to a hero who specialized in fighting them. "Monsters always seem to like you, Naofumi," she added.

"It's just because of my weapon. I could do with less of the licking though," I told her.

"Raph!" said Raph-chan. I had nothing else to do while they were getting set up, so I was stroking her.

My work on modifying the accessory for Therese had also seen some good progress. With a little more work, I would be able to complete an exclusive accessory for her, which sure sounded romantic.

Sadeena and Shildina were helping with the ceremony. They had both served as priestess of the water dragon, so they likely knew a bit about rituals.

"Divine liquor, ah, divine liquor! The little Demon Dragon loves drinking, correct?" Sadeena said.

"If not, we'll drink it," Shildina replied. It looked like they were only helping out in order to get their hands on some booze.

"Right, shall we get started?" Ethnobalt finally said, all the preparations finished. "If you are to be the owner, Kizuna . . . I'll need some of your blood on this sealing ofuda."

"Okay," Kizuna replied, a little uncertainly. Kizuna followed Ethnobalt's directions over to the ofuda attached to the egg. As instructed, she cut the tip of her finger and pressed it to the ofuda. So far, the ritual was similar to the one our world.

"That should be enough to hatch a normal dragon's egg . . ." Ethnobalt said.

"But this is a Dragon Emperor. Let's do everything we can before it hatches," I said. Kizuna was carrying the Demon Dragon core and placed it on top of the egg. Things would be a lot easier if that caused a change . . . but even as I thought that, the Demon Dragon core slipped inside the egg. The egg looked like it had successfully managed to absorb the Demon Dragon core.

"Now we'll start the egg hatching. Everyone, please take a

step back," Ethnobalt said. He knew what he was doing with this stuff. Even when he didn't have sufficient combat abilities, he still was a big help at times like this. Now he could also fight, so he was quite the significant asset for Kizuna's allies. Quite honestly, I wanted to trade him for Filo.

"Hey! Master, you're thinking something rude!" Filo chirped up. Bah! Her instincts were on the money, I'd give her that.

Itsuki was playing music to provide support to Ethnobalt. It looked pretty effective. Itsuki had been playing a lot recently, and it was showing in his playing. Practice really did make perfect.

Even as I thought about Itsuki's music, the egg started to crackle and spark, floating up into the air.

"Is this all okay?" I asked.

"Yes. It should be . . ." Ethnobalt said. I hoped he was right. I had everyone ready with their weapons, just in case we had to respond quickly to whatever happened next. The egg floated for a while, and then wind gathered around it before it created some water. The earth beneath the stand below rose upward, and fire erupted from the divine liquor placed on it. The killer whale sisters looked a bit displeased with that particular development.

After a blinding light, darkness gathered around the egg . . . and a faint shadow started to appear from within. Something formed into a shape inside, and the egg cracked. With a splitting sound, a female baby dragon—a purple palette-swap of Gaelion—poked out her face. After keeping just her head outside the egg and blinking a few times, she looked around. Spotting me caused her to make a noise for some reason.

"Kwaa!" She sounded exactly like Gaelion. What did this mean? Maybe we had messed up somewhere along the way. I was overcome by a feeling of disappointment and despair . . . "Bah! Damn you! How dare you do this to me!" The dragon proceeded to speak. They were real words, but with a squealy dragon voice. She said this while breaking out of the rest of the shell. Seeing everyone arrayed around her, weapons ready, the dragon proceeded to raise her two front paws. "You seem prepared for the worst given how small and weak I am," the dragon commented. "Hunting Hero."

"Are you the Demon Dragon?" Kizuna confirmed, speaking for all of us.

"I am. Allow me to ask you what prompted the insanity of reviving me. I only know the background to the Shield Hero's side of things," she told us.

"The background of my side?" I asked.

"Yes. The Emperor Dragon from the Shield Hero's side was being unreasonably stubborn in his attempts to do something to this body. I was almost overwritten," she explained. *Overwritten, huh?* I wondered what Gaelion had tried to do

too, but whatever it was, it was probably at least somewhat deserved. "I've been somewhat influenced by that. From what remained of the core, I was able to perceive facts about the shield, so I have some memories from the Shield Hero's side of things. Like the fight with these 'vanguards of the waves' and the power of the Dragon Emperor on their side."

"What did Gaelion do?" I asked.

"Let me see. When you were coming over to this side, you had to select your party members, correct? The Dragon Emperor was displeased with being left behind. Predicting that this current situation may come about, he attempted to over-write the fragments that were meant to return to me," the baby dragon explained. I shook my head in surprise. I hadn't realized Gaelion had wanted to come that badly! He must have disliked the fact that Filo got to come while he got left behind. He had been glaring intently at Raph-chan too.

"It sounds like that might have been for the best," Glass muttered, glaring at the Demon Dragon with a pretty foul look.

"Don't get too full of yourself, holder of the fan vassal weapon!" the Demon Dragon retorted, giving a glare back that was just as fierce. That seemed justified, given she had almost been wiped from existence. Still, appearance-wise, she was just a Gaelion palette-swap. But from the look in her eyes, she seemed to have a pretty bad attitude. She had a different aspect again from daddy Gaelion, but you could tell at a glance that both of them harbored a lot of ill will. On that point alone, it could be said that daddy Gaelion was actually doing pretty well to not fall out with us completely. I'd never seen him turn such a look of disrespect onto a human, not like this.

"Tell me, Shield Hero. Why have you awoken me?" the dragon asked.

"Why are you only talking to Naofumi?" Kizuna questioned.

"Because I'll never get straight answers out of the rest of you," the dragon responded. It was such a pain to get caught in the middle of this, and I was impressed by the gall of her thinking that she could have any kind of discussion with me she wanted. She was treating everything she had done to us like it was water under the bridge.

"I don't like your attitude. You attacked me and even tried to take me over," I said.

"Hah, Shield Hero. I understand a little of your ways. If you just destroy me now, what will all of this have achieved? I will listen to what you have to say, at least," she said.

"Still, I'm not sure I like her attitude," Raphtalia said. I strongly agreed. This dragon really seemed to think she had my number, and I both didn't like it and wasn't sure why . . . but standing around bickering about it wasn't going to solve anything.

"This doesn't mean I trust you, and in light of your past deeds, I don't really want to rely on you either," I said.

I proceeded, however, to explain to the Demon Dragon everything that had come to pass and proposed our strategy for the future. Once I was finished . . .

"Seriously . . . it brings dragon tears to my dragon eyes to see you, the great Shield Hero who defeated me, now reduced to this." The Demon Dragon placed her front paws against her head and muttered sadly to herself.

"I hope you aren't looking for sympathy," I said harshly.

"Just think about it for a moment. The same bunch who shouted about defeating me and saving the world are now back, having screwed everything up, relying on me—their sworn enemy—to save them! Take a look around. Does this world look like it's at peace to you? Well?" the dragon said, really coming for me now. What was worse, I didn't really have a reply. This world was still plagued by humans fighting each other and had been ravaged by the vanguards of the waves. Everything the dragon had said so far had been so on the money that Kizuna and Glass probably didn't have any response either. "Can you see how this might feel like something from your own past? Having been chased as a criminal, and then having to clean up after those very weaklings who were chasing you after they had been beaten down by the waves and people from another world?" That punch really landed hard. I wanted to call it a low blow, but she was basically providing a stunningly succinct summary of my life in these other worlds.

"So, Demon Dragon, just what do you actually want to do?" I asked.

"A good question. If I simply turn you down, I can tell you are prepared to kill me pretty quickly," the dragon responded. *No shit. That's why all these weapons are pointed at you.* "More than anything else, though, I do hate the idea of becoming the plaything in a world I should have obtained for myself."

"If you are about to propose we split the world in half or something, we're not going for that," Kizuna muttered. The dragon would probably need a mustache to twirl if she was going to go that hard into a traditional villain. Or did she fancy herself the queen of the monsters? The Dragon Emperor in our world called himself the King of the Monsters, but it was a title he had applied to himself.

"Hah, I don't expect you to agree to anything so obvious. I will give you a hundred years before I act. In that span of time, all of you should die out anyway. Then I will realize my world of monsters," the dragon said.

"Those still don't sound like conditions we can accept . . ." Ethnobalt said, somewhat distressed. The Demon Dragon looked over at him and her eyes widened.

"What? That cursed library rabbit has been revived too? I can imagine a situation no worse! Not to mention, this flow of power I feel . . . the sworn enemy of my lifeblood!" the dragon exclaimed. Of course, the dragon was sensing the potion that

Ethnobalt drank. "That said"—the dragon calmed herself—"you originate on the monster side, and if you live that long, then you will surely come to realize the foolishness of humans."

"You need to watch what you say," L'Arc growled. For once, even he had his hackles up. As fine an indication as any of the bad blood between these two groups.

"What did this dragon try to do in this world, anyway? I'm still not really following this," Sadeena asked.

"He commanded monsters within his own area of influence and used humans like slaves, basically," I told her. Thinking about that now—

"That's it? Just a race war?" Sadeena replied. "Just" might be pushing it a little, but sure, it could be boiled down to a pretty simple conflict: monsters versus humans. Quite honestly, I admitted to myself, I was a little jealous of how simple that all sounded. We had our hands full with a far more convoluted mess.

"Are we sure the goals of that war are to be rejected out of hand?" Kizuna said.

"It sounds pretty bizarre to say it, doesn't it?" Raphtalia replied in agreement.

"Indeed. I'd expect no less from a hero from a therianthrope nation," the dragon said. "I was pretty sure you would display a higher understanding of culture and awareness."

The Demon Dragon seemed pretty friendly toward me. So I decided to capitalize on that.

"In our world, the humans see demi-humans and theri-anthropes almost like monsters, due to religious reasons," I explained. "That's why they treat them like enemies. From the human perspective, I'm basically a hero on the side of the monsters, and I've been through my fair share of trouble because of it." More than my fair share, when I thought back on it all.

"There are also conflicts between races," Raphtalia pointed out.

"That's true, but if you consider 'monster' to be a race, then those are just conflicts between their leaders," I said. The issue that Kizuna and her allies had here, as I saw it, was the monsters having used humans like slaves in the past. That would certainly look evil to Kizuna and her allies, but in our world, you could find examples of that everywhere; just take Siltvelt. The opposite was also true. The relationship between Filo and myself, strictly speaking, was that of owner and slave.

"I'm not going to get all friendly with those who promote the arrogant idea that humans are the leaders of the world," the dragon stated.

"So? What do you want to do?" I asked.

"Like I told you. I will concede that you can have a hundred years before we take dominion over the humans," the dragon replied.

"Meaning you'll do whatever you like in a hundred years, but until then you'll play nice?" I asked.

"Stop making me repeat myself. What can any of us gain if this world gets destroyed? We need to prioritize overcoming the waves. Do not place things out of order," the dragon admonished. I hated to admit it, but the dragon was right. It sounded like she wasn't ready to let the ill feeling between her and Kizuna's faction go for the time being and was also willing to cooperate when it came to the waves.

"That should do for now," the dragon said. "Hmmm, and this is a female body. Excellent. Shield Hero, under the condition that you will ultimately mate with me, I shall provide even greater cooperation." So *that* was how long it took for things to take a crazy turn.

"Right, sounds like we're done here. Kill the Demon Dragon," I said, gripping my mirror as I curtly gave the order to Kizuna and her allies. They all just looked confused.

"You lack skill in negotiation, Shield Hero. Look at the concessions I have already made. Why do you flinch now?" the dragon asked. I was happy she seemed to have given up on the idea of taking me over completely, but I wasn't sure where bestiality fit into this.

"What kind of sick joke is this?" Raphtalia exclaimed.

"Sick! That's not allowed!" Filo chirped in.

"Raph!" Raph-chan was bristling with anger too.

"Why are you trying to do . . . that with Naofumi?" Kizuna asked. The dragon crossed her paws and looked back with condescending eyes.

"Don't you understand how good that raging anger that boils so deep inside the Shield Hero felt when I was inside his shield?" she asked. Of course, none of us understood that! Kizuna and the others had looks on their faces signaling they didn't have a clue what she was talking about. "That was fine indeed. Bottomless anger, a blazing hatred directed at everything in the world. You can see why it might get me hot and bothered, no?" She had a longing expression on her face, even as she said it.

"Oh my!" said Sadeena.

"Oh dear!" said Shildina. It sounded like Itsuki was keeping them in the loop.

"Looks like you've picked up a dangerous new admirer, kiddo," L'Arc jibed.

"That's why our negotiations end here. Just kill her, nice and quick," I said.

"Indeed. We can't accept this." Raphtalia was on my side. I was in the right here. Hatching this egg had clearly been a big mistake. We made Kizuna her owner and she didn't care about her at all. She was still just coming after me! That didn't solve anything! "We should have hatched a male," I said.

"You are so naive, Shield Hero. You think you can control me using my gender?" The Demon Dragon smirked. "You'll have to do better than that against a dragon." I remained impassive. That kind of love-conquers-all phrase wasn't going to have any effect on me.

She continued. "First and foremost . . . no, I think I'll keep that to myself. It will be more fun as a surprise."

"What are you talking about? What are you hiding?" I asked.

"If you want to know, you'll have to agree to my conditions," the dragon shot back.

"Never," I snapped.

"Either way suits me." She chuckled. I wanted to just end this by taking the dragon out. I'd had enough of all this sexual harassment focused entirely on me.

"Rat said that dragons pollute the environment, but now this one is even trying to pollute Mr. Naofumi," Raphtalia bemoaned.

"Hah. I'm not aiming to take the virginity of the Shield Hero. Young lady—Katana Hero and Heavenly Emperor, if that's who you are—you may foster your love first. Is that your intent?" the dragon replied.

"Twist my words all you like. We won't accept your conditions," Raphtalia said.

"That's right! That's right!" Filo shouted. *These happy-go-lucky fools!*

"How intensely stupid you humans are. If you see an excellent partner, isn't it your natural-born instinct to allure them and seek to leave children? There is no question that a pairing with the Shield Hero would leave powerful progeny," the dragon said. I'd almost been caught up in this kind of "breeding" issue in Siltvelt. I certainly didn't need it again now.

"Can't you make do with Kizuna? She's one of the four holies from this world. You'll just have to overcome the gender barrier," I said.

"Why me?!" Kizuna exclaimed.

"What are you planning on doing to Kizuna?" Now Glass turned a hostile gaze on me too. I'd had more than enough of all this. The Demon Dragon had already caused more than enough trouble!

"Hmmm . . . I do understand the nature of the Shield Hero. For now, then . . . I can give a little on this matter. I certainly don't want to talk myself into getting killed," the dragon said. She didn't look happy about it, but she seemed to have decided to back down. "Right. Let's get things back on track. I will help you. What exactly is it you want to do?" I didn't really feel like we'd achieved much with our negotiations, but the Demon Dragon seemed willing to cooperate and so it felt like we had no choice but to press on. Personally, I still hoped it would end up with us killing her.

"Do you know the method to break the level cap in this world?" I asked.

"I do. Among the Demon Dragon fragments that the Hunting Hero once shattered, there is one that contains that information," the dragon confirmed. I shook my head, wondering if I was the only one pissed off by hearing this. In our world, that information had been held by Takt's Emperor Dragon, but here it had been in our hands the whole time. I can't believe the key to raising all non-heroes' levels past the cap was just sitting there . . .

"Seeing you make that face, Shield Hero, it really gives me a thrill! I am enjoying this immensely!" the dragon crowed.

"I'm gonna rip your stinking wings off!" I raged. It was rare to encounter a creature so capable of causing such direct damage to my mind. What pissed me off even more was that her approach wasn't based in anger or hostility, but more like . . . lust. She reminded me of the killer whale sisters a little. If the influence of the Water Dragon had brought that out in them, it might mean all dragons were a crazy, sexy bunch. That meant educating Wyndia carefully or there could be trouble. Ren and Rat would need to be warned too . . . but I was moving off topic again.

"So you wish to use the limit break to overcome some hazard in this world. Or maybe it's just to control the flow of information. In any case, give me my remaining fragments," the dragon said.

"We still don't fully trust you, okay? As soon as we hand the fragments over, you might get all big and nasty and attack us," L'Arc said, pretty aggressively. The Demon Dragon shrugged her shoulders and gave a sigh, eyes half closed.

"Like I already told you, I have no plans to fight with you heroes at the moment. What do you think I could even do with this freshly born weak little body and so few of my fragments?" she asked. There was some truth in what she was saying, but I didn't feel like sticking up for her. "You heroes are about to fight me with weapons that came from my fragments, are you not? I would like a little respect for that, if nothing else." That was another reasonable point. There were quite a few decent weapons among those that used Demon Dragon materials, and Kizuna and her allies were generally using Demon Dragon weapons. Thinking about things like that, she was the source of some pretty nasty weapons for me too.

"I won't accept you relying on me completely," the dragon said. I just grunted. "Think about it for a moment, anyway. You have the Hunting Hero on your side, one who boasts unmatched strength when fighting monsters. If you can't overcome any little tricks I might try to pull, how can you call yourselves heroes?" she asked. I really hated her condescending attitude.

"How about we just kill you, raise a new dragon, and let that one get overwritten?" I suggested.

"Like I said, naive. That won't change the potential for you to get your head bitten off while you sleep. There's no monster-sealing ofuda for an Emperor Dragon, not when you get down to it. No matter how kind you are, once it has all the information, it will reach the same conclusion," she said. I wondered how she could be so sure of that. She probably had her reasons, but she was definitely spending too much energy hating humans. "Shield Hero, the reason Dragon Emperors like you is because of your innate good nature. You should be proud of that." I didn't feel especially proud. It wasn't even something that made me happy.

"Look, this is all getting a bit too much for me," I said, shaking my head. "Let's not get too jumpy, but be ready for the worst and give this a try. If it doesn't work out, we'll just kill her. Again."

"Excellent, Shield Hero. Your ability to prioritize so easily is surely another reason I have taken such a liking to you," the dragon said.

"Sure, sure, whatever," I replied, just brushing her off.

"I guess that's the approach to take, Naofumi, but I can't say I like it," Kizuna said and looked at the Demon Dragon with hatred still in her eyes but sounding half resolved to the plan.

"Will this really be okay?" Raphtalia asked.

"Fighting here won't solve anything, that's for sure. And haven't you heard about this kind of thing in stories? A punishment that falls on humans due to their arrogance. We've a grace period of a hundred years, so we just have to create a world that the Demon Dragon won't have to attack," I said.

"You're making a lot of trouble for us, or maybe for our kids," L'Arc said.

"Maybe, but it's also a fact that we never knew when the scattered Demon Dragon fragments might cause her to revive. Even if we collected them up and sealed them in your castle, L'Arc, one day they may eventually pass back into circulation . . . Ultimately it might prove more productive to make use of her now, while she is here offering her neck for the collar, than wait for a rampage in the future," I reasoned. I recalled the Tyrant Dragon Rex and the monsters that had been sealed in Q'ten Lo. Botching the sealing and having to deal with a revived monster somewhere down the line would really suck.

"You'll find me quite giving," the dragon said, "but I need to take as well. Hurry up and get them ready for me."

"That said, Romina and other blacksmiths have been using them when making all sorts of gear," I mentioned.

"I'm impressed you even thought of using the fragments from such a beast," Kizuna said.

"That's just how great a material they are," I replied. With that, we set about collecting the Demon Dragon fragments that were in the possession of Kizuna and her allies. The Demon Dragon proceeded to absorb her fragments that Kizuna and the others had gathered and regain her powers.

"I also want the fragments in the heroes' weapons," she said. "Heroes, hold out your weapons. That will allow me to just take the fragments from inside." As requested, all the heroes present who had a weapon using Demon Dragon materials held them up to the Demon Dragon. The weapons started to glow, and then a sparkling droplet from them flew over to the Demon Dragon.

"Hmmm . . . now I can perceive most of what has been happening. I've achieved common intent between all the fragments too. No more issues. I am reborn!" the dragon proclaimed, throwing both paws up in front of her with a look on her face like she'd just answered a quiz question correctly. I really needed her to stop doing stuff like that, or I was going to burst out laughing. I wondered for a moment if she was observing my memories.

"Well, simply taking so much from you will affect my reputation. Here is something of a thank-you." With that, the Demon Dragon clicked her . . . claws, I presumed. Upon doing so, all of the heroes' weapons—including mine—started to glow.

True Demon Dragon Mirror conditions met!

True Demon Dragon Mirror
<abilities unlocked> equip bonus: skill: "Multiplying Mirror Fragment," enhance power of combination skills, dragon magic disposition awakened, dragon growth adjustment (massive), enhance power of curse weapons.
special effect: Dragon Scale (large), C Demon

Bullet, all resistances (medium), magic power consumption reduction (medium), SP consumption reduction (medium), power-up success rate up, magic incantation shortening (large), Demon Dragon's protection, growth power.

Exclusive attached soul: Demon Dragon.

"Wow, this is incredible! It's made my trusty old Demon Dragon weapon easier to use and stronger too!" L'Arc said, immediately sounding happy.

"Dragon magic disposition awakened? It sounds like we've got something new to use," Kizuna said, also sounding pretty enthusiastic.

"Use it to your heart's content . . . the power of monsters . . ." the dragon said. She made it sound like we'd been given permission to use some kind of forbidden technique. The vassal weapon holders seemed pleased with it, so I wasn't going to complain.

"These properties could make quite a difference, Glass," Kizuna said.

"Indeed . . . but should we really be using them?" Glass replied.

"I share your concerns, believe me," Raphtalia sympathized. I could understand where the two of them were coming from.

"This looks so easy to use that I should be able to handle

most of the upcoming combat with this alone," Kizuna said. She seemed very pleased with her new weapon, happily swinging it around. In my case . . . the Spirit Tortoise Carapace Mirror had better stats. It was like the Mirror of Compassion, the transformation of the Shield of Compassion, was auto-mixed in.

"Bleh. It's not like the horrible feeling I get from Gaelion in the other world, a different . . . strange feeling," Filo said, upset about something.

"Humming fairies don't have the whole racial hatred of dragons, after all," I said. Filolials didn't exist in this world, making it hard for her to draw out her innate hatred. It sounded like Filo was being affected by some emotions other than her genetic hatred.

It was worth noting that putting some of Filo's feathers from this world into our weapons had turned out a lot of gear with musical abilities, none of which was really useable for anyone apart from maybe for Itsuki.

"Shield Hero, I can add some rage if you desire it. The mercy within you is not well matched with my power, after all," the dragon said.

"Sorry to break it to you, but I can't use the Shield of Rage at all due to the Shield of Compassion," I told her.

"And I'm telling you that I can let you use it again. I showed reasonable control of your rage, did I not?" the dragon said.

"Stop trying to allure Mr. Naofumi in strange ways!" Raphtalia chided.

"Raph!" agreed Raph-chan. I did want to avoid that if possible.

"If that is your wish, Shield Hero, very well. I've also boosted the stats of your favorite Spirit Tortoise gear. If you encounter a need for it, then you may turn to my power," the dragon said. That was a nasty proposal—and it sounded like foreshadowing too. Forcibly activating my sealed rage, perhaps. I really hoped I'd never have to rely on that overly enhanced shield ever again.

"Well then . . . it feels like I've recovered a sufficient volume of my intelligence and strength. Now I just need to increase my level and I should be reasonably powerful." The Demon Dragon lifted up into the air and crossed her paws, as though she was thinking, while choosing to land—without permission—on my shoulder. I swatted at her with my hand, but she nimbly dodged it!

"Get off me! That's Raph-chan's spot!" I said.

"I'm not sure I agree with that either!" Raphtalia commented.

"Raph!" said Raph-chan.

"Boy, I wish I could ride up there," Filo complained. I shook my head, really wishing they would pick their moments better.

"We can use the limit break now. What we also really need is a way of dealing with having our support enhancement magic removed," I said.

"That's right," Kizuna chimed in. "When we fought, you removed the magic Therese cast on us, right? How did you do that?"

"I am the Demon Dragon, the master of all magic in this world. You would think that I know about dispel magic, but . . . in any case, I sense that even if I shared it with you, it would not lead to a complete resolution of your problem," the dragon stated.

"Why not?" I asked.

"There's something from a memory of a Dragon Emperor who fought a hero long ago—a technique that denies dispel magic . . ." the dragon replied. That sounded like something that might be useful in our situation.

"So do you know which weapon it comes from?" I asked.

"We only fought, I'm afraid. So I don't know that much. That said, if you search, then I'm sure you can find more information. Holder of the fan vassal weapon . . . it was something used by those who originated your style," the dragon revealed.

"My style?" she replied. Fighting as she did with a fan, Glass did seem suited to that kind of delicate work.

"I don't know if it is simply a technique or if it is a skill, but if it originated with your style, then there might be some hints for you there," the dragon said.

"I see where you're coming from," Glass agreed.

"We will investigate it later. It could become a trump card for defeating our enemies," Ethnobalt said.

"Still, Shield Hero. If you mix that technique you called 'life force' with magic, aren't you capable of achieving a similar effect?" the dragon suggested.

"Life force, huh?" I replied. I looked over at S'yne and she shook her head. So she didn't know anything. Fair enough . . . but it also looked to me like she was making a stuffed doll of the Demon Dragon. It seemed nothing more—again—than a palette-swap of Gaelion. I wondered if it would be useful for anything.

"With all your intellect, do you know anything about the power-up methods for heroes' weapons?" I asked.

"There are lots of gaps in my memory around there, so I can't provide anything useful," the dragon responded. I had expected as much. "In any case, for the sake of our hundred-year treaty, I will now lend you my strength for the sake of this world. Make sure to give your all to raising me up nice and strong, heroes." With that, a really nasty piece of work joined the party.

Chapter Eleven: Volunteer Soldiers

It was a few days after the Demon Dragon joined us.

Going to the place where Glass's style originated was going to be quite a trip, so we decided to prioritize performing the limit break procedure on the most trustworthy among our companions. We also had to raise the Demon Dragon, meaning we had plenty to keep us busy. The way things worked differed for wild monsters and the Demon Dragon. Suffice it to say, she had to collect a fair volume of experience before she could level up. Even worse, she was a monster from this world and so couldn't level up using earth crystals. I just wanted to give her a big boost and get it over with.

In regard to our overall levels, L'Arc and the others had reached as high as 135. They were pretty up there. I was currently 110, Raphtalia was 115, and Sadeena and Shildina were 105. By this point, it was getting harder to earn more for all of us. Kizuna and L'Arc had provided details on a super-hard labyrinth packed with powerful monsters, and in consideration of the future, we started to plan a serious expedition.

The Demon Dragon also displayed quite an interest in my fighting style and started asking me questions about it. One of the moments I was quite proud of recently was when I reflected that magic back at Bitch, and the dragon seemed very interested in that moment in particular.

Then there was the subject of what to do next.

Ethnobalt's ship had been stolen. That meant we had no idea when the enemy might attack. It also meant we had to keep security tight while continuing to work on powering ourselves up, which was not an easy balancing act. To make things even worse, the reduction in the number of the four holy heroes meant the frequency of the waves had greatly increased.

At least the enemy hadn't chosen to attack at the same time as a wave. Not yet, anyway. If we got lucky and the wave matched up with our world, then our levels would jump up, which was probably the reason why they weren't risking it, but that being said, none of that would apply if they had been leveling up too. In the worst-case scenario, though, Itsuki and I could return to our own world and then buff up with magic and take care of anyone who came after us.

It would have suited us better if the enemy was a bunch of morons. It was annoying that life never worked out quite so easily. We had no idea how bad it was going to get with the waves, so we had to plan our moves carefully and move to prevent this "fusion of the worlds," whatever that meant.

Regarding the dragon hourglasses in locations away from human habitation, a force that might be called the "Demon's Army," who were subordinates of the Demon Dragon, was apparently taking care of things. I was pretty jealous of that level of control. In our world, that was probably all being handled by Fitoria.

In any case, we were using the Demon Dragon's limit break to enhance our forces while moving via my teleportation skills toward the place Glass's style originated. The only baggage we had to take was a mirror, so it was pretty easy. We were working on enhancing our strength as we went.

Itsuki and Rishia were again helping Ethnobalt decipher the ancient texts. It seemed they were close to understanding a passage that had eluded them until now, so they were holed up in the Ancient Labyrinth Library like it was some kind of research laboratory. Itsuki, who was really just helping out the best he could, had reported that they were close to a complete understanding.

On this particular day, I was preparing a meal in the kitchen.

"We have quite a number of volunteer soldiers gathering. How should we handle them?" Glass came and reported to Kizuna and me. The rumors had been spreading fast that we now had access to the legendary limit break.

"How are these rumors spreading?" Kizuna pondered.

"You don't exactly run a tight ship around here," I commented. There were concerns about Yomogi and Tsugumi having at least one spy in the ranks, for one thing. "Do you think your allies from when you fought the Demon Dragon will turn up?" I asked.

"I think they will," Glass conjectured. "We've been able to keep the waves under control due to the allies we spread across each region."

"I wonder how they'll react when they find out that the same Demon Dragon is now alive again," I said.

"You never know what's going to happen in the world," Kizuna muttered, looking distressed.

"I'm surprised to hear you say that, Kizuna. I thought you could get along with anyone," I said.

"Just what do you think I am, Naofumi? Honestly?" she asked me. If I had replied honestly with "an airheaded dummy," she would probably have gotten mad. I wasn't mocking her when I thought that either. It was great having a hero like Kizuna around. In fact, she was perfectly suited to carrying the expectations of other people.

"Volunteer soldiers, huh? We might have some vanguards of the waves mixed in. Sadeena, Shildina," I called.

"We know the drill, little Naofumi," Sadeena confirmed.

"No problem!" Shildina added. The killer whale sisters could—according to them—spot the vanguards, so we'd have them take a look over this fresh crop of volunteers. That said, the word had been spreading to be suspicious of self-styled "geniuses" who had a harem of women. So things depended on whether our enemies were also picking up on that.

If we just started adding people to our forces without

checking them out, something like the loss of the scythe could easily happen again.

L'Arc and the others had been using diplomacy to spread information to other nations about people who had been told since they were born that they were geniuses—those like Kyo, Takt, and Seya—and to spread word that they were highly likely to be vanguards of the waves. The other nations had immediately responded, and rarely positively. L'Arc's nation had gathered quite a bunch of heroes, after all, and so any warnings coming out of here tended to be taken in a cautious, if not downright distrusting, light.

Furthermore, few countries would be willing to easily give up the advantages that having one of these geniuses around could bring them. Of course, we could just leave those types in play and then use whatever drama they stirred up as a reason to go in and intervene. Best-case scenario, we might even lure out those behind all this.

If it could be proven that Sadeena and Shildina really could spot them, then it might be time for a serious hunt for the vanguards of the waves hiding in Kizuna's world. As for our world . . . something tickled my memory. I kind of recalled a report saying that Takt had been doing something similar. Maybe the vanguards of the waves also had a tendency to fight each other.

We didn't understand all of that stuff yet . . . but when I looked at Kyo and at Takt, neither of them seemed like the type to cooperate with others. They had both thought they were the best, and both had no time for anyone other than cute girls. Anyone else like themselves, they had considered trash and immediately wanted to kill them. There was no way the vanguards of the waves were going to get along if they all acted like that, even if they were on the same side.

Something was still tickling my memory there . . . I tried to recall it but couldn't. It didn't matter at the moment.

In terms of checking the volunteer soldiers, however, everyone was pretty busy with their own work and so we didn't have many bodies to apply to the task. Itsuki, Rishia, and Ethnobalt weren't even here; they were off deciphering the ancient texts. If anything happened over there, S'yne had gone with them and would let us know. She hadn't really wanted to tag along, but she was the one who could move the quickest when it was needed, so she'd been left without much choice.

L'Arc and Therese, meanwhile, had left the nation to attend a council relating to such matters as the Demon Dragon. The Demon Dragon herself was at the dragon hourglass, preparing for the ritual. Some additional materials were apparently required. The exact method probably differed from the one in our world.

That left me, Raphtalia, Raph-chan, Chris, Kizuna, Glass, Sadeena, and Shildina to go look at the volunteers. Filo had gone out on a walk. I'd glimpsed her earlier, walking around the castle moat while humming to herself.

And so we arrived to check out the volunteer soldiers gathered in front of the castle . . .

"Oh my," Sadeena said at once.

"We've definitely got some," Shildina confirmed, both of the sisters shaking their heads sadly.

"Okay. Point them out," I said.

"That one there. Then that one behind him. And that one making adjustments to something over there." One after another, Sadeena reeled them off.

"Guilty until proven innocent is my stance here. They've been kind enough to come find us, so let's set a trap for them. You two sisters had better be right about this," I said, checking with them.

"Of course we are," Sadeena replied.

"There's no doubting it," Shildina confirmed. They sounded absolutely positive, but I still gave them a bit of a suspicious look. Then I ordered the guards to pick out the ones that had been identified. That was the moment that Raphtalia and Raph-chan pointed at a single spot in the line.

"Hiding right there, it's—" The moment after Raphtalia drew her katana, however, none other than S'yne's very own sister suddenly appeared from among the throng, a smile on her face. This was the enemy that all the enhancement cooking and the Demon Dragon had been for. It was all to become strong enough to defeat her. That deadly threat had now just walked up to the castle gates. One of the enemy leaders just sauntered up to our main base! Security around here really was a joke.

"Well, well, well! I'd say I'm impressed, but then again, I expected you to spot me," she taunted.

"You!" I shouted. If she unleashed her unknown techniques at us again, we would have trouble handling her. She had really picked her spot to strike too—right where our security was weakest.

"As I had heard, Iwatani, your right-hand girl is skilled at detecting subterfuge or impediments to awareness," S'yne's sister said as the party she had brought with her spread out into a ring around us. The actual volunteer soldiers realized something was up and backed off. "Nice to see you again, anyway! How have you been? I'm just popping in to have some fun."

"To have some fun? Are you joking?" I raged.

"Oh, I wouldn't exactly say that I'm joking . . ." S'yne's sister replied tauntingly.

"So these are the guys, are they? The ones with the remaining holy weapon and the vassal weapon holders?" said one of her minions. It was a guy standing at S'yne's sister side, giving off vibes just like Kyo, Takt, Miyaji, and Seya . . . basically a vanguard of the waves in spades. It sounded like he didn't think much of us either. *Why do I feel we've just encountered our next enemy of the week?*

I was getting a bit sick of this now. They had to have quite a stock of these guys to keep dragging one after the other out like this.

"This is your new boss? Forget him, anyway. Where's Bitch?" I asked.

"Yes, he's my boss," S'yne's sister replied, furrowing her brow and flicking her hand in a way that this enemy of the week wouldn't spot. It looked like she wanted me to be quiet. At my question, however, a woman appeared behind Mr. Enemy of the Week.

"You used that name again! I told you, didn't I? All he does is insult Lady Malty! Unforgiveable!" the woman said.

"He must be really bad for you to say that about him," Enemy of the Week commented. I'd seen this woman before somewhere, I was sure, but I couldn't quite place her. I tilted my head to the side, squinting my eyes, and she started to shout at me, anger and disgust on full display.

"I'm a former ally of the Spear Hero! I'm not Elena. I'm the other one!" she shouted. I was still puzzled for a moment, but yes, there had been someone who looked like her, always at Bitch's side. It did look like her. Okay, mystery solved. I hadn't even known her name. I just knew her as "Woman B," someone in the background.

Maybe Elena had been Woman B though. I hadn't really decided for sure, and by now I had totally forgotten.

"What's this? You look like you've completely forgotten me!" the woman exclaimed.

"What if I tell you that's exactly what I've done?" I said to her.

"What?! If it wasn't for you, Lady Malty would never have suffered so harshly! You inhuman animal!" the woman shouted.

"Whatever. All I hear from you and Bitch is the howling of defeated dogs. Howl on, dog," I taunted.

"You fiend! I will purge you, I swear it!" she raged. I simply didn't care. The more she talked, though, the more fitting the title "Bitch II" seemed to be for her. She'd never really stood out before, perhaps because the real Bitch had always been there.

"You seem to have a real thing for Bitch too. You respect her, do you?" I asked. It came as a bit of a surprise to me that anyone could get along with that shitty bitch. Even Elena had only teamed up with her for her own mutual benefit.

". . . I do!" Woman B exclaimed. There had been a noticeable pause there though. She needed to think about her answer. She went on. "If only you hadn't shown up! If only you had never shown up, our happy existence could have continued forever!"

"I've heard it all before, honestly. So? Where is the real Bitch?" I asked. She didn't seem to be here. If she'd been hiding among the volunteers, then I'd been hoping to finish her off for good this time, but I couldn't see her here. She didn't seem to be concealing herself among the crowd either.

"She's recuperating from the terrible wounds you inflicted on her!" Bitch II shouted.

"Recuperating, is it? Sounds like a lovely time. What a shame you didn't get to 'recuperate' with her," I retorted. My reply seemed to have hit a nerve. Woman B started shaking with anger, her face bright red.

"Silence! You are the one causing all these problems! You are the infection consuming this world!" she shouted.

"Sure you aren't talking about yourselves there? You are parasites, the trash of this world, latching onto power and feeding from it," I spat.

"I see again why you were selected as the Mirror Hero," Glass said, nodding her head. "You are just reflecting what she says back at her." I could have used some support, not jibes. S'yne's sister ignored the screeching Woman B and replied.

"Well, well, well," she said. "Indeed, she has been through a lot and is recuperating at the moment."

"You'd be better to just chase her off as quickly as you can. To be quite honest, there's nothing good about her at all. It would greatly benefit the world if you just killed her," I said, speaking as directly from the heart as I could. Bitch was the woman who really made you feel that there were some people who were just better off dead. There was no way she could possibly bring about anything of benefit to this world.

Then S'yne's sister gave Woman B a disparaging glance before turning back to us as though nothing had happened.

"We can't do that. In our illustrious leader's world, we had the last of the holy weapon holders subdued and held captive. During a wave, however, those blasted terrorists almost destroyed that weapon holder, which meant that world would have been wiped out by the waves. As this was happening, we happened to encounter your little friend and her allies, and they helped turn the situation around in the nick of time. That's why she's earned such favor," S'yne's sister explained, as heavy with the exposition as ever. The thing that surprised me most about this reveal was that S'yne's sister's forces had also faced circumstances that they considered dangerous. I really wished they had just been wiped out. "This was before meeting with you, Iwatani," S'yne's sister confirmed. Maybe that was why S'yne's sister didn't seem that happy about Bitch and her allies being around and hadn't been all that cooperative with them during our last encounter.

"What are you talking about?" Enemy of the Week said, glaring at me. Maybe he was feeling a little left out in the cold.

"You'd be better off not to consider these guys your friends," I warned him. "They specialize in betrayal."

"Hah, you must be joking! They believe in me, trust me implicitly! They would never do anything like that to me!" he replied.

"Of course we wouldn't," S'yne's sister said slyly.

"Never." The noisy Woman B now turned on the sexiness, pushing up to Enemy of the Week and placing her arm around him . . . pretty low on his body too. Talk about "sex appeal." Enemy of the Week was pretending to stay calm, but his eyes were fixed on her tits, and below them. They had him under their thumb, clearly, while he looked like he thought he'd just bagged another chick.

I had to wonder, though, if they didn't feel depressed at having such a bitch among their allies.

"Little Raphtalia! Show them we've got the goods too!" Sadeena shouted.

"That's right. Give them the works!" Shildina chimed in.

"Ah, well . . . okay," Raphtalia responded uncertainly. The killer whale sisters continued to rile Raphtalia up, trying to get me to act like them. Now I was starting to feel depressed.

"You're really draining the tension from this situation!" I chided them.

"Hah. Showing off your harem, are you? Unsightly," Enemy of the Week said. He was quick to pick up on this, at least, and his eyes were particularly sharp. Like he had a leg to stand on though—he was surrounded by women himself!

"You don't have to play along, Raphtalia!" I told her. "Make some barbed comment like normal!" Getting hooked into the foolishness of the crazy whale sisters would really harm Raphtalia's reputation. I had become a bit more tolerant after Atla's final wish, but I still wasn't going to play along with all this sexy stuff.

"Okay," Raphtalia said, looking confused. That just depressed me more.

"You just aren't bothered about sexy stuff, are you? I sympathize," Glass said, getting involved for some reason.

"I'm starting to feel sorry for Naofumi," Kizuna agreed.

"He probably thinks you two are in the 'harem,'" I told them.

"I really don't like that," Glass responded. "No, I don't. I don't like that at all." I wasn't sure why she said it three times, but I didn't like it either. Just for the record.

"Naofumi is a friend and a comrade, but we're not like that!" Kizuna retorted. I wondered if she really understood the situation. She was the type who needed things to be said directly to her face.

"A shame we don't have Fohl here. Even L'Arc would have worked," I said. Just a few guys mixed in might have broken the group up a bit and prevented it from looking like a harem.

"Naofumi . . . even if we did have some guys, it would probably just give them some different ideas. Like . . . boys love?" Kizuna said. It sounded like, whatever the composition of the party, they would presume a lewd relationship with me at the center. I might be better off just surrounding myself with monsters.

Then I thought how much the Demon Dragon would probably enjoy that. Fresh fodder for more misunderstandings.

"What do you want me to do?!" I shouted. Still, we had been bantering for a while and S'yne still hadn't shown up yet.

"Oh, S'yne can't come help you right now," S'yne's sister said, stroking her chain. She must have noticed me looking around. "We're jamming her abilities."

"Jamming, huh?" I said.

"We also understand the problem with your transportation skills too," S'yne's sister continued. "You can't use them if the vicinity has been warped by magic or something similar." She really had our number. This was all such a pain in the ass. I could feel the acid reflux boiling in my stomach. "Then there are means of transport in this world. You need to interact with a dragon hourglass to bring them in, and do you really have time to be calling reinforcements?"

"Aren't you forgetting my transportation skills?" I said. I had Transport Mirror and Movement Mirror in my back pocket and could easily bring in some allies using them.

"But you understand what will happen here if you run away, right? Iwatani, the way I see it, you need to use those skills to travel away first before you can bring anyone back with you, correct?" she snickered. At that, I grunted. That was a painfully precise observation. She wasn't just a moron woman after all. She was smarter than Bitch, that was for sure.

"Even if you do get away, we can just leave. Being on the attack is so easy. You got one over on us last time too. That obviously makes us want to fight back," she said.

"I'm sick of you already," I replied. She was throwing every trick in the book at us. Right when our defenses were weakest too . . . it was looking more and more like we had a spy to worry about.

"That's the sister of S'yne I've been hearing so much about?" Kizuna asked.

"That's right. You must be the Hunting Hero. I think I preferred you as a statue," S'yne's sister jibed at Kizuna. The two of them locked eyes for a moment. They both looked pretty mean.

"You got lucky. If a wave had occurred with the world of our illustrious leader, we were planning on shattering you. That's the problem with this system; that's the only way to get the reward for destroying a world," the sister explained. I'd heard this talk about rewards for destroying worlds before, I vaguely recalled. I had no idea where that reward came from.

"Indeed, I feel pretty lucky," Kizuna said.

"That would have been . . . truly terrible," Glass agreed. She could say that again, but I could hardly imagine what a world being destroyed would be like.

"It's a pretty stunning sight," the sister said. "The sun suddenly vanishes and everything is turned into a lifeless, barren plain. Sometimes everything just crumbles into dust. All the life on that world just withers and dies too. All of it." I didn't need to hear her tales from the apocalypse either.

"Kizuna, you should fall back," Glass said. "If you die, this is all over."

"Oh my! What a suggestion. We would never do that without a wave. Why ever would we want to destroy this world?" S'yne's sister asked.

"What are you talking about? I can't understand you," Enemy of the Week said, furrowing his brow.

"We're speaking in a language only they know," S'yne's sister replied with a dollop of treacle in her voice, stroking the gemstone on her chain again. "I'm telling them to stop spreading lies about the waves destroying the world." It looked like she could turn off the translation function on her weapon and was using that ability to spread lies about us!

"I see. There's really nothing that scary about the waves, is there? In fact, they are quite useful for making us stronger," Enemy of the Week replied. He saw no threat in the waves at all, that much was clear. No wonder he had no desire to listen to us at all. It would be pointless to try and explain things to him.

There were so many people in the world, and yet S'yne's sister and her forces were able to pluck out these vanguards of the waves with so little trouble. Maybe they had abilities similar to the ones Sadeena and Shildina had been displaying.

"You are the enemy of King L'Arc Berg! Defeating you will earn us great reward!" one of the volunteer soldiers shouted, and a bunch of them pointed their weapons at Enemy of the

Week. Choosing to mingle with the volunteers might have turned out to be a stupid idea . . . but this was S'yne's sister we were talking about. We could not afford to drop our guard.

"You'll make the perfect gift for our king! Hands up, let us take you into custody! For our own sakes!" another volunteer shouted.

"Wait, please! You can't handle—" Kizuna started shouting.

"Hold it! You're not on the same level—" I also started shouting, pretty much the same thing. The volunteers paid no attention and charged at the Enemy of the Week. The other two that Sadeena and Shildina had spotted, along with their own companions, had fallen back and were just pretending to be normal people.

"Bah! Pathetic dogs, only able to fight in a pack! Learn your place!" Enemy of the Week raised his hand and a clear wall appeared, trapping the volunteer soldiers who had been crowding in toward him. The wall was shaped like a cube, with a hole in the middle for Enemy of the Week and his entourage. The soldiers shouted from inside, imprisoned.

"What the hell is this?!"

"It's like defensive-wall magic, almost . . ."

"Dammit! What is this? It's incredibly hard!" The volunteers sounded suitably bewildered as they hacked at the wall together, but to no avail. Then something like a transparent floor rose up from beneath Enemy of the Week's feet, lifting our foes up to a vantage point from where they could look down on us.

"This is self-defense," he proclaimed. "You attacked us, and you will now pay for that with your lives!" He tightened his fist in the air, and then the walls he had created started to draw together, with the volunteers still trapped inside. They started screaming and shouting at once. I'd seen this kind of attack, but only in manga—or movies. The old "trash compactor" maneuver. Those inside got pressed and squished. Heroes normally got out of it. I hadn't expected to see someone actually using it.

"Come on," I said. "We have to get them out!"

"Okay!" Raphtalia agreed.

"I wasn't expecting combat so soon! I'm not really ready!" Kizuna said.

"You'll be fine. We just have to do it," Glass assured her. Kizuna took out an ofuda and summoned Chris, while Raphtalia and Glass sprang at the walls . . . the barriers that were still closing in on the volunteers.

"Formation One, Formation Two: Glass Shield!" I shouted, placing Glass Shields inside the compressing barriers in order to provide some protection. With a scraping sound, the walls stopped shrinking.

"Huh? Don't get in my way! Those who dare attack me have no right to life," Enemy of the Week ranted.

"Sorry to say it, but anyone who would attack you is an ally

of mine. I can't let these good people die. Come on! To action!"
I shouted.

"I'm with you! Raph-chan!" Raphtalia called.

"Me too! Chris, lend me a flipper!" Glass called. The two
cuties replied accordingly, and with Raph-chan on Raphtalia's
shoulder and Chris on Glass's, they started to attack the barriers
Enemy of the Week had created.

"Dream Illusion: Mist Single Strike!" Raphtalia unleashed
her illusion-wreathed Mist Single Strike over and over.

"Circle Dance Destruction Formation: Frozen Turtle Carapace Cracker!" Glass unleashed a combination skill that ignored
defense with a shot of ice magic. By turning her Mist Single
Strike—normally just a single blow—into a combination skill,
Raphtalia had achieved the ability to unleash multiple strikes.
As for Glass, her attack had properties to slow down the enemy
and also sometimes turn them into ice. The two of them were
really acquiring some pretty vicious little attacks, which was also
thanks, in part, to the Demon Dragon.

The attacks Raphtalia and Glass unleashed barely managed
to open a hole in the surface of the barrier.

"This stuff is tough," Glass said.

"Indeed. But we've finally shattered it! Hurry up and get
out of there!" Raphtalia shouted.

"Oh dear! I'm not about to allow that!" Enemy of the
Week shouted back, applying his power to close the hole my

two party members had ripped open. The opening in the barrier was gradually closed, changing shape as it did so.

"And you think we're about to let you do that?" I shouted in what was perhaps not my best comeback ever. I moved up and used two Float Mirrors to block the closing hole.

"Come on, get out of there!" Kizuna shouted. The men replied with a ragged cheer and started to escape through the hole.

"You're just getting in our way! Fall back!" I shouted. These might not be normal civilians, but considering what had just happened, we could hardly count on them in battle. If we were going to keep having to save them, we'd never get any fighting done. Not having them around was the best solution. Grasping my words and the situation, the volunteers quickly backed off.

That created another issue. The other two vanguards of the waves that Sadeena and Shildina had spotted had used this fresh chaos to make a run for it, and so I'd lost track of them. If they came back, the sisters would spot them again. That was the best I could do right now.

"Hah! It looks like all you can do is defend," Enemy of the Week crowed down at us. He was just making a fool of himself. Our attack was about to begin.

"Don't forget about us," Sadeena said, starting to incant magic with a gemstone in one hand.

"That would be a mistake," Shildina added, taking out an ofuda and incanting magic.

"I'll show you the results of all my recent training! This is magic I learned from little Therese, rearranged using the Way of the Dragon Vein! Have a taste of magic cast using the same method as little Naofumi!" Sadeena shouted. Even during her long-winded explanation, her gemstone accessory was sparkling brightly, and then it launched some magic. "Jewel Aqua Blast!"

Shildina, meanwhile, seemed to have completely mastered incanting using ofuda.

"I now command you. Ofuda! Respond to my words! Cut these foes to pieces! Wind Weasels!" While Sadeena summoned a massive chunk of ice, Shildina created blades from the air. All their attacks headed directly for Enemy of the Week, S'yne's sister, and Woman B.

"What?! But also pathetic!" Enemy of the Week threw up a barrier to protect himself and his allies from the sisters' magic. The magic crashed into his barrier and vanished without being able to penetrate it. I'd kind of been hoping they would just bust through it.

"Oh my. It's so hard," Sadeena said with a suggestive tone in her voice.

"We cut into it a bit with life force . . ." Raphtalia said.

"Indeed, I first thought it would be easy to break, but it wasn't very effective," Glass added, everyone offering their thoughts on this new barrier problem. A barrier that even life force couldn't completely break. There had to be some kind of trick to this.

"Oh wow! You're so cool! Hurry up and kill the Shield Demon King! He's right there!"

"I want to see blood fly!"

"I'm so impressed!"

Enemy of the Week's women were all shouting. I wondered how he wasn't embarrassed, having women like that following him around. S'yne's sister remained silent. It didn't look like she was going to get serious about fighting us this time either. I wasn't sure if that was lucky or not. If she did get serious, I really wasn't sure we could win. If possible, I wanted to get them on the ropes—just like last time—and chase them out of here.

If we did run for it now, it was clear that L'Arc's country would be overrun. That would not only take out our base of operations, but the pressure we were already feeling from surrounding nations would get stronger. We had to avoid running away.

"Stardust Blade!" Raphtalia launched a long-range star at Enemy of the Week and his entourage, but the attack was unable to penetrate his barrier.

"Hah! As if I'm going to let that attack through," he scoffed.

"I added even more life force and mixed in a Point of Focus, and it still wasn't enough!" Raphtalia bemoaned. I was beginning to think these barriers were based on some factor other than just pure durability. I had to think of some way to break through them.

"Hah! Die!" As Enemy of the Week shouted, sparks suddenly scattered around my Stardust Mirror. Position-wise, it looked like he had been aiming something at my neck.

"What? I can't do it inside the barriers? What a pain!" he said. Based on the attack he had just used, it looked like he could use the barriers to perform cutting attacks. That made sense of everything, then; the barriers were primarily a means of attack.

"Raphtalia, Glass, his barriers look like defense, but they are actually used as attacks. When your attacks grind against them, twisting in some life force might make a difference," I told them.

"Understood! I'll give it a try!" Raphtalia quickly responded.

"Okay," Glass affirmed too.

"Hey . . . I can't just stand around watching either," S'yne's sister said, picking her moment to speak up, and then took out . . . something. Something that looked like a round ball, which she then threw. Another something then emerged from inside it. It was something that looked like it had been patched together from a lion's body and a cow's head. Looking more carefully, I saw there was a steel bar like a visor across its eyes, from which burned two red lights that looked very much like eyes. Its chest area was also covered in similar-looking metallic armor. The name popped up as . . . Artificial Behemoth. The beast gave a growl, emitting a miasma-like cloud of breath as it landed. It looked around and immediately fixed its gaze on us.

"Now, rip them to pieces!" S'yne's sister commanded. The beast accepted at once, emitting the deadly intent of an animal as it closed in toward us with a far more enthusiastic growl than before. The next moment, it was leaping at us! This thing was fast!

"Formation One, Formation Two, Formation Three: Glass Shield!" I shouted, quickly deploying multiple Glass Shields as I leapt forward to protect Raphtalia and Glass. However, the Artificial Behemoth just ignored them completely, smashing through all of my defenses and leaping directly at me. It proceeded to shatter even my Stardust Mirror in an instant!

The three of us gasped and cursed as it closed in. It was so fast we could hardly keep up. And we certainly couldn't react in time. I could see it coming, but my body couldn't respond! I was using life force to push my body to the limit and I was still too slow.

We were knocked away, flying through the air, but just before we crashed into the wall . . . we started floating in midair. It was a light and fluffy feeling.

"Look at you. We leave you alone for a few minutes and you get into all this trouble."

"Master, are you okay?"

Chapter Twelve: Double Reflection

I turned at the voices to see both the Demon Dragon and Filo there. They had saved us, just before we—quite literally—hit the wall.

"Well, well, well, reinforcements? I guess you do have the home-field advantage. Just floating there makes you lovely targets though," S'yne's sister shouted.

"Eat this!" Enemy of the Week launched a barrier right at us. He was persisting in using these barriers for a range of cutting attacks, making me think they were fundamentally something else entirely.

"Stardust Mirror!" I said. The cool down had already finished, so I put my own barrier back up and stopped his attack. Sparks proceeded to grate out around us. I had stopped the barrier itself, at least. What was the original purpose of a barrier, anyway—to defend? But he could use them to attack all he liked. There was no way he was going to break through my own barriers. They were focused entirely on defense.

The Artificial Behemoth had landed and followed up its attack with more nasty growling. Its claws slashed down at us.

"Enough of this! Universal power of my core! Respond to my call and materialize your magic power! I am the Emperor

Dragon who rules this world. Create walls that block my foes! Demon Dragon! Encompassing Mirrors!"

The Demon Dragon unleashed the same protective barriers that she had used against us so long ago. The Artificial Behemoth crashed through them one after the other, but the speed of its attack was definitely slowed down.

"Hey! Watch out!" Filo didn't really need to shout, as we were all already moving out of the way. This wasn't an enemy that I was equipped to face head-on! It had to be extremely enhanced—to a crazy level! All our hard work enhancing ourselves recently just felt completely pointless!

"It reaches us so quickly there isn't time to imbue enough magic to make a spell that can stop it," the Demon Dragon analyzed.

"Leave monsters to me! Instant & Massive Monster Exclusive Pit Trap!" Kizuna thrust her hunting tool into the ground and a pit trap suddenly appeared right in front of the Artificial Behemoth. It fell in, burying itself up to its middle. Kizuna immediately made a surprised noise.

"What's going on? It's so powerful! It's going to force its way out!" she exclaimed.

"Well, well, well, I don't think you'll be able to hold it for long," S'yne's sister mocked. The Demon Dragon perched on my shoulder and stared at the chest of the Artificial Behemoth.

"Indeed. You've created quite the twisted creature here,"

the Demon Dragon spat at S'yne's sister, her voice twisted in anger. The Demon Dragon always looked down on humans but generally seemed to think of monsters as allies.

"I don't know about any of that. I just brought it along to test it out," S'yne's sister replied.

"Toying with monsters in such a fashion . . . you have exceeded the level that I, ruler of all monsters, can possibly permit!" the dragon raged.

"I bet we have! This is an artificial monster, created using all of the holy weapon and vassal weapon power-up methods from this world. It was developed as an experiment by my people," S'yne's sister explained. I gave a start in surprise. That meant this monster had all of the heroes' power-up methods applied to it!

"That's pretty much what I was expecting. Shield Hero, let me tell you something interesting," the Demon Dragon began. Then she looked at the Artificial Behemoth's chest again. "That part there houses a corrupted holy weapon from this world, which has artificially turned the monster into one of the four holy heroes and has allowed it all the power-up methods. It's basically the monster version of a holy hero."

"What the hell?!" I exclaimed. No wonder it was so strong! I might be the Mirror Hero, but I still had high defense—even if it wasn't as high as with the shield. This monster had to have some serious firepower to be breaking through my defenses so easily. If we had to fight a monster that had the power-up methods of twelve weapons, the vanguard of the waves with the cutting barriers, and S'yne's sister and all the other women present, any amount of home-field advantage wasn't going to be enough!

"This is still just a prototype, of course. We haven't been able to replicate skills or magic yet. I just wanted to see how well it would fare against you," S'yne's sister explained. Human testing seemed a bit extreme for something so dangerous!

"Do you think I could revoke its authority, Naofumi? That thing you were talking about?" Kizuna asked.

"Probably not. It's pretty corrupted. We have to destroy the source first," the Demon Dragon warned. Taking that under advisement, Kizuna placed her hand on the hunting tool.

"You're right. I can hear a voice from the hunting tool. It said it's impossible," Kizuna replied.

"This is the best you heroes can do?" Enemy of the Week said, laughing maniacally. "You're far weaker than I expected!" He cackled down from his perch.

"This monster being so strong doesn't mean you're strong yourself!" I shouted back.

"The weaker the dog, the louder the bark! If you have a problem with that, prove your strength! You moron!" Enemy of the Week shouted.

"That crap again! Survival of the fittest is your base

template, is it?" I retorted. These guys just thought so little of us. I was sick of these vanguards of the waves and their cookie-cutter personalities! They were all the same! Maybe they were like the monster that caused the waves, something other than a human—they just looked like one.

"Hmmm, they seem pretty confident that they can defeat us. That said, I will brook no insult of the Shield Hero," the Demon Dragon said. I wondered why the representative of all monsters was sticking up for me—a representative who had a pretty similar attitude herself.

The Demon Dragon floated up into the air and raised a claw.

"Shield Hero's humming fairy, lend me your strength," she said.

"Huh? What are we doing? I don't really want to help you," Filo responded.

"You and your friends are being supremely mocked! I am still weak. I need your strength to achieve this," the dragon admitted.

"Don't want to!" Filo retorted.

"Gah! You annoying wretch!" The Demon Dragon was glaring intensely at Filo. It was like she had completely forgotten what she had done to her.

"You're planning on absorbing me again? I don't want that, no way!" Filo retorted.

"That's not what I'm talking about. I just want you to lend me some strength! Sing like you always do and bring out some magic! Sing something close to the 'Hero's Melody.' The one the Bow Hero always plays," the dragon said.

"Huh? Okay," Filo finally agreed. She landed on the ground and started singing.

"If I'm seeking raw power, your shikigami will also be quite efficient. Do you both understand the situation?" the dragon asked them.

"Raph!" said Raph-chan.

"Pen!" said Chris. Both of them nodded in response to the Demon Dragon and moved over toward her. The two of them then became semitransparent and appeared to be bolstering the power of the Demon Dragon. I really had no idea what she was planning.

"I still don't have enough participants or magic yet to cast a high-level incantation. You sisters, the water dragon's miko priestesses, also lend me a hand," the dragon demanded.

"Oh dear. Little Naofumi, what do you think we should do?" Sadeena asked me.

"Oh my! Getting ordered around by a dragon feels a bit too close to home!" Shildina said. The two of them turned to me for advice.

"Go ahead. Help her out," I told them.

"Okay. But what exactly should we be doing?" Sadeena asked.

"I'm going to perform something close to ritual magic. While I'm doing that, use your gemstone and ofuda to incant your own magic," the dragon instructed. This was all starting to feel like we were working under orders from the dragon—a bit of a risky proposition. "Hunting Hero, you understand full well which weapon has selected you! You defeated the Demon Dragon, a mighty beast seeking to dominate this entire world! If you can't defeat one pathetic little creature like this, you aren't worthy of the title of hero!"

"Come on!" Kizuna gasped. "You're really asking a lot with that one!"

"Just so arrogant . . ." Glass also complained.

"I am the Dragon Emperor and Demon Dragon! If you're looking for humility, look elsewhere!" the dragon shot back.

"Kizuna can't handle that thing alone, surely," I said.

"Huh. Shield Hero, you don't seem to understand what the Hunting Hero means to this world," the dragon said. Kizuna squatted down, readying the hunting tool in dressing knife form. The Artificial Behemoth roared, dragging itself out from the confinement of the hole. It had looked ready to leap again at any moment, but seeing Kizuna's stance, the beast suddenly dropped back.

"Oh, sorry . . . my gathered power was leaking out a little. I've still got a lot to learn," Kizuna muttered. I wondered what was going on. The Artificial Behemoth was clearly incredibly powerful, and yet it looked concerned about the prospect of fighting Kizuna.

"Well, well, well. Whatever has gotten into you? You shouldn't be afraid of anything. Perhaps your specs aren't as high as we thought?" S'yne's sister said.

"The hunting tool has given up the ability to fight humans in exchange for unmatched power when fighting monsters. That includes in regard to defense and speed," the Demon Dragon replied. When fighting Kyo, at least, I hadn't really felt that Kizuna lacked in strength. Glass and the others obviously placed a great deal of faith in her. She just couldn't fight humans. "Shield Hero, you should concentrate on protecting those others around you."

"Yeah, I'm on it," I said. Even in that moment, Enemy of the Week unleashed another barrier attack toward us. It didn't look like he was interested in mixing it up with a little close combat. I could imagine that any trouble he had faced so far, he had resolved with exactly the same attacks he was using right now.

"Don't forget about us!" Enemy of the Week taunted.

"That's right, that's right!" Woman B added. I was already wishing she'd just blend back into the background.

"I've got this! Stardust Blade!" Raphtalia shouted.

"I'll help too! Circle Dance Empty Formation: Moon Break!" Glass joined in. The star Raphtalia's Stardust Blade unleashed and the slice Glass's skill unleashed landed squarely on Enemy of the Week's barrier attack and shattered it.

"Bah! I didn't put enough into that one. But that won't work again! Don't underestimate my barriers!" he snapped back. Then he unleashed a second barrier, and the same attacks from Raphtalia and Glass were unable to stop it this time.

"He changed the pattern . . ." Raphtalia mused.

"These barriers are so hard it's going to be difficult to shatter them all head-on," Glass confirmed. I cursed to myself. I'd managed to use Stardust Mirror to block the position he could place the barriers, but that still didn't mean he might not get lucky, pop one out neck-high, and lop off someone's head. Fighting this guy was going to be a real pain. I also had to wonder if he was a feminist like Takt, because he seemed to only be attacking me.

In any case, the fact he wasn't going for Kizuna and the others actually suited me quite nicely. If all he was going to do was long-range attacks from behind his barrier, it was actually easy to defend against him. He also probably didn't want to make a wrong move and kill the prototype monster that his female companion was so happy about.

Glass was providing some support to Kizuna in her battle with the Artificial Behemoth, while Raphtalia circled in to give aid.

"Glass! Watch out!" Raphtalia drew her second katana and

defended Glass from the attack of the Artificial Behemoth using haikuikku state. The three of them were buying me some time with the formation of Kizuna on the front line, Glass in support, and Raphtalia defending.

Someone shouted, "Heroes!" Then I saw some soldiers from the castle come running toward the battle.

"Don't try anything, you guys!" I shouted. "If possible, just stay out of this!"

"But—" one of them started.

"Who knows what L'Arc will say if we get all you guys killed? This isn't even a good enemy for some supporting fire," I told them. Picking up on my thinking, the soldiers obeyed my warning and fell back, starting instead to quell the unrest in the rest of the town.

"Talk about bad timing," I muttered. Why couldn't we have Itsuki, Rishia, S'yne, or Ethnobalt come running up to help us? It would be harder for L'Arc and his party to sense that something was going on. As I stood annoyed at the situation, the Demon Dragon spoke to me.

"It is time for you to fully understand exactly what I am. I am the Emperor Dragon, ruler of evil, the one who knows all about the magic in this world. Now I will show you the truth of magic. Magic in its ultimate form!" The dragon started to incant magic on my shoulder while also looking at me at the same time. "In your world, Shield Hero . . . I believe this to be a technique that the staff seven star weapon is most proficient with. This will give you something to tell people about, a story of how wonderful magic truly is!" At the same time, I heard a voice in my head. It was the telepathic conversation technique that Gaelion sometimes used. "You told me about this before, didn't you, Shield Hero? That technique you pulled off recently on that woman who you hate so much. That is what we are about to do here," the dragon told me. Something I had done to Bitch . . . the dragon had to mean reflecting Bitch's magic using a mirror. Bitch had launched fire magic at me, full of hatred and anger, and I'd reflected it back at her and turned her into the burning version of a snowman. Seeing her rolling around on the floor, literally cooking by her own fire had felt exceptionally good.

Putting that aside, anyway, it seemed the Demon Dragon wanted to go for the same effect.

"You can use Float Mirror, correct? I will perform an attack first and some support second. You must make good use of what I give you," the dragon said. So now she needed my help too. That said, the plan was actually a pretty good one. Confirming my acquiescence with a nod, the Demon Dragon raised her right claw and lightly rotated it, then started to incant the magic.

"My universal collaborators! Respond to my call and materialize your magic power!" I felt a powerful field of magic deploy, and a raw lump of magic power formed in front of the Demon Dragon's eyes. I could feel a vast volume of magic being sent to the Demon Dragon, presumably because of my understanding of the Way of the Dragon Vein. Power was flowing to her from somewhere. We all felt the Demon Dragon take the magic she was receiving and start to mold and shape it, almost like clay. This was very different from when we had fought her back in our world. She was also borrowing power from Sadeena and Shildina and constructing some kind of magic that was similar but ultimately different from cooperative and ritual magic.

"You'll never break my almighty defense, no matter what tricks you try to pull!" Enemy of the Week cackled.

"That's right. Give up now or you'll regret it! Eat this!" Woman B was still entwining herself around Enemy of the Week while she taunted the Demon Dragon's incanting. Enemy of the Week launched a barrier attack at Kizuna, Glass, and Raphtalia, but the three of them were too quick and moved out of the way before they got sealed in. He wasn't aiming for their necks, but their legs and arms, which was why he couldn't hit them. That said, he couldn't try the trash compactor again because the Artificial Behemoth was still in the mix and because that same Artificial Behemoth's attacks would break the barriers.

"You've stopped doing the shield attack that blocks the barrier's movements," S'yne's sister noted. She was starting to read what we were planning! I willed the Demon Dragon to get to the point quicker!

"Your power of blazing flame, the truth of magic that eradicates all, now become the technique to eradicate my foes! The Emperor Dragon, ruler of this world, commands you! Burn like the sun!" Even as the first spell was cast, I heard another one at the same time.

"Your power that foreshadows victory, the truth of magic that eradicates all, now become the mercy that I lay upon those beneath me! The Emperor Dragon, ruler of this world, commands you! Receive all of my power!" I wondered if I was the only one thinking this was all very much like when Shildina used magic.

"Oh my, very impressive. Simultaneous incanting," Sadeena said.

"I can do that too," Shildina muttered. The two of them were chatting even as they incanted themselves. I could feel different flows of magic coming from that being handled by the killer whale sisters, by Raph-chan, by Filo, and by Chris.

"Here we go, Shield Hero! Don't make me waste these!" the Demon Dragon shouted.

"I'll do the best I can, but don't expect too much!" I replied. At my shout, the Demon Dragon tossed the first burning hot cluster of magic right at me.

"Oh man! They can't work together for shit! They are

treading all over each other's feet! Morons!" Enemy of the Week crowed.

"I think they are fighting among themselves now!" Woman B cackled. "What idiots!" They both pointed and laughed, but that clearly wasn't what was going on.

"Well, well, well," S'yne's sister chimed in and turned her chain into a ring and . . . stepped through it. Immediately after that, she vanished. That was a movement skill. No doubt about it. Her instincts were on the money, I would give her that. Still, I was more focused on wiping out the annoyances she had left behind.

"You had better make good use of this!" the Demon Dragon roared.

"I will!" I replied. I adjusted the two Float Mirrors that I always kept out during combat . . . and then smacked away the incoming magic ball with a roar of my own. I'd never really played baseball, but the feeling of impact was maybe like getting a solid hit on an incoming ball. It felt quite good.

Basically, I filled the mirror with power and swung it like a bat.

Then I placed Float Mirrors to adjust the angle of its flight. The first one reflected the magic, and the second one sent it flying.

"Formation One, Formation Two: Glass Shield!" I shouted, creating Glass Shields imbued with sufficient life force to intercept the magic unleashed by the Demon Dragon. The angle looked good too. Still, the whole process had really zapped my life force.

The magic hit the first Glass Shield with a cracking sound, and even as the mirror shattered, it reflected the magic in the desired direction, leading into the second shield. Each time the magic the Demon Dragon created hit a mirror or Glass Shield, it grew larger. The expression on the face of Enemy of the Week did become more serious for a moment, but when he eventually saw the magic flying off toward the horizon, he relaxed again and started laughing.

"Formation Three: Glass Shield and Transport Mirror then . . . Mirror Cage!" As the finishing move, I used two Glass Shields along with a third . . . and this time I was able to place one inside the enemy barrier! I had been thinking that wouldn't be possible. But I'd pulled it off. So then I changed the one inside the barrier to Transport Mirror, which turned into Mirror Cage.

"What? Inside my barrier—" Enemy of the Week started, and then he and Woman B vanished inside the Mirror Cage.

"Hey, Bitch's minion!" I shouted. "When I reflected Bitch's magic, it increased in strength, didn't it? And that was when I used just one mirror. If you really know all about Bitch, you should have proposed running away." The complete failure of these two to realize what we were planning showed the marked difference between them and the cunning of S'yne's sister. If they had dropped the barrier and made a run for it right away, they might have gotten away from this. Woman B, in particular, had been given plenty of time to warn Enemy of the Week, since S'yne's sister had already evacuated the area.

"This is the magic I have incanted for you! The magic that filled this world with despair!" the Demon Dragon cackled. "Demon Dragon! Flare of Nine Heavenly Suns! Let this magic multiplied by the Shield Hero burn your very bones to ash!" The dragon seemed pretty pleased with herself. There was still a ball of remaining magic hovering in front of her. I felt like reminding her that I was the one who had got her first magic ball to land on target. It hadn't been that hard, after all, because our enemies had just stayed there, unmoving inside their barrier.

A moment later, a thudding impact resonated out from inside the Mirror Cage. It was accompanied by some pretty loud screaming and shouts of things like "It burns!" and "Save us! We're dying!" Quite unpleasant, all things considered.

"The screams of humans are like music to my ears," the Demon Dragon purred. She really did sound evil. And yet, in this case, I was inclined to agree with her!

I hit the magic back myself first, then reflected it from two Float Mirrors and further boosted it via a Glass Shield . . . then turned two more Glass Shields into Transport Mirrors . . . and then sent it inside the barrier! *Just how much did all that increase its killing potential?* I pondered to myself. Transport Mirror was a movement skill, but at the same time, it was a defensive skill that could shorten distances. It had a tricky side, relying on the medium of the mirrors for movement, but it also offered a wide range of uses. I just had to be careful of how an attack came out of the mirror, especially at this distance. Still, applying some life force had at least increased the distance I could deploy the mirrors. Not to mention, I created a cage completely made of mirrors suddenly appearing around them, with the magic exploding inside it, bouncing off all those mirrors again and again! Even as I finished my explanation with a flourish, the Mirror Cage split and cracked apart and a massive pillar of intensely compressed flame rose up into the sky. Once it cleared . . . as expected, there was nothing left at all.

Eradication complete! Then I noticed the Demon Dragon draw in a deep breath . . . and start chewing on something.

"Human souls garnished with despair and pain are so delicious. These souls of people from other worlds are such a delicacy too. They have a different flavor from those of this world," she mused. She ate souls! I almost slapped myself. Sure, getting rid of the souls removed the risk of them reviving, so that was actually quite useful, but it also made me want no association with her at all.

"If you get possessed or controlled because you eat the wrong thing, I'm putting you down in a flash!" I warned her.

"It will take more than a bad meal to take control of me," she retorted. She was so evil I didn't want her among my allies at all.

"Wow . . . that was nasty," Kizuna muttered, barely avoiding another attack from the Artificial Behemoth.

"Kizuna! Watch out!" I shouted.

"Phew . . . even so, this monster seemed a lot faster when I first saw it," Kizuna said. She used the smallest possible movement to avoid the descending claws of the Artificial Behemoth, then hopped up onto its arm and tried to jump onto its back. She was hit by a follow-up sideswipe, impossible to avoid because she was in the air, but she skillfully caught it and deflected it, almost looking like a leaf dancing in the air. I was impressed and tried to recall what her hero power-up was.

That said, she had support from Filo and the others also in play, so that was probably really helping her out too.

I continued to watch her, furrowing my brow, and then Glass and the Demon Dragon stepped in to explain.

"Kizuna's hunting tool . . . makes her a hero specialized for fighting monsters," Glass said.

"That is why I was defeated, after all," the dragon added.

"If she employs deflection, and is only fighting monsters, her defense is probably close to yours, Naofumi," Glass continued. I was impressed. It looked like S'yne's sister—and whoever it was she represented—had underestimated Kizuna.

"So they're testing out all the power-ups . . . but they can't use skills and magic yet, right? We also don't know if they've worked out the mirror and musical instrument power-ups. And they can't use those power-ups that need you to master the weapon first. Maybe that's why this beast isn't any stronger than it already is? Intellect-wise, it looks like just a simple beast," I analyzed. Kizuna landed with a sigh, while the Artificial Behemoth gave a roar in frustration. Its attacks weren't really working. I wondered for a moment why Kizuna looked like she was bored of the whole thing. The attacks from the hunting tool weren't hitting her target either. Or if they were, they were just bouncing off.

"Your attacks are so simple it's like you're asking me to avoid them. Formation One, Formation Two, Formation Three: Tiger Trap!" That was all Kizuna had to mutter to make tiger traps appear on the ground, one right where the Artificial Behemoth's front legs came down after it leapt forward and the other right where its back legs landed. Both traps bit down deep into flesh. The beast roared again, in pure rage, swinging its remaining free front paw toward Kizuna.

"You don't give up, do you?" Kizuna said with a shout as she repelled the paw attack from the Artificial Behemoth with her dressing knife. However, the impact of that downward attack also caused the ground under Kizuna to crumple beneath her. Part of the jacket she was wearing was also ripped to shreds. That had certainly been a powerful attack, almost as strong as the one that had first sent us flying.

"Shall we end this, Hunting Hero?" the Demon Dragon said to Kizuna. Then she threw the remaining magic ball at me. "Make sure to hit the Hunting Hero!" the dragon warned me.

"Easy for you to say!" I retorted. I still had a lot of skills on cool down. I called out the Float Mirrors that had been broken when I reflected the magic ball. Then I reflected the second ball of support magic, adjusting the angle and sending it toward Kizuna.

"Beasts really are simple. Because it looked like its remaining front leg could reach me, it decided not to break the traps, but attack me instead," Kizuna said. She jumped backward, right into the support magic that I had boosted and sent toward her. The magic flashed white and enveloped Kizuna. We had been aiming for the reflection boosts again, but it would have been a nightmare if the enemy touched it first. If it got the effects of stolen power-up magic, that really would have sucked.

"Demon Dragon: Songbird's Protection!" the dragon said.

"Now to finish this," Kizuna said and turned her weapon into a fishing rod and tossed out her lure. I matched her by tossing out a Multiplying Mirror Fragment. That was the end of my SP. I needed to use some soul-healing water or other item to recover it.

The Artificial Behemoth gave a raging roar, muscles

popping up all over its body. It destroyed the traps on its legs and charged right for Kizuna. I could tell right away that it was going even faster than when it had sent us flying. There had to be a reason for that, like maybe its rage had drawn out the power of the weapons further. Its body was so massive the charge attack was going to be powerful indeed—like getting hit by a dump truck. Surely her only choice was to avoid it, but that wasn't the route Kizuna took. She hunkered down and prepared to counterattack.

"The final blow!" she declared. Kizuna dropped her stance low, returned her weapon to the dressing knife, and charged forward.

"Universal power of my core! Respond to my call and materialize your magic power! I am the Emperor Dragon who rules this world. Unleash pure darkness to cull this ignorant, contemptible monster!" the Demon Dragon intoned, already having started providing magic support for Kizuna. "Now, Hunting Hero, prove you are worthy of that title! Demon Dragon: Abyss Bullet!" I was impressed with the volume of magic this dragon could pull off in quick succession.

"I never expected to be combining my strength with the Demon Dragon and unleashing a combination skill," Kizuna said. An arc created from jet-black darkness curved down the entire body of the Artificial Behemoth.

"Dark Formation: Blood Flower Strike!" Kizuna shouted.

With a slashing sound, Kizuna flicked off some of the darkness from her dressing knife. The Artificial Behemoth gave a guttural cry and in the same instant was enveloped in the darkness and shredded to pieces. All the bouncing between mirrors and fragments had quadrupled the support magic's power, which itself had already been a triple-header under the direction of the Demon Dragon and the "Hero's Melody" from Filo, creating the perfect combination skill to perform the final blow. Even a monster with the power-ups of the heroes couldn't withstand something quite so potent.

"Right! We pulled it off . . . but I could use some healing magic over here," Kizuna said, turning around with a smile, and then blood erupted from her entire body.

"Kizuna!" Glass exclaimed.

"Kizuna! What is this?" Raphtalia shouted.

"I used skills to delay the damage . . . might have gone too far . . ." Kizuna managed to explain.

"Oh my!" Sadeena exclaimed.

"This is terrible!" Shildina added, both of the sisters also rushing over to Kizuna. Shildina took out an ofuda and started to use some healing magic.

"Raph!" said Raph-chan.

"Pen!" said Chris.

Perhaps to have them concentrate on the incanting earlier, the Demon Dragon had turned the two cuties semi-transparent with a click of her claw. Maybe it was in order to stop them from thinking about anything else. But now they came back to normal, surprised at the turn of events and rushing over to each of their mistresses.

"Master, do I still have to sing? So much of my magic has been drained off. I'm exhausted," Filo said.

"Keep going a little longer," I told her. It was a copy of "Hero's Melody," which itself was a support song, but having it going was better than nothing.

"We've got you now!" someone shouted. The two other apparent vanguards of the waves who had slipped away earlier now chose this moment to attack, along with their accompanying parties.

"We've been expecting you!" Raphtalia replied.

"That's right!" Glass added. The two girls faced the newcomers down, attacking with each of their respective weapons.

"I'm not going to allow such sneaky tactics," Sadeena said, turning into her therianthrope form and spinning her spear around before plunging it into the chest of an oncoming enemy. Her first target screamed, and then another, as the women surrounding the new vanguards of the waves were smashed and sent flying away by one pissed off Sadeena and her whirling spear.

They really had picked the worst possible moment to attack. It would have been far more effective, for example, to attack

while the Demon Dragon was still incanting. That suggested there had been some kind of connection between the groups.

"Cowards, seeking to seize the initiative in such a fashion! Learn your place. I have nothing but disgust for you," Sadeena spat.

"These are the 'winner writes the history' types," I commented.

"I'm sure they are. Little Naofumi, maybe we should use the people from the castle to capture them," Sadeena said.

"You bet," I replied. There was no room to drop our guard at all—a point S'yne's sister proved by suddenly reappearing from somewhere.

"Well, well, well, so you wiped them all out. Prototypes can only get you so far," she muttered. Then she extended her chain and drew out something from the body of the Artificial Behemoth that looked like a core of some kind. I guessed that was probably the corrupted holy weapon.

"Hand that over!" I shouted.

"You really think I would?" she replied. Of course, she wouldn't. She gave me an incredulous look while she slung the core, still wrapped in her chain, over her shoulder. "I'm thinking that S'yne and your other little friends will be arriving by hourglass pretty soon, so I should probably leave you to it. You've highlighted some real problems for us, like avoiding pitting our creations against the Hunting Hero." Kizuna had pretty much kicked the thing's ass. "I am even more upset that we let you get away from us in the first place."

"Well, it'll be you who won't be getting away this time!" Kizuna said, staggering to her feet and selecting Hunting Weapon Zero. "This weapon is effective against that accessory, I can tell . . . and I'm going to release it."

"Well, well, well, that sounds very scary," S'yne's sister mocked, but I wondered if it might actually work. In either case, it felt like she was going to get away.

"Oh my," Sadeena said, looking at S'yne's sister from the sidelines, suddenly interrupting their conversation. "I can tell this is all very serious, but can I ask a question?" I had no idea what Sadeena could possibly want with this woman. Maybe she had noticed something important about her.

"Whatever do you want?" S'yne's sister asked.

"You put on quite an attitude, but I'm starting to wonder how much of it is what you are truly thinking?" Sadeena asked. S'yne's sister did not reply, quitting her normal arrogant act and glaring at Sadeena with an offended face. "In the very least, you seem pretty different from the girls who were just here. Pretty different from the girl that little Naofumi hates too. You have a different intent from them. I can sense it. What did you really come here for today?"

"Well, well, well. Playing detective isn't in your best interests. You might get all sorts of funny ideas," S'yne's sister replied.

"Do you really think so? The longer we talk, the more certain I become that I'm not imagining things," Sadeena said. S'yne's sister had no response to that. Perhaps pissed off by this assessment, S'yne's sister dropped her comedy routine and just glared at Sadeena some more. The two of them glared at each other for a while, and then S'yne's sister just let her menace fade and turned her back to Sadeena.

"I've lost my taste for this. I was leaving anyway," S'yne's sister said.

"Really," Sadeena replied.

"To be perfectly honest, I don't get along well with people like you," S'yne's sister admitted.

"Oh my, is that so? I don't dislike people like you at all. In fact, I think we could get along quite well," Sadeena responded. This was taking a strange turn.

"I hate being knocked off my game. I'm leaving now," S'yne's sister stated.

"And I said . . . that's not happening! I'll grab her! Everyone, back me up!" Kizuna still had the support magic on and charged at S'yne's sister at considerable speed. However, S'yne's sister easily detained Kizuna with her chain. Kizuna slashed it off and dashed forward again, but S'yne's sister stepped lightly on Kizuna's back—clearly just toying with her—and jumped over behind us all.

"She's too fast!" Kizuna gasped. "I can't hit her at all!"

"Ah, something else I should mention. You seem all hopped up and happy with your magical buffs, so I need to warn you about those again. I have the power to nullify those, remember?" She proceeded to perform an incredibly fast incantation. Her own innate speed was probably factoring into it.

"What?!" The Demon Dragon looked surprised to see this magic being used.

"Disarming Shot: Earth Evasion Explosion 4!" S'yne's sister shouted. I'd seen magic like this somewhere before from the first guy we encountered in the force behind S'yne's sister! It seemed to be an area-of-effect spell, because a band of magic appeared and then passed over all of us.

"Huh? The effects of the support magic . . . have gone?!" Kizuna exclaimed.

"Oh . . . I can't even sing 'Hero's Melody' anymore. What kind of magic is that?" Filo said, who had still been singing up until that moment.

"Even if you've debuffed us . . ." Raphtalia started.

"We're still taking that back from you here!" Glass finished. The two of them moved to leap at S'yne's sister.

"Please. Give me a break. You do look stronger than when we last met, but you still aren't a match for me. If I stay and play with you though, S'yne and the other heroes are going to show up. Then I might be at just the slightest disadvantage, so I'm leaving before that happens. You should think yourselves lucky," S'yne's sister taunted, glaring at Sadeena again before waving her hand in the air. "Bye-bye now!" The next instant, she was gone. Just as she had declared, she had used a movement skill or something of the like to leave.

"That is the foe we face," the Demon Dragon said. "She certainly does have some fearsome powers. Right now, we are only alive at her whim." I couldn't really disagree with that. Not to mention, I didn't think S'yne and the others turning up would have been enough to make a difference. Based on Sadeena's reaction to the proceedings, S'yne's sister did seem to have some kind of method to her madness . . .

"I wonder," Sadeena muttered, still looking at the spot where S'yne's sister had been standing.

"Wonder about what?" I asked her.

"I hadn't talked with her for very long, so I can't make a definite statement on this, but she doesn't have any intent to kill. Just like she said, she was just here to play around with us," Sadeena replied.

"You almost sound like you're talking about yourself," I said. Sadeena rarely displayed any strong intent to kill during battle either.

"Oh my," she replied. Maybe her nature as a drunk who was exceptionally hard to read meant she shared something with S'yne's sister after all. I'd thought S'yne's sister was just an overly strong moron, but maybe she did have some kind of secret.

That was that, anyway. Onto other things.

"Raphtalia! We finally rubbed out one of Bitch's allies!" I gave a thumbs-up and a victory smile. She hadn't been a major player, perhaps, but eradicating such a shitty woman from this world, as well as one who had a long relationship with Bitch, really did feel good! I wasn't celebrating murder. She had tried to kill me and my friends on many occasions. Not to mention, there were a number of victims she had actually managed to kill. So she wasn't worthy of my pity.

"I'm not sure that's something to boast about . . . but they are causing all sorts of problems. It's a difficult situation," Raphtalia said. I took that as an endorsement and allowed myself an evil smile, and then an evil chuckle.

That was when the Demon Dragon started to laugh with me. I stopped, without even thinking about it.

"Stop that! Why are you laughing too?" I asked her.

"If I can't laugh when some foolish humans have been wiped from this world, when can I?" she inquired back. She was originally a ruler on the monster side, after all, standing in opposition of humans. I couldn't fault her on the "foolish" part, either. We were looking at a guy who spouted some extreme ideal of survival of the fittest while being manipulated by stupid women. These were women who tricked men for their own convenience and then threw a hissy fit when they couldn't get their way. The worst possible people I could conceive of. "Not to mention, I'm laughing alongside the Shield Hero. How could I not feel anything but pleasure?" The dragon really did have a thing for me. I wondered if that might become a problem in the future. "Laughing together like this shows how well matched we are. Let us crush the foolish humans together and create a better world!"

"Hey, come on. I don't consider all humans to be foolish," I replied. The dragon chuckled.

"We'll see how long that lasts, Shield Hero," she commented. I wasn't going to get lured over to the dark side so easily . . . but I would concede that there were a lot of stupid people in the world. "Don't you think that becoming a Shield Demon King with me might be best for everyone?"

"Stop giving Mr. Naofumi strange ideas!" Raphtalia warned the Demon Dragon. The dragon shot back a thorny glance.

"That is for the Shield Hero to decide," she spat.

"I'm not really bothered about becoming a Demon King. However, from our enemies' point of view, I guess I already am," I pondered. Those connected to the Church of the Three Heroes had been big on calling me demon this and that.

"For now, let's just laugh together!" The dragon broke out into fresh evil chuckling.

". . . The moment has passed," I said. I shook my head, wondering why I had to be surrounded by so many people—and creatures—intent on whittling down my motivation.

"You two seem to be getting along well," Kizuna said. That was a comment that perhaps struck me as the most painful of all.

Chapter Thirteen: The Reborn

A little after the fighting had ended, S'yne, Itsuki, Rishia, and Ethnobalt came rushing up. Those who had participated in the battle were watching the cleanup of the damaged castle courtyard. S'yne's sister seemed to have been planning to keep the battle short from the start, but S'yne looked distressed at not having made it in time. Her sister's decision to leave before S'yne arrived spoke again to the precision of her skills in situational assessment. Sadeena seemed to think there was some other intent behind her actions . . . but I couldn't see anything yet.

The vanguards of the waves themselves hadn't been that strong, and the main threat had been the artificial monster housing the power of the holy weapons.

Maybe they really had just come to taunt us a little and feel us out. I wasn't sure how things might have turned out if they had brought the Harpoon Hero with them.

"About the two vanguards of the waves we captured alive . . ." I said. Sadeena and Shildina were looking over at the two who we presumed were also vanguards of the waves.

"Dammit! Let us go!" one shouted.

"What are you claiming we even did?" said the other.

"You attacked us, pretty plainly," I replied. These guys didn't seem to come fitted with standard functions like a sense of guilt or common sense. They never listened to anything you said to them either. Once defeated, they always claimed they had never done anything wrong, lashing out at the ones who had defeated them. They didn't give a moment's thought to what might happen to themselves, or the countries that were supporting them, if they came and attacked the holder of a holy weapon and the vassal weapon holders. That was exactly why this world was having so many problems right now.

We had at least made it so that those considered "geniuses" were having a harder time of things. That was a direct result of the things the allies of these two had pulled off. The issue was, apart from the crazy things they did and the horde of female followers, there was no way to spot these guys just by looking at them. If they played possum, it would be hard to punish them. Sadeena and Shildina, however, could apparently spot them at a glance.

"Is there really something different about them?" I asked.

"Yes, something . . . tingly," Sadeena said. Shildina just made a noise of agreement or perhaps deep thought.

"Raph!" said Raph-chan, looking pleased with herself as she rode on Sadeena's shoulder. It looked like she could spot the difference too. That was impressive, but with Raph-chan it seemed to take her a bit of time to make the identification, so the killer whale sisters were more reliable in this instance.

"I'm sorry I—" S'yne started.

"Lady S'yne regrets not having reached you in time," her familiar explained. She made a little noise, showing signs of that attitude she had of clinging to me. She had displayed it when we were campaigning in Q'ten Lo. She often stood guard while I slept too. I kind of wanted her to stop that, as it made it harder for me to get to sleep.

"She knows you too well. So we can't expect that you can outsmart her. Relax. Just be happy we didn't take any serious damage," I told her. She didn't seem to want to accept that though. I was going to be stuck with her again for a while. I looked over at Raphtalia to see sympathy on her face.

We really hadn't lost much though. That much was true. S'yne's sister had been the only one we probably couldn't have taken, and we had learned about a dangerous new threat that the enemy was developing to use against us. If we sat around without acting for too much longer, we could find ourselves facing a whole army of those monsters. That placed us in a dangerous situation, but at least now we could prepare for it. We needed to take the next step forward, without wasting that intelligence.

It would only be a little longer before we reached the origin of Glass's style.

"It sounds like you've had quite a day," Itsuki said, light and casual.

"Indeed. No need for you to feel bad about not making it in time either," I told him. To be quite honest, I wouldn't have been able to protect any more bodies using Stardust Mirror. I was really hoping that one would change into the equivalent of the higher-level skill soon, like Shooting Star Wall. "Keeping everyone in one place just in case the enemy attacks would be just as foolish. They just picked a good time to attack us."

"Does this confirm we have a spy?" Raphtalia asked.

"That is a good question. There's also the possibility they are using a movement skill like S'yne that lets them see their destination. To be honest about it, S'yne, I need your help. Rather than protect me, I would like it if you helped me make something to stop them from being able to run away," I told her. S'yne nodded at my request right away.

It was a good idea. Even if we did get the upper hand, it would be pointless if they could just run from us so easily. Something completely unexpected might happen. If we couldn't block their movements, they would get away and we would be back to square one. We needed a solution to address the root of this problem.

Also . . . we needed some way to handle any vassal weapon holders we might bump into from S'yne's sworn enemies. If they were proceeding as we were, they would be implementing all of the holy weapon and vassal weapon power-up methods. The buff magic that we had hoped would fill that gap could also be used by the enemy, and they had tech that could just cancel it out. The main problem we definitely faced right now was how to cover the fundamental handicap of the weapons that had been captured by our foes. We needed to do something about that as quickly as possible.

"Going back to this problem of having a spy in our ranks . . . what can we do about that?" I asked.

"I'm good at spotting people like that!" Sadeena volunteered.

"Me too!" Shildina chimed in, the two sisters both putting up their hands.

"They didn't call me the priestess of carnage for nothing!" Sadeena said brightly.

"I'll bring carnage to them all." Shildina nodded. I had no reply. They remained so light and bubbly, no matter the situation. They probably had performed torture and stuff like that in the past. They had been like internal auditors, something like that—just with a bit more carnage.

"I'm not sure I really want to give that job to you. Seeing as you don't fully understand the language, I'm not sure it will be easy for you either," I told them. They could talk if a Jewel like Therese or when a holy or vassal weapon holder was present, but not the rest of the time.

"In which case, let's work with little Therese and little L'Arc and interview them all one at a time. I'll pull my weight. You can count on me!" Sadeena said.

"I mean, if you think that's going to work . . ." I said, still unsure.

"Oh, little Naofumi. Your kindness brings warmth to my heart," she replied.

"I'm not being kind. I'm thinking of all the hassle this is going to cause," I said. Having vanguards of the waves mixed in among the volunteer soldiers was bad enough. Wasting time looking for a spy we didn't even know was there felt like a bit too much. Rather than that, I'd prefer they went out and raised their level, even by just one more.

"Ah, that reminds me. Rishia and Ethnobalt have finally deciphered that key part of the ancient texts," Itsuki informed me.

"They have?" I asked.

"Rishia did say that there may still be some mistakes in the translation," Itsuki muttered. This was Rishia and Ethnobalt we were talking about. They weren't pushy people and probably didn't want to make a big declaration and then eventually have it proven false.

"Rishia," Itsuki called, beckoning Rishia and Ethnobalt over. "Come on, both of you. Share with everyone what you just found out."

"Honestly, these are just fragments that Itsuki pieced together," Rishia said.

"Indeed, we haven't translated the entire thing yet, so there might be mistakes. We hurried over here because of the enemy attack too," Ethnobalt said. Neither of them appeared especially confident. It sounded like Itsuki had led them to this, whatever it was.

"Just think of it as a progress report. Come on," Itsuki said.

"You can't hold out on me now," I added.

"Hey! What's going on here, Naofumi?" Kizuna announced, who had also come over to listen.

"You should hear this too, Kizuna," Itsuki said. "Go ahead, Rishia. Tell them."

"Okay then . . . first, we'll tell you what we've discovered about the waves themselves. If worlds are clashing together with considerable frequency, then it means something is probably causing them to do so. Sometimes the floating worlds do impact with each other, but it is very rare—very bad luck—for that to happen," she said.

"The Shield Spirit and Atla told me that," I replied. The key thing here was the existence of someone behind all this, and we didn't have any details on them.

The idea of it being rare for the worlds to collide was easy to understand if you thought of the worlds like the stars in the sky. It was pretty rare for large stars to hit each other. I'd never heard of planets with living creatures on them hitting, ever. I mean, in my world we didn't even know about any other planets with life on them.

Maybe that meant that someone like Kyo was lurking somewhere, causing the waves.

"Up to that part, we can translate with confidence. It's what comes next that is the problem," Rishia continued.

"Go on," I prompted.

"The ancient text says that it is one who assumes the name of a god who is causing the waves," she revealed.

"Wow. That sounds like bullshit," I replied. I could see why the translators didn't have much confidence. So now, after everything else we'd been through, it turned out we were fighting a god. Talk about a riveting plot twist. That said, if we were talking about a being with the power to cause something as supernatural as the waves . . . maybe "god" wasn't so far off the mark.

"The ancient text also says that the holy weapons and vassal weapons can only suppress the damage caused by the waves, and the only solution is to get the one causing them to stop or wait for help to come from elsewhere," Rishia continued.

"The Shield Spirit and Atla told me all that too. They called this god the 'World Eater,' I think," I said. It caused the waves in order to wipe out worlds and eat them.

"I'd heard that much too," Itsuki said. "But that was still just a hypothesis, and we have no details on exactly what this being is. That answer, it seems, is in the next part." He looked like he was pretty sure of this information, at least. "Naofumi, you seem to also have a lot of experience with Internet games and the like, so I think maybe you can work this out for yourself. Do you have any ideas?"

"Huh? About what?" I asked.

"Think of those we have called vanguards of the waves, starting with Kyo, and then Takt, Miyaji, Seya. Think of their shared characteristics, and then try to consider things from their point of view," Itsuki said.

"Think like them? No way," I said. To me, they seemed like a totally different, totally evil form of life that just happened to speak the same language.

"Sorry, I didn't explain that very well. We heroes were summoned here from other worlds by the weapons. That is the correct process. So this World Eater . . . this one who assumes the name of a god is interfering with the heroes and giving strength to the vanguards of the waves. Does that sound familiar to you? Think about their histories and their abilities," Itsuki continued, seemingly keen to continue the guessing game.

"Hold on." It was like that one tricky puzzle piece finally slotting into place, and I didn't like the picture it made in my brain. I turned to look again at the two we had caught who appeared to be vanguards of the waves. One was a kid no older than seventeen. He still had a youthful look to his face. We had investigated his background and found, as expected, a master of a singular art form who was now an adventurer.

"Raph-chan, lend me a paw," I said.

"Raph?" Raph-chan queried. Then I looked at Raphtalia, who had Raph-chan on her shoulder. I should have paid more attention when Shildina had talked about souls having different shapes.

"Do you have any weapons or attacks that can draw out someone's soul?" I asked her.

"Let me think . . . yes, I do. The weapon from the Soul Eater materials can do that," she replied.

"Do it. Even if this counts as torture, I need to check this," I said.

"Check what, exactly? What are you about to do?" Glass asked, coming over with a frown on her face.

"This is how we find out the truth about the vanguards of the waves. Just stay quiet and watch," I told her. She looked puzzled but did as I asked.

"What's with you people? What are you going to do to me?" the kid shouted. Without replying, Raphtalia changed her weapon to the katana that had been made using the Soul Eater materials, thrust it at the vanguard of the waves, and drew out his soul. A scream filled the air, but it wasn't coming from the mouth of the kid.

There had been signs of this with Kyo. It wasn't that I'd stopped myself from thinking about it when the idea first came to me; it was just that I wasn't confident in the idea. It made sense though. If they could summon heroes, then why not this too?

The soul that Raphtalia had pulled from the vanguard of the waves was not much like the body it had come from. Instead, it was a gloomy, Japanese-looking guy who was probably in his thirties.

"Raphtalia, that's enough. Take them away and finish them off," I told her.

"Okay," she replied. She withdrew her weapon and the soul of the vanguard of the waves started to return to the body. Then the Demon Dragon grabbed the soul and started to chew on it.

"Why let it go to waste? It's still a delicacy," she said.

"Stop it! That hurts! What have I done to you? Just because you are heroes, you think you can—" the soul spouted but then just descended into screams and cries for help. I took Raph-chan down and hid her from the scene using my body. It wasn't an especially nice thing to watch, but he was a vanguard of the waves. We could not hesitate when it came to our enemies. People would be people. I'd seen plenty of death so far. It wasn't anything to get worked up about.

I gave them a calm analysis.

"I know who the vanguards of the waves are," I said.

"What? You do?" Kizuna asked.

"I guess from how you came here, your gender, and your

age, you might not be as clued in as us," I said to her. Kizuna was a girl, after all. Even girls who liked games might not have knowledge on this kind of subject. "The vanguards of the waves arrive in this world with the protection of this one who assumes the name of God," I said.

"What? You mean like Miyaji?" Kizuna asked.

"Kyo, and those guys we just fought too. All of them. It seems certain to me," I said. Just assuming it was true, I assumed the ones the name of God brought over would likely all have similar personalities. This supposed god would be choosing people who would be easy to control. Maybe even just churning them out, mass-production style.

Everyone other than Itsuki was looking at me with a puzzled expression, including Kizuna. We were pretty similar, after all. The difference was, though, that we were heroes who had been drawn here because the world wanted us around. The vanguards of the waves were the enemies of the world. That was why we were never going to see eye to eye.

Prior to actually coming to another world, I'd had a bit of a thing for stories about adventures in another world, so this made me feel a bit strange.

"You asked me something before, didn't you, Naofumi? About where I met a god and obtained my cheat abilities?" Itsuki reminded me. That made sense too, then. No wonder this being would assume the name of a God, if they could do things like that.

It was like a being that appeared in stories about being reborn or transferred to another world.

"The vanguards of the waves are people who have been reborn or transferred over here after being selected by the one who assumes the name of God. They are given all sorts of abilities, such as the power to steal holy weapons or seven star weapons. They come into these worlds and start causing chaos," I explained.

"Reborn? You mean like having spare bodies, like Kyo?" Raphtalia asked.

"No, something else. Just their souls were led to this world from Japan, and then they were reborn here as someone from this world. With their memories of the past," I said. For example, they are people who died in unfortunate accidents—people like Ren, Itsuki, and Motoyasu. This "god" would whisper to them that they had died an untimely death and offer to reincarnate them in any world they liked. They were already dead and so had no reason to reject such an offer. If they did, the "god" probably claimed to be taken with their resolve and promised to give them additional cheat powers, basically forcing them to accept. In some cases, maybe they were just forced to be reborn, no matter what they felt. I'd read books like that, loads of them. Now that they knew being summoned to another world was actually a thing, why not getting reborn or transferred over? Then, what if these ones selected by this "god" turned out to be like Takt. Their creator could then move these reborn souls around like pawns, whittling down conditions that were disadvantageous to the waves. The queen and old Hengen Muso lady had both said it: genius was a symbol of both prosperity and decline.

Take the Hengen Muso Style, for example. If that style spread across the entire world, it would clearly present a threat to the waves. So the reborn had been sent to put an end to the style. No one could state for sure that there wasn't something out there, repeating that kind of attack. Further proof was that records about the waves in each world were systematically being erased. Information had been lost in this world, in exactly the same way. Or even worse, it was replaced with lies. This "god" was clearly at work in multiple worlds. That was just a fact.

"If we consider the barrier in Q'ten Lo that wouldn't allow souls to pass through it as a means to prevent these reborn, the vanguards of the waves, from getting out, that also makes sense," I said.

"I see! Yes, that's another piece of the puzzle!" Raphtalia agreed with a nod. That said, she didn't seem to quite understand the "reborn" concept yet.

"You might well be right." The Demon Dragon alone seemed to be getting it. "There are monsters like that too. Monsters with bodies and souls that don't match and that need to be culled. A dragon would never allow such abominations to last, of course. I didn't know why they existed, because it seems that fragment was lost, but this explanation does seem to make sense." The lifecycle of the dragons was, when you thought about it, quite similar to this idea of being reborn. We'd basically done the same thing, without really thinking about it, when we revived the Demon Dragon.

Raphtalia seemed to have picked up on the same thing, because she pointed at the Demon Dragon and looked at me.

"Yes, it feels similar to her. Being reborn in a new body, in a different world," I agreed. In our world the Demon Dragon had taken over baby Gaelion, so perhaps that felt closer to being transferred. "That reminds me. L'Arc, Glass, you were talking about a nation that used to worship a strange god long ago, weren't you?"

"Yes, that's right. I'm sure this is the same in your world, Naofumi. But because the four holy heroes have saved the world so many times, they have become the subject of worship. This country had a religion that was based on a different god," Glass said. This world definitely had cultural similarities with ours. There might be some new religions like that here too, just unable to expand too far because of the four holies and vassal weapons.

The next question, though, was exactly what kind of world needed the intercession of these reborn to be destroyed. It couldn't be easy to destroy a world in which the hero system was operating smoothly. But it was also hard to believe these reborn would ever fight for the sake of the world. Indeed, it seemed likely that the very kind who wouldn't do that were being selected on purpose. It would depend on the abilities of this "god," but in every age, place, and world, there was always going to be at least one or two people who were just crazy in the head. I wasn't about to call myself a paragon of positive intellect, but I'd already seen plenty of whacked-out crazies in my time. If this "god" was only collecting people like that, it would definitely cause some chaos. There was also the potential that they had been subjected to some kind of brainwashing, making them think the waves were not a threat to the world, for example. That the waves were a minor inconvenience, nothing more. Now I definitely had experience with people like that.

I recalled that time that Ren and the others had said we were fighting an event battle and that we wouldn't die even if we lost. Maybe these reborn had that kind of mentality. The reborn we had encountered were all very aggressive toward others and couldn't accept not being the leader. Kyo and Takt had banged on about being the ultimate one all the time.

"Kyo, Takt, Miyaji, Seya, all of these guys had very similar personalities. But maybe that's because this one assuming the name of a god is selecting and sending in people who are similar. Wouldn't that also explain how religions about strange gods got started?" I suggested.

"If that is the case," Glass pondered, "then we don't want this to get out into the world. It will create an age in which everyone is terrified of each baby that is born."

"I can see it. Some of them have definitely been messing with you," I said. If the battle with the waves extended decades into the future, that would bring with it the terror of fresh vanguards of the waves being mixed in among all the children being born. A Spirit might be able to spot them, but attacking the soul would not be easy. That kind of thing led to infanticide. Not to mention, all information about this rebirth process would have been eradicated as well. It also didn't help that the technological developments that these vanguards of the waves realized were particularly delicious for the nation on the receiving end. No one would want to admit that they were actually a corrupting poison. L'Arc was already struggling in his negotiations with other nations based on just the information we already had.

I looked over at S'yne, wondering if she had known any of this, but she shook her head. I guess this was beyond even her knowledge.

"It all seems to line up," I said.

"But wouldn't this mean that the preparations for causing the waves started years, even decades ago?" Glass said. She was right. Eradicating records on the Spirit Tortoise and Phoenix, wiping out the successors to the Hengen Muso Style, sending in more vanguards of the waves, all took place over decades—if not hundreds of years—slowly corrupting and consuming the worlds. If this being we were facing was capable of all of that, I could see why the ancient text would choose the word "god" to describe them.

"In any case, I think this interpretation is highly likely to be correct. Please continue your research, giving consideration to there still being other possibilities. You may even find a solution to the waves," I said.

"Understood," Rishia replied, a little hesitantly. We were still facing a battle without any solution in sight. I was prepared for that. But if a solution could be discovered, it was worth having them continue to decipher the materials.

"This is all getting a bit convoluted," Kizuna said.

"It always has been. For now, we need to proceed with wiping out the vanguards of the waves, those who have been reborn here," I said.

That seemed to bring the trouble with the volunteers to a conclusion. L'Arc and his party returned a little later; he looked disappointed at having missed the battle and surprised at learning the truth about the enemy we were facing.

Epilogue: The Video Game Knowledge Pitfall

It was later that same night. We were eating a buffet-style meal, set out on the terrace in the castle courtyard and illuminated by both torches and magical light.

"Hey! That's mine!" Filo squawked.

"Hah! Dinnertime is a battlefield! If you wanted it so badly, you should have put your name on it! But even that wouldn't stop me from eating it!" the Demon Dragon retorted.

"Bleh! I really do hate dragons!" Filo and the dragon were bickering over a massive pile of food. For all the words coming out of their mouths, strangely enough they looked like they were getting along quite well. The Demon Dragon had certainly pulled her weight in the battle earlier. The biggest immediate problem was her continued attempts to sex me up. Every time she saw me looking over, she would throw a saucy wink my way, so I was making it a habit not to look at her at all.

Everyone was eating their evening meal in their own way. After a while, amid the natural flow of things, I found myself sitting with just Itsuki and Kizuna, the three heroes who held holy weapons. We were eating together.

"Reborn souls, huh? Do you think we could find some kind of common ground with them?" Kizuna asked.

"They are dangerous individuals, handpicked by this one who assumes the name of God—our ultimate enemy. Do you think that enemy would select anyone who might listen to what we have to say?" I asked her.

"They are still human. I think there is a chance," Kizuna replied.

"Which is how they lured you into that trap in the first place," I reminded her.

"Hey, too soon!" she shot back.

"I mean, I don't have a problem with the idea of wanting to try talking with them. I can understand it," I said. It was one of Kizuna's strong points. The point she was making was that wiping them out without even trying to talk to them first wasn't especially human on our part. However, I didn't expect them to give us time for such a strategy.

"What if . . . and just hear me out . . . what if this one who assumes the name of a god is somehow responsible for my game knowledge?" Itsuki quietly suggested. That sounded possible to me now. Even if being summoned was the correct process, having some prior knowledge would change your actions once you arrived.

"The other three heroes, the dead ones, all seemed to treat this like a game too from what I knew of them," Kizuna said. This being like a video game could very well be another trap placed by this "god." Ren, Motoyasu, and Itsuki had all basically placed limits on their own strength because of their game knowledge.

"That gives me a thought . . ." I looked at Itsuki and Kizuna, who both gave puzzled replies. "Itsuki, you thought this was the world from a commercial game called *Dimension Wave*, right?"

"That's right," he said.

"Hold on. They have the same name?" Kizuna spoke up. At Kizuna's comment, Itsuki looked over at her.

"Does that mean we played the same game?" he asked.

"I doubt it. You have some kind of special powers in your world, right, Itsuki? I don't have that in mine," Kizuna replied.

"And you don't have any game knowledge about this world, correct, Kizuna?" Itsuki asked.

"That's right. I was about to play a game called *Second Life Project: Dimension Wave*. It was a VR game and I'd never played it before. I got summoned right after getting into the pod, so I started out thinking this was just a very realistic game," Kizuna explained. That experience was definitely going to cause some misunderstandings, timing-wise. "Do you think this god being was involved in that somehow?" she asked.

"That's a tough one. Even if they were, you wouldn't have any preconceived notions and power-up methods," Itsuki mused.

"There's a difference between a game you are playing for

the first time and one you've devoted your life to," I added. On that front, Kizuna was pretty lucky.

"You read a book, right, Naofumi?" Kizuna asked.

"That's right. According to the Shield Spirit, summoning that way never fails," I replied. I still wished they had considered the place more carefully.

"Thinking about it now, I'm quite jealous of you both. Whoever thinks that having some knowledge is going to lead to such failures, after all," Itsuki said.

"You might be right. If this was all set up by the enemy, then it's quite a nasty trick," I replied.

"You said it. The VR game you were about to play, Kizuna . . . was that different from the one Ren played?" Itsuki inquired.

"From what I've heard about them both," I said, "they are two different things. Ren played on a helmet-type machine while Kizuna used a machine prepared by a company—a pod filled with liquid."

"There sure are a lot of Japans," Itsuki commented. At least five of them, for sure. I could only think of mine as the "normal" Japan, but to the others, it was probably just as weird as theirs were to me. "Knowledge being the pitfall placed by our enemy . . . that sure is dangerous."

"A trap that already killed three of the four holy heroes in this world," I said sadly.

"Please, don't remind me. Ah, and we have a wave tomorrow

as well," Kizuna moaned. That made me feel annoyed too. It was for the sake of the world, true, but they really were too frequent here. I wondered if there was any way to spread them out more . . .

Then it hit me—an idea that would later be confirmed by deciphering more of the ancient texts.

"What would happen if you used Hunting Tool 0 to attack the crack in the waves? If it has the power to severe illegitimate power, it might have some effect on it," I suggested.

"Ah, that sounds interesting. Ideas like that just take a bit of trial and error," Kizuna replied.

"I think it's worth giving it a try," Itsuki added.

"Well then. We've still got a lot of work ahead of us. You guys need to eat up and prepare for the next battle," I told them.

"We know, we know," Kizuna said.

"Indeed. With delicious food, a clear objective, and the combined strength of our allies . . . we can overcome any troubles that may befall us," Itsuki said.

"Even someone calling themselves a god," I replied.

"You bet," he said.

The scale of the foe we faced had just got a whole lot bigger. I also needed to let the guys back in our world know about this as quickly as possible. This feeling in my heart, I couldn't explain it. Each of us from our different Japans settled down for a brief moment of respite.

The Rising of the Shield Hero Vol. 18
(TATE NO YUUSHA NO NARIAGARI Vol.18)
© Aneko Yusagi 2017
First published in Japan in 2017 by KADOKAWA CORPORATION, Tokyo.
English translation rights arranged with KADOKAWA CORPORATION, Tokyo.

ISBN: 978-1-64273-082-1

Written by Aneko Yusagi
Character Design Minami Seira
English Edition Published by One Peace Books 2020

Printed in Canada
1 2 3 4 5 6 7 8 9 10

One Peace Books
43-32 22nd Street STE 204 Long Island City New York 11101
www.onepeacebooks.com